THE
HISTORY OF
NOW

Jesse Darnay

June 25-26, 2011

Camille listened to the click of her heels against the sidewalk. Mused how each footstep was commanding attention, advertising her pseudo-celebrity persona. *Summer in Chicago makes the city likeable, livable. Especially cool, dusky evenings like this.* It was amazing to her she'd lived in Chicago most her life and yet each summer, usually the beginning of June, it came to feel like the first summer she'd ever experienced here.

She stood at Inner Lake Shore and Belmont, waving her hand in the air.

A road-worn Yellow Cab pulled to the curb. She clicked open the back door and crouched in, looking through the square opening of the Plexiglas partition at a short, unshaven, Turkish man. The man stared back at her through his rearview.

"Lion's Head Pub," she said. "Lincoln and Belden."

The cab moved forward with a fierce jerk before she could finish her second sentence; the driver had already ceased looking at her and was eyeballing the road.

She leaned back, staring out the window at small, brown-brick shops that cruised past. Watched groups of people walking up and down the sidewalks, animated, laughing, drunk. Throw into the shifting city tableau the occasional twenty-something in a suit, with iPod headphones plugged into his ears, coming home from his company where he'd had to stay late and work. Throw in an aberrant, homeless nomad or two, three, studying the ground, talking to it, stumbling, shuffling. All of them people who would again disappear come winter when these same streets would be as glacial and barren as some uncharted corner of Antarctica.

4

College dreams, once so vivid, tangible, exciting, bearing so much promise, have become this over time. This dull, thirty-one-year-old woman that is me. With a bullshit job. No fame, husband. Nothing. I'm nothing. She snickered at that cavernous disconnect between her once hopeful conception of the future and what the future had actually brought her.

She could feel her scrim purse vibrating by her leg. Reached down and pulled out her BlackBerry, which read "Mere-Bear" on the caller ID. She clicked the talk button and put the phone to her ear as the cab swung left on Halsted.

"Where are you, bitch?" her friend Meredith said.

"On my way." Cam fished into her purse to find her Camel Lights.

"Smelly-guy's here."

"You're kidding."

"He just came up to me and tried to tell me he was sorry for breaking up."

"*No,*" Camille said. She lit a Camel and rolled down the window. "What'd you say?"

"I told to him to go fuck himself. Don't talk to me."

"Oh, Mere." Camille gave a deep, raspy cackle.

The cab turned right onto Lincoln from Belden and began to slow down. "Where you want me to stop?" the driver said, gazing at her in the rearview, his voice strained, lilting.

"Mere, I'm here," Camille said. "See you in a second." She clicked off the phone, dropped it in her bag and leaned forward. "Right here's fine," she said, looking at a small crowd of DePaul undergrads - the multi-ethnic, baby-faced nightcrawlers who'd all had their private and impassioned trysts with the Gods of Hairspray and Pomade - all smoking cigarettes outside a bar across the street. She was trying to pull out a small stack of tens and twenties when the cab whipped to a stop.

"I really don't appreciate you driving like a maniac," she said.

"No-no-no," the driver said back, flickering his eyes at her in the rearview, squinting. "No speak to me like that, please." He wagged his index finger.

"Excuse me?"

"I said you no tell me how to drive." He was staring at the windshield now, shaking his head.

"Why not? I'm the customer. This *is* a transportation service. Isn't it?"

"The woman should never talk like this to the man," he said, almost inaudibly. "Never. Never-never-never."

"What was that?" she said, now noticing a lackluster picture of Necmettin Erbakan scotch-taped to his dashboard. "You-know-what, nevermind." She thrust twelve dollars through the opening in the partition, which he took without looking at her. "Fucking terrorist," she muttered, clicking open her door, stepping out.

The neon lights, most of which beer signs from lines of bars across Lincoln Avenue, would just not seem to let this mid-American night rest, seemed to keep it alive, but in a malevolent way, as though it was one of Victor Frankenstein's clandestine experiments.

Two miles east of these benighted buildings, a 300-mile-long lake was slumbering, waiting to wake with the first wink of sun and share its salmon with local fishermen in an endemic, summerlong exchange. To the west, a careful lacework of long and short roads, some of which were illuminated by columned street lamps casting the city in a moody, film-noir orange, guided the iterant eye through hushed neighborhoods, where multicultural inhabitants snored away the woes attached to their daytime jobs. Those glaring bar lights of Lincoln Avenue were the deceptive signals of weightless, libertine freedom smack dab in the middle of a society fueled by aged and refined Puritan blood.

Cam's cab had long since turned down some small street, disappeared. She was striding across Lincoln now, looking at a quartet of DePaul girls standing outside Lion's Head Pub, smoking cigarettes, texting, all of them flipping their eyes left and right and giving inane smirks at no one as though they were in an interminable state of excited terror, as though they'd all long since sold their humanity for a one-way ticket into the inferno of American capitalist culture and this was what was left of them. The girls so engrossed in their phone relationships they didn't even realize their shoulders were brushing other shoulders. Camille looked down as she passed, thus evading the way in which she could relate to them. She gazed back up when she stood before a bouncer by the bar entrance.

Bouncer's face round and smooth-skinned though mostly obscured by a small, feral beard. He flashed his light brown eyes at Camille, but continued to sway his heavy body back and forth, gesticulating the shape of a card with his thumb and index finger. "ID."

She fished through her purse, found it. The bouncer glanced at her license, nodded, handed it back and she began moving through the darkened doorway. The wide, dim pub filled with Led Zeppelin music. Young Robert Plant screeching out "Hey, hey, what can I do?" in a drunken euphoria. Someone had played the song on an iridescent, neon juke box in a far right-hand corner. She continued to walk past gatherings of DePaul kids all crowded around circular, wood tables with large tubes of beer or medleys of diverse glasses atop. At one point, on her way to Meredith, who was sitting on a stool at the far end of a long bar toward the back, she got shoulder-bumped by a lanky guy in a Cubs cap.

She whipped her face at the guy, thin brows turned down, eyes glistening. "Watch where you're going!"

The lanky guy stuck his arms out and thrust his chest at her, pint glass sloshing, spilling. He looked left, right, then at her, snickered. "Why don't you chill?"

"Don't tell me what to do!" she said, pointing her finger at him.

The domineering intonation caused two girls chatting beside them to stop and look over. The lanky guy noticed this, looked at the girls, shrugged. "You got issues," he said, turning back to Camille. He walked off, disappeared.

She continued to gaze in his direction long after he'd gone. Shook her head, turned, continuing on course to Meredith.

Meredith Santini now on her fourth Raspberry Stoli and soda, about finished. Had taken seven and a half bong rips of Blueberry Kush before she'd left to come here. She knew there was a point in her life when she'd had a clear justification for getting so obliterated on booze and drugs, but it had now become such routine she couldn't even remember. All Mere knew was that she had the intoxicants: the cynical, little friends with whom she could fly away from a private, sober sorrow about being misunderstood by her domineering mother. Sometimes Mere would just drop things on her way home -- groceries, trinkets -- without even realizing it. She'd get perturbed about the items having disappeared and blame life for inundating her with more responsibilities than one human being could handle. She didn't notice Camille's approach, was instead leaning toward the muscular bartender in front of her, bantering.

"…it's because all men think about is their dick," Camille overheard Meredith saying as she walked up and touched Meredith's back.

"Looks like I came at the perfect time," Cam said.

"True, though," Mere said back, reaching up to hug her friend. "Men just wanna' get off." She was still hugging Cam and gazing at the ceiling with those large, glassy, brown eyes. "That's why they treat us like shit." Meredith released her grip, gawked the bartender, who was gazing back at her and sniggering. "They don't care about romance or calling you back or…" Mere shut her eyes and made like she was going to burp. When she flipped them back open, she'd forgotten she'd been talking. She began to sing something indiscernible and gaze at the countertop.

Cam looked at the bartender. "How many has she had already?"

He held up four fingers, his smile emphasizing his inchoate dimples. He nodded toward a wood wall in the near distance. "You know her hipster friend over there?"

She turned round, locked her eyes on a slender guy in a Super Mario Brothers t-shirt with long, snaky hair, black-rimmed glasses and shapely sideburns. The guy slurping his pint and listening to his friend, beaming, tucking strands of hair behind his ears. She turned back to the bartender. "That's her ex-boyfriend. Why the hell is he here?"

"Why do you keep dating these chodes?" the bartender said to Mere.

Days go by and still I think of you, Meredith sang, bouncing her shoulders. *Days when I could live my life without you.*

Bartender, smiling, turned to Camille: "I'm Jake." He pressed one hand on the bar and reached out with the other to take hers.

"We used to work together at Old Town Social," Mere said while they shook. "What are you drinking, bitch?"

"Hold on," Jake said. He walked off toward the other end of the bar.

"Why are we *here*, Mere?" Camille said. "I graduated college ten years ago."

"Jake's gonna' hook us up."

They both looked over and watched him as he filled a pint glass, now with a concentrated look on his face that accentuated his serpentine brows, slightly protruding jaw.

"How do you know him again?" Camille said, turning back to her friend.

"Old Town. He was a bartender."

"You guys ever . . .?"

"We kissed, once; I was wasted."

Jake had now come back. "Sorry about that. What'll it be, ladies?"

"Do you have anything *fruity*?" Camille said.

"Four Chocolate Cake shots," Meredith said.

"I can't drink all that, Mere."

"Got it, ladies," he said. "No se preocupe."

The three of them chatted awhile after Jake had poured Belvedere and Pineapples and a couple sanguine shots. He spoke of his unrelenting hatred for Old Town Social between the coked-out general manager's sudden temper explosions and the capricious scheduling from week to week, how he'd just walked out one Friday night and how he'd had to take this silly job here in "collegeville," because he had scant spending cash and dared not touch the modest savings account. Camille and Mere laughed in accession. They continued to look behind them at "Smelly-Guy," trying to decide whether to go annoy him or just keep making fun from afar. Mere finished her drinks and began looking around, looking toward the exit, batting her eyes, yawning. Took Camille almost an hour to drink hers. Never touched the shot.

"Time to get this little loco home," Camille said to Jake. Both were watching Meredith as she was falling asleep against her palm. "How much?" She put her purse on the counter, unzipped.

"Don't worry about it."

"Sure?" Still gazing into his eyes.

"Actually . . ." he said, "you could come over to my place with cleaning supplies. Crib needs a good scrub. While you're at it, please kick my roommate Tommy out and find some way to make him pay half his rent each month, from a distance. Also wouldn't mind a ticket to Japan. Any of said forms of payment would be acceptable."

"Ha-ha," she said, cocking her head.

"No, really, please. My pleasure."

The sudden kindness coming at her like an unexpected birthday present. Last time she'd had such a pleasant encounter with a stranger was with that dreadlocked girl behind the check-out counter of Whole Foods the other week -- Ramey. How it had seemed to her from Ramey's stoic facial expression and eagerness like Ramey was such a hard-working, humble girl. How she'd kept trying to make eye contact with Ramey that day and smile at her, but only managed to connect gazes after all the groceries had been checked through. "Thank you" and "you're welcome" the only two words exchanged between Cam and Ramey then. Camille still yearned to go back to Whole Foods when Ramey was working, try to do it again, better.

"This is refreshing," Camille said, much more audibly than she'd wanted to.

"Refreshing? Don't worry," he said. "It's a recession."

She chuckled. "No, refreshing to meet such a nice person."

"Feeling's mutual, dear."

She glanced at her friend. "Really better get this one home."

"Be honest," he said, smiling at Camille, "it's been a long time since I've been around people who actually thought about things other than themselves, like their friends."

She blushed. "What do you mean?"

"I come from a small town. It's different. Much as I love Chicago, I'm turned off by the sense of pervasive individualism here."

"Good phrase."

"What?"

"'Pervasive individualism.' Your phraseology. Sorry, I'm a huge literature dork."

"I prefer reading," he said. "Actually just finished

up *Cien Anos de Soledad*."

"You kidding? Epic. One of my all-time favorites."

He nodded. "Marquez: genius."

"You gonna' do some work over here, hon?" a voice called out over the bar's roaring din.

They glanced over at the other bartender, pulling a Stella tap, her spike-hoop earrings twirling against her neck as she shifted eyes between Jake and the beer.

"Not really," he said back. He gave the co-worker a smug smile, then turned to Camille. "Labor calls . . ."

"Course, course," she said. She turned to Mere, began shaking her.

"Really nice to meet you, though," he said, winking. "Grab my number from Mere." He turned to Meredith, just now coming back to consciousness. "Later, Santini." Leaned over to pinch Mere's cheek, then walked off to the other end of the bar.

***

Mere lived in an old, three-story just off 94 and Armitage. The building, which had initially been sunshine yellow, had long since become the color of blanched corn soufflé from years of merciless, wayward Chicago weather and from lack of maintenance. The white paint around the building's four front windows was chipped and cracked and looked like it was riddled with dismembered spider webs. None of this could be seen beneath the drape of night as Camille and Meredith pulled alongside a street curb in Mere's old, red Celica. Camille was driving. She had the driver's seat shifted forward so that her tall, slim body towered above the steering wheel and positioned itself as equal to the windshield.

"Trust me, Mere, Smelly Guy is no one to be concerned about," Camille was saying as she hit the brakes. "Look, every time I start dating someone, it doesn't work. I know not all men are assholes. It's not always their fault. But something's wrong. Look at everyone else we know. So many people happy, married . . ." She put her hand to her chest and shook her head at the windshield. "Maybe there's just something horribly wrong with me." She squeezed the wheel and looked down.

Mere leaned over and began whispering monkey noises in her ear.

Camille giggled. She let her head fall against Meredith's shoulder. "Let's move to an island. Away from all this bullshit."

"You've *got* to stop bitching," Meredith said, head back against the headrest, eyes shut, voice moaning. "Men suck. Get over it."

"So why continue the ill-fated mating dance? What's the point? Procreation?"

"You think too much."

Cam's eyes wandered upward toward Mere's jawbone. "What's your solution? Not giving a shit? Getting hurt again and again and not caring?"

Mere, the eyes still shut, rocked her head back and forth. "You can either be alone or keep the faith, keep trying to find the right person."

"If only it were that simple . . ."

"It is. You make it too complicated. Just date. Love. Take risks. Live your life. Stop asking so many fucking questions."

"Please, Mere. You complain about not being able to keep a guy in bed for more than two minutes after he cums."

Mere gave out a breathy sneer. "It's too complicated for you because you're too complicated, Cam. You need to find someone who can help you start dealing with all your shit. A therapist, I don't know. You certainly don't share anything with me, even though I'm supposed to be your best friend."

Camille shot upward and poised her back against the driver's side door. "You have a lot of nerve saying all that to me, Mere."

"Truth hurts."

"Why are you being so mean right now?" Camille's tone high, roiling.

"Sorry," Meredith said. She twisted her head toward her friend, opened her eyes. "I can be a bitch. Probably more a reflection of me than you."

"What do you mean?"

"I'm the one who needs help. A lot of help. I'd rather not deal with it, so I just try to ignore it. You're being introspective and that's totally healthy, but it's reminding me I need to be introspective, too, and I'm getting pissed off. I'm taking my frustration out on you."

Cam looked down again. "We're both so bitter. Really sorry I said what I said about the whole cumming thing."

"It's all good, you know I love you. Do yourself a favor and call him, though. I'll give you his number."

"Call who? What are you talking about?"

Mere shut her eyes. "Don't play dumb. I know you like Jake. Give him a call. I'll give you his number."

"Jake the bartender? I do not. What on earth gave

you that impression?"

"You're a lying bitch. I heard you guys talking."

"Shut up. You did not. You were sleeping at the bar, Mere."

"You thought I was."

A breath-stuck silence between them, like that which falls upon a circus audience when they watch a tightroper about to take a leap at 150 feet.

"So refreshing to meet such a nice person," Mere said, mimicking her friend.

Cam whacked Meredith's arm. "Can't believe you were listening."

Mere flicked her hands at the windshield. "I'm fucking James Bond." Her face turned serious, brows furrowed. She turned back to her friend. "Why we still in the car? Let's go in."

Camille giggled.

They ambled out and walked along a concrete pathway, Mere reaching into her black purse, fumbling for her keys. "What the fuck? Where--"

"I have them," Camille said. "I drove. Remember?"

Meredith gawked at the ground, silent.

Cam jangled keys in search of the one that would open the door, found it, did it. They moved past a winding staircase with a dilapidated wood banister, toward a dark, plywood door. Keys rattling, they let themselves in. Door opened to a narrow hall with shoes scattered all over. There was a strange yet faint yet unpleasant odor of marijuana and half-eaten Ramen noodles. They continued to walk, single-file, toward the rectangular window at the end of Meredith's small living room, which, during the day, looked out onto the disheveled back yard of Meredith's neighboring house -- a two-story gut rehab occupied by a middle-class, Puerto Rican family of five -- but now only glowed with the soft, cigarette-ember hue from distant streetlights.

Camille fell onto Meredith's vintage couch, sighing. Mere sat on the matching couch, leaning over to unscrew a small jar half-filled with Blueberry Kush on her glass coffee table. She packed her tie-dye pipe, put it to her lips, roasted it with a Bic. Said nothing, but leaned forward with the bowl and let out a chimney of smoke as she passed it to Camille. Cam lit up, sucked, coughed a smoking stream back at Mere. They expressed themselves in a remedial language of carbon monoxide.

"He is really cute, though," Camille said.

"Who?"

"Jake," Camille said, giggling. She looked toward the living room window, staring at it now like it was the center of a poignant Faulkner novel. Bowl still smoked in her left hand. For a moment she could feel that same tingling in her stomach she'd felt when she was eleven and running through Mitchell Park with Michael Parker -- the two of them falling into a shrub, bouncing off. The sun setting that day. The sky gone to ash.

She remembered her callow lust for Michael emerging when their game of tag had become more intense. "Michael!" -- that echo from twenty years ago still ringing in her mind. *Michael, slow down!* Still she could feel the feverish breath and stifled laughter as she chased little Michael, full-speed, across an open field, toward a dark, barn-like church on the corner of Wilmot and Deerfield. Not that she'd planned to express her swelling feelings for Michael at that moment, not that she'd had any idea what those feelings were, but that it had all just happened when she'd tackled him by the bush and they'd rolled, stopped, panted. How certain it had been to be with Michael and to kiss him.

We've all grown and changed and experienced and Michael's sixteen year-old figure is still buried in the earth, she thought.

Her eyes became hot with tears. She gripped the bowl. "Life's so cruel, Mere," she said, almost whispered. "It's so hard for me. What's the point?" The ensuing silence seemed to last too long and she looked over to find Mere sprawled out, snoring. The sight of Meredith's half-open mouth, her frizzy, sable hair running across her small cheek and over her chin like a series of cat scratches made Camille smile. She took a deep breath and wiped her eyes, shaking her head, taking another hit of the bowl.

***

When Camille awoke on Meredith's couch, Meredith was still asleep across from her. Cam could feel a dry, sticky heat at the back of her throat, which inspired her to look down at the pipe that was still in her left hand. Its contents had spilled over and there was a small, blackened hole in the couch cushion beside her amongst a wind-swept sandbank of marijuana ash. She stood up. She dusted off her belled jeans. She began to take fast, shallow breaths as she looked around. She strode, while conscious of the noise she was making, into Meredith's condensed kitchen. Realized it was probably eight or nine in the morning. A muted light from the living room window was filling the areas on both sides of the kitchen and had brightened up the kitchen's darkness so that she could see the shadowy shapes of a gas stove, a plump refrigerator, a laminate countertop below paneled cabinets. She hesitated before flipping the light switch. She couldn't wake Meredith -- have Meredith see her like this, in this naked moment of neurotic stealth. She began to open cabinets below the sink, quietly, flashing her eyes at various cans and bottles of detergent in the semi-dark until deciding Lysol was best. She took the can and then picked up a ragged dishtowel from the countertop, smelled it, tiptoed back to the couch from whence she'd come. Rubbed and scrubbed and brushed but that stain just wouldn't disappear. Now the stain looked like a faded, apocalyptic sunshine. There was nothing she could do about the hole. Her cheeks became hot, red: *Nothing I can do*, she thought. *Careless, Cam! You're fucking careless!*

She began to tap Meredith's shoulder.

Meredith's eyes fluttered open. She let out a noise that was a cross between a panicked gasp and a lazy moan. Looked up. "What?"

"Meredith, I fell asleep on your couch. I accidentally burned a hole in one of your cushions. I'm so sorry. I'll buy you a new one. I ..." Camille was on the verge of tears.

Meredith sat up, closing her eyes, opening them. She began to look around, gazing at her small dining room table just beyond the other couch, which was covered by a mussy pile of old *Cosmopolitan*, *Rolling Stone*, *Playboy* magazines and dotted with half-eaten, black, Target bowls of Lucky Charms, the shriveled green clover and yellow moon marshmallows still drifting atop dyed ponds of expired whole milk. She looked back at Camille. "What?"

19

"Your couch -- I burned …"

Mere glanced at the couch across from her, back at Camille. "No worries."

"I gotta' go, Mere," Camille said, reaching down and hugging her. "I'm sorry. I'm so sorry. I'll call you later." She turned and strode back through the hallway, out the plywood door, back out onto the street.

A desiccated quality to the early morning air around Wicker Park. A handful of birds could be heard chirping in the distance, between the intermittent whish of cars back and forth across the highway. Camille was moving toward Armitage. The sound of her heels on the sidewalk now annoyed her, as did all the other sounds of a city that had just woken from sleep and commenced another industrial workday: the faint growling of trucks, the random, angry beep of a horn … She raised her hand for a cab at the corner of Armitage and Sheffield and envisioned herself a flunky, a floosie, a dirty girl wandering the streets of Chicago in the early morning, un-showered, without an impressive career, smelling like old couch and bud. A girl who'd slipped so far beneath the expectations placed upon her during her upbringing in Deerfield that she'd almost become invisible. She started to become angry and her airborne hand tensed. *What are you doing here? People like this, places like this. Got to do better.* Then she felt remorse for disparaging Meredith in her thoughts. Felt fearful she would lose Meredith's friendship because Meredith would pick up on her energy from a distance. Thought maybe she should call Meredith and apologize for having those thoughts, but didn't.

A white taxi stopped across the street. Cam shimmied her way to it, gripping her arms, her purse swinging back and forth against her upper body.

The cab ride home silent, bumpy, cold. She put her head against the window and watched the city at fifty miles an hour. She was going back to a cramped apartment she still didn't really have to pay for:

"Don't worry about the cost right now," she remembered Mom saying six years ago. "You're sure this is what you want?" Her mom had been nodding manically and pacing around the empty apartment. She'd stopped to turn the kitchen faucet on, off. "Your job is just to figure out what you're going to do for a career." Their rental agent chuckled.

Over the years the apartment had become a semi-furnished space empty of human warmth, without someone there to understand her and make the place feel safe. She was all alone. Would throw on some Portishead when she got home, lay on the couch, stare out her filmy, single hung window, chain-smoke, become one with Beth Gibbons' astral voice. She'd convince herself she was too spiritual to be burdened with mundane issues like money. Or, she'd crank up Steve Angello's Subliminal mix and start stripping. Strut around in a red g-string and pretend she was a tan-skinned stunner from a Fellini film, as light and free and unencumbered as a stray leaf in a New England fall. Do whatever she could with the help of music to transcend this lot of hers. Then she'd have to be at work by five. That crummy Lincoln Park restaurant she'd applied to and made herself a part of one week to feign a life of financial independence.

"Thanks," she muttered to the cab driver as he pulled alongside the Belmont street curb. She paid, got out, walked into her building and went up the grated elevator. When she got to her place, she fell down on her padded sofa. Was about to fall into a deep sleep, a

21

consuming sensation that seemed to be swallowing her will to stay awake and put her life together, when she felt her purse vibrating by her legs. She shot upward and unzipped it to find a text from Meredith:

"Jake: 3126512217. Call him. Love you, bitch."

She responded "Thanks. I love you, too!" because she felt that type of response was compulsory. Felt if she didn't say something back to Mere, she'd be abandoning her -- she'd be a bad person.

I'll never call Jake. Never, she thought, standing, chuckling. She flipped hair behind her ears. *Of course I'm beautiful. Of course I'm wanted.* She pictured Jake's bulky figure and his little dimples when he'd smiled at her the night before as she walked into her bedroom.

Her closet closed off by a pair of sliding, glass doors. She now found herself posing before one of those doors, looking at her lean body from the side, making a kissy face, she didn't know for how long. Privately, she considered herself to be "special." Had always considered herself this way. It was something about how her face was put together. The ancient mysticism that came through her eyes.

Just feels nice to be back in the game or whatever, she thought as she disrobed and laid down, spread-eagle, atop her queen-size mattress. She closed her eyes and began to run her fingers up and down her stomach, strumming her protruding ribs. Could feel the brightening sun of late morning coming in through the blinds, pressing her face, invoking resplendent shapes into the blackness behind those closed eyes. That sobering mid-week sunlight that sought to shun the dusky aura of her apartment or any ambiance she could try to create. That assertive sunlight, which, if it had a voice, would say:

"You should be ashamed of yourself, Camille -- lying here with no purpose, sucking on your own existence to get high and numb while everyone you know and respect is busy working, being dedicated, wise. This aimless laziness is who you are, Camille." She wanted to respond to that Apollonian voice, but didn't. Wanted to get up and find a career, have a full life, but didn't. Kept her eyes closed and let her fingers slide between her legs. She began to feel heated and blissful as she pictured Jake taking her from behind: his large frame, his violent will to give her pleasure, the sheer naughtiness of that type of exchange. *Maybe I could just be sexual with him*, she thought after she came. She rolled into fetal position and reached for a crunched pack of Camel Lights on her nightstand. Lit up and puffed, flicking ash into a small, blue ash tray in the shape of a leaf. *We could have fun*, she thought. She rolled over and touched her breasts and blew smoke at the ceiling. *It wouldn't mean anything. It would be easy and exciting -- like a drug.*

April 23, 1976

Martin Carlyle was so late. He'd promised Rick he'd be over for dinner by six.

"Don't fuck this up," Rick had said to him when he called that morning.

"Relax, Ricky, my man," Martin had said. "I dig, I dig."

Martin looked down at his silver watch, shook his head. He pressed the elevator button at the fore of a modern apartment building on the corner of Pine Grove and Irving Park. Held a bottle of Chablis in his right hand and muttered profanities to himself, cursing his own tardiness, the empty promises he'd become known for by his colleagues at Foote, Cone & Belding. Then, as was his peculiar ability, he seemed to laugh it off, patted himself on the back. *Rick's no one to worry about*, he thought. *Just a copywriter on the Kleenex account. I'm the exec. I'm not expendable to FCB. He is.*

Ellen Teatzer was walking behind him as the elevator was opening, her downward eyes dancing for the floor, gleeful face like a cartoon sketch because she finally had time to spend with her old high school friend Katrina in 11D.

Martin did a double-take and then held the door for her. They both stepped in, pressed buttons and stared at the door as it closed. Martin noticed Ellen's slim legs from the corner of his eye. The way her legs accentuated themselves through those charcoal Levi's. They way they spoke, violently, confidently, about the mysteries of her femininity.

"Kind of sad things, aren't they?" Martin said as they began to ascend. He was still staring at the door.

"What?"

"These elevators." Martin shrugged, now looking

25

at her, pointing his Chablis toward the closed door. "I feel they tend to remind us how little we are in the scheme of things. That we have to be lifted up distances our little legs just can't handle the strain of."

"That's morbid," Ellen said, looking back at the elevator door and snickering.

A brief quiet passed, then both looked at each other and smiled.

Just as Martin was about to continue defending his analogy, the elevator came to a halt. Door opened at the eleventh floor.

"Cool meeting you," she said, glancing at him one more time and chuckling as she stepped out.

Martin walking behind her. "This is your floor, too?"

The elevator now closed and both standing across from each other in the hallway.

"We both know this isn't your floor," Ellen said.

"What do you mean? Of course it's my floor. I should know -- I live here."

"You pressed sixteen when we got in the elevator."

"Did I do that *again*? Bummer. Must've been a long day."

Ellen gave him a serious look. A smile then lit her face. "You really live here?"

"No," Martin said, breaking into a laugh. "Friend lives here. I was supposed to meet him -- double-date sort of thing, but I'm already way too late."

"That's not very nice of you."

"You know what would be nice? Going to dinner with you."

Ellen chuckled. "I don't even know you. You

26

don't even know my name."

"Martin," Martin said, sticking out his free hand. "Ellen."

"Chicago girl, originally?"

"What would make you say that?"

He pointed to her waist. "The gold stretch belt. Every corner I turn, I see girls your age wearing them. Mostly upper middle-class migrates from the suburbs. Trend is blazin' in this city right now. "

Ellen looked down at her belt, back up at Martin. She let out a muffled laugh. "These are hip everywhere. Girls have been pointing attention to their waists ever since Brigitte Bardot, before. You're either a writer or an ad-man. Not a very good one."

Martin staggered backward, looked up at the ceiling and let out a Shakespearian groan. "Right through the heart." He recovered his gait with sangfroid and stepped toward her. "I'm in advertising. Must've been so taken by your supernatural beauty that I lost my wits for a second."

Ellen smirked, blushed. She tilted her head and contemplated him in a strange silence. "I think I will have dinner with you. Might be cool. Want to take my number?"

He'd already put the Chablis on the floor and was patting his back pocket, digging up a bulky, brown-leather wallet, pulling out a card from First Chicago Bank and flipping to its blank side. He jabbed the white space at her. "Can you write it down? I don't have a pen."

She continued to stare and smile. Pulled a blue-marble fountain pen from her purse and inscribed the digits, then took a moment to study what she'd written, as though she was sitting beside a reading lamp in a metropolitan library. "Better get to your guy," she said, handing it back.

"Really looking forward to this," Martin said. He stared into her vivid, brown eyes, waved the card.

"Highland Park," she said as he bent down to pick up his wine.

"What?"

"I'm from Highland Park."

He pointed the bottle at her. "See! I'm awesome at what I do. That's why I do it."

"Goodbye, Martin."

"Bye, Ellen. See you real soon."

July 8-9, 2011

Camille didn't know why she was about to do it. It was impulsive. The long night at work; her loneliness. A fleeting yet body-numbing sensation of freedom as the Yellow Cab took her toward home in the early Chicago night. She began typing the text on her BlackBerry:

"It's Camille from Lion's Head Pub a couple weeks ago. What r u up 2? Wanna' grab a drink?"

From the moment she'd sent the message, she'd began to regret. Way too obvious she liked him. Why else would she want to have a drink with him? *What if he doesn't respond?* She began to feel pangs of rejection without even giving him the chance to get back. This creeping, stinging feeling of dismissal and sadness seemed to intensify as she made her way out of the cab and into her building, into the messy living room of her apartment. She lay down on her couch, kicking her long legs over an arm rest, gripping the phone in her left hand, dying to feel it pulse. *Stupid*, she thought. *You're so stupid. Why'd you send that text?* She coasted off into sleep.

When she awoke it was about six in the morning. The time of day her first thought as her heavy lids batted open and she looked at the living room window. That pale and subdued light of the sky which announced to all underneath that night's time had just now come to an end -- that all things pass and must again be re-born.

She looked down and noticed her phone had fallen to the floor, right beneath her open, dangling palm. Remembered she'd texted Jake and wiggled herself upward. The phone's red light flashing -- she picked it up, clicked in her password. There'd been a text from Jake at 2am:

"'The world must be all fucked up when men

travel first class and literature goes as freight.' Awesome, right? Marquez: prophet. So great to hear from you! Just getting out of work. Can I call tomorrow?"

Reading the message, reading it again and again, Camille was at once heartened, frightened, detached. *I'm an adult; he's an adult. We're two adults about to engage in friendship. Everything else is just silly.* She stood up and stretched, yawned. The day was so young. She was so young. Had her whole life in front of her. She still smelled like quesadillas from the restaurant: she grimaced. Walked into her small bathroom, humming "The Last High" by the Dandy Warhols.

Camille began to think about Jake naked as she twisted and fidgeted with the squeaky nozzles to her shower. That big, heaving body, wrapping her up, protecting her. She got in and masturbated. Eyes shut tight, tepid water trickling along her shoulders, she let go -- lost in a devious world where Jake and she had become one, where she was in control. When she regained senses and balance -- the froth from her coconut shampoo now slithering down her temples -- she became cautious again. Body stiffened. She began to scrub her scalp systematically. One thing to exist with Jake in fantasy, quite another that the two of them were actually in contact. *This is just going to be like all the others*, she thought, now tilting her face up at the water. She began to glide a bar of mint soap up and down her lengthy contours. *Such a nice moment we had. Why ruin it by dragging it out into something it shouldn't be? That's life, people come and go. But you texted him.*

For a quick minute or two, she completely regained composure. Put the soap down and was now just listening to the faint smack of water against skin. Every part of her body seemed to be soothed by holy calm. This feeling now came from her sudden realization that she'd been picked out by Nature for a divine purpose which involved making the world better, a purpose she'd have to carry out alone and that made everything else, like dating, less important.

The passion left her. Water began to have an uncomfortable, nails-on-the-chalkboard sound. The shower stream felt like razor blades. She gripped herself and tried to breathe, taking rapid breaths. Shut her eyes. *Breathe, breathe,* she told herself, over and again.

By the time she'd dried off, wrapped a fluffy, white towel around her waist and another around her head, ambled into her bedroom, she felt she was returning to a place of Zen. *Zen?* she wondered. *Or is this the willing of my mind to be something it naturally isn't? It's all so confusing.* She sat at the edge of her bed, reached for the little, half-packed bowl on her nightstand.

The marijuana didn't get her high -- just put some of those voices in her head to sleep. *Whatever*, she thought. *Doesn't matter. I can do whatever I want and be whatever I want with Jake. Mind as well use him for a little fun.* She grinned, watching herself in that closet mirror.

She hoisted off her bed and tottered to and fro like a zombie, then shuffled back to her living room. She picked up the phone from her couch and began replying to Jake's text:

"Good one," she wrote. "I'll be free tomorrow tonight."

This time his response was instant. She heard the phone buzzing as she began walking back toward her room in a languid haze of giddy self-satisfaction. The

sound of the phone stopped her, stiffened her. She turned
and rushed back to it as though it was her lover's train
leaving from a station during WWII.

"Can we do Wednesday night at 8, if you don't
have to work?" Jake had written. "Have you been to
Wilde on Broadway, over by Intelligentsia?"

March 20, 1977

Lana Teatzer, Ellen's mom, looked down at her blue-rimmed plate and speared a piece of turkey lasagna with her fork. She continued to look down as she chewed. "I still don't understand what you're doing," she said, looking at Martin who was sitting in the cushioned chair across from her.

"Mom," Ellen said. "Please . . ."

"That's okay," Martin said. "Simple. I'm starting my own advertising business."

Lana, looking back down at her plate, contorting her wrinkled brow: "It's a profession that has always puzzled me." She looked at her daughter. "Samuel felt that way, too. He never had any friends who were in the business." Back at Martin. "I guess the question wasn't what you're planning to do, but how you're planning to do it? A business, any business, even the *advertising* business, requires some start-up capital. Where are you planning on getting that?"

"Mom . . ." Ellen said.

"Valid question," Martin said, puffing his lower lip. "I was working for a large agency in Chicago. Saved up a little bread for this venture."

"Bread?" Lana said.

"Money," Martin said, smiling.

"How much is a little?"

"Mom, stop."

Lana looked down at her plate and carved another corner of lasagna.

"Martin's been in advertising for ten years," Ellen said. "There are plenty of people he knows from FCB who will back him on this -- financially, with advice. Also, a bank loan. I think it's exciting."

They all became quiet and chewed. Silverware

clinked softly against plates. Beverages were gingerly sipped from tall, notched glasses. Even the airy hum from a ceiling fan in the adjoining room seemed like the heartbeat of God as they all grappled with their private thoughts.

Martin gazed at Lana. "Ellen tells me you're planning on moving back to Chicago."

"Yep," Lana said, focused on the pasta.

The collective food-nibbling, quiet sipping, secluded thinking resumed, this time for what felt like thirty minutes. Ellen had been staring at Martin for awhile before he noticed.

"I'm sorry," she mouthed.

He smirked at her.

"Can you believe this whole Roman Polanski thing?" Ellen said.

Lana stopped eating. Her face soured. "Disgusting. Absolutely foul, putrid behavior." Lana went on to condemn Polanski, at length, for the way he'd sexually abused poor, little Samantha Geimer. "Reminds me of a joke," she said, chuckling, her huddled shoulders jouncing. She shifted glances between Martin and Ellen and smiled for the first time since dinner began. "A priest calls his altar boy into the church undercroft . . ."

Martin and Ellen gave out hearty laughter at her punch line, even though neither found it funny, even though Ellen's face had tensed and reddened from embarrassment, even though Martin continued to smirk at Lana because he actually loved Polanski and found the whole scandal to be blown out of proportion.

Lana, now rejuvenated, recited more jokes. Martin and Ellen offering up their affected laughter, some of which genuine. When the jesting waned and began to transform into another disagreeable silence, Martin stood up and took dishes to the kitchen.

No dessert -- just coffee, mixed with Nutra-Sweet and sipped out of petite, porcelain cups. Lana had forgotten all about her interrogation of Martin. She told a final joke about an ugly princess and her guests tendered their perfunctory giggles.

"You're all right," Martin said.

Lana took another sip of coffee, stood. "Bedtime for Bonzo." She grabbed her cup and saucer and reached for miscellaneous plates on the table.

"We'll take care of it," Martin said, standing, nodding. "Thanks for having me. I had a wonderful dinner."

Lana gave Martin a half-smile and put her cup back on the table. She gave her daughter, now standing beside her, a hug and kiss. "See you in the morning." She turned and walked down a narrow hall, opening up one of the closed doors, letting herself in.

"She's a little rough around the edges," Martin said after a few minutes, as he and Ellen were cleaning the table.

"That's completely inappropriate," Ellen said, not looking at him. "How dare you say anything like that about my mother."

He glared at her, even though she wasn't observing. He felt crushed, abandoned, deceived. Thought they'd been working as a team to assuage Lana's acrimony during dinner and had agreed she was indeed a bitter old woman. He felt like he'd just been thrust into the outside of the loving family circle he'd forged with Ellen, into some vacant, public square where he could now be shamed and ridiculed by all and sundry. This stinging sensation of hurt stayed with him as he finished off the table and was now staring at Ellen in the middle of Lana's luminous kitchen.

"You should apologize for talking like that," he said.

"Like what?" she said, crossing her arms.

"The way you just spoke," Martin said. "About your mom." He shuffled to the doorway, stopped, peeked his head into the living room.

"We're not doing this now," she said, pushing past him. She clicked the light below a ceiling fan and then took a seat at the end of a beige couch in the living room, by a green-plated reading lamp on top of a nightstand. Reached for her hardcover copy of *Carrie*, which had been sitting below the lamp, began reading.

Martin remained at the kitchen door. *Not going to fight*, he thought. *It's her nature. Live and let live.* He turned and began walking down the hall in front of him. Opened up a door to his right, stepped in, closed it.

This room had a strong odor of cinnamon air freshener. In the middle, against the wall, a queen-sized bed raised up and situated center of a black, metal frame with tall posts. Martin's timeworn, russet attaché lay at the bed's edge, white paper with storyboard sketches sprawled out of it. His and Ellen's puffy, black, half-unzipped luggage sat on the white carpeted floor, on both sides of the bed. The bags still swollen with clothes and varied items that Ellen and Martin had brought with them for this trip, Ellen's bag a little more deflated than Martin's because she'd already begun folding her garments and filing them in the sandalwood dresser against the wall, below a curtained window.

He sat down on the bed and began organizing

papers. Lay back against a large down pillow and closed his eyes. *Doesn't matter,* he thought. *Love's messy. Better or worse. All that shit.* His eyes flickered open as Ellen opened the door and closed it behind her.

"That was quick," he said.

She said nothing. Lips pressed together, eyes fixed in front of her, she knelt down beside her luggage and began taking out her remaining clothes.

"Elle," Martin said, swinging his legs around the side of the bed and then pressing his feet to the floor. "What's your problem? Mellow out."

She snorted, shook her head, continued to pull out clothes.

"Seriously?" he said, scowling. "You brought me all the way to Florida and now you're going to pull this shit?" He stood up and began walking to the door.

"You're not going anywhere," she said. Glaring at him, pointing her index finger. "I told you I won't do this now. We're at my mother's. Have some respect -- or we're through."

"Aren't you over-reacting? You're the one who belittled me about your mom. Now you won't even listen. You're threatening me? I thought things were going really swell with us."

She turned and continued tending to her task. Martin returned to the bed and lay back down, closing his eyes. They were enshrouded by suffocating quiet, within which Martin shifted from pose to pose on the bed and Ellen became more focused on her bag. It lasted ten minutes, until Martin rolled over, stared at the back of Ellen's head and said:

"It can't be like this."

"Maybe it shouldn't *be* at all."

39

"I don't know why you're so pissed. I'm the one who should be pissed, but I'm not. What's your story? Talk to me."

"Just fucking buzz off."

He sighed. Pulled between the will to walk out the door without concern and inertia born of pity for what he perceived to be his lover's personality flaws. He decided to lay in the bed and try to sleep. Sleeping within five minutes, giving out hoarse snores within ten. He was just starting to dream of his father's white-haired face looming large against a disorienting blackness, snarling, when he was roused back to consciousness by Ellen swatting his arm. He felt his mind being ruptured as he rapidly forgot the ethereal world he'd come from and began to make sense of the pale darkness around him, cushy mattress beneath him, lavender-scented body beside him. He noticed Ellen was half-naked now and had their quilted blanket over her. "I'm sorry, Martin," he heard her whispering, her soft breath still permeated by the stench of Colombian coffee.

"It's okay," he whispered, batting his eyes. "What time is it?"

"Two-thirty."

"What are you still doing up?"

"I couldn't sleep . . . I finished un-packing . . . I felt so bad about the way I acted . . ."

"It's okay. Just forget it."

"I hate when you brush things off like that."

He rolled over, took a long breath through his nose. "Okay. Talk to me. I'm listening."

"I don't want to say anything *now*. You're patronizing me."

"Goddamnit," he said. "Just speak."

She became quiet and rolled over, gave him her back.

"Elle," he said, "seriously, baby…" He was spooning her, nuzzling her nape. "Please say what you wanted to say. Sorry I got mad."

"I never had a good relationship with my father, Martin. I just didn't. I have a small family. It's all I really have."

"You have me."

"I'm very protective about my mother," she said. "Just don't talk about her. I guess that's what I'm saying. Please don't."

"I don't understand."

"My dad died of a massive heart attack when I was fourteen, okay. It was sudden. I was at school when he was rushed to the hospital. He was dead by the time I got home."

"Jesus, Elle. I'm sorry. I didn't know… You never really spoke about him, how it happened." He felt her body begin to tremble and listened as she cried.

"I was glad," she said after another minute or two, sniveling.

"What?"

"He was a vicious, alcoholic asshole. He used to get drunk and knock Mom around. I would lock myself in my room and put my fists to my ears, rocking back and forth, while it was happening. Paula was always sneaking out with the older boys. She was never there. I hated myself for not having enough strength to stop him. I hated Paula for not being there. I was thankful when Dad died because I knew Mom would be safe. I promised myself I'd never let it happen to her again."

In the silence that ensued, both let information hit

them like rocks in an aluminum bucket.

"I left home when I was seventeen," Martin said. "Got fed up with the old man telling me what to do with my life. Dad was a head chef at this classy, seafood joint in downtown Cocoa Beach. Mom didn't work. She wanted to, but the poor lady didn't have a voice in that house. No one did. Old man ran the place like it was the Spanish Inquisition."

"Where'd you go? What did you do?"

"It's a long story, Elle. We'll talk about it some other time."

"You're brushing me off again."

He rolled over, sighed. "I worked while I was high school, saved. I hitched my way to New York two days after graduation with a backpack and about five hundred in cash. Never looked back. Did film school at NYU, worked in the city a couple years and then I moved to L.A. It's been a hard road, sweetness, but *my* road -- no one else's. Dig where that's at?"

"Why didn't you tell me this before?"

"You never asked."

She turned to face him, even though they could barely see each other between their hunger for sleep and the room's obscurity. He could hear how her breathing had slowed with didactic expectancy.

"They're things I just don't like to think about," he said. "I haven't really talked to my dad in over thirteen years. Mom died when I was fourteen. It's the past. It's done with. I'd rather focus on what I have right in front of me, which just so happens to be this incredibly foxy lady who I love and who loves me back. That's what's important." He touched her arm, rubbed it, leaned in and pressed his lips to hers awhile. "Let's go to sleep," he said as he pulled himself away. "I'm tired."

"I love you, Martin."

"Love you, too, baby."

They held hands until both were asleep.

July 12, 2011

Camille's manager stood on the sooty sidewalk of the parking lot behind Tilli's, hands flipped backward and pressed against his flanks. He stared at Camille, smirking. "How do you think you're doing?"

"What do you mean?" she said. She puffed her Camel. "I thought I was doing good."

"Okay," he said. He looked down, nodded.

"I'm always happy to know how I can improve, Richie."

Richie staring at her again. "I hate doing this stuff. I don't like confrontation . . . You need to move faster."

"What do you mean?"

"Watch for food in the window," he said. "Run it."

She took a last drag of her cigarette and let it fall to the ground. Stepped on it, put her head down.

"I'm sorry," he said. "I hate doing this."

"It's cool." Smiling at him. "I'll definitely watch the window from here on out."

They turned and walked, single-file, through a rusty, silver door, going their separate ways at the back of the low-lit restaurant: Camille to the kitchen window center of the space, her manager to a small office at the end of a slim hall where he closed the door behind him.

She saw tickets dangling in front of the kitchen window, but no food beneath the lamps -- just three, portly, Mexican men in chef hats behind those lamps, all intently involved in cooking this, that. She turned to Rodrigo, one of her co-workers, who was slouching against an elongated tabletop, palms outspread behind him and pushed against it.

"Richie just told me I wasn't doing a good enough job out back," she said, rolling her eyes. "He's such a

45

douche bag."

"He did the same thing to me last week," Rodrigo said, lifting his brows. "He sucks. Don't worry about it."

"Yah," Camille said. She walked past him and made her way through a wide, wood doorway, into a dining room ornamented on all sides by high-reaching windows. Stepped up to a circular booth at the corner of the room, packed with middle-age women, their jade, glass-tile tabletop a war-torn village of smeared dishes, half-eaten chunks of meat, displaced silverware, depleted martini glasses.

"Can I get any of this out of your way, ladies?" Camille said.

With the exception of one, the women, all wrapped up in an engaged conversation about the best Groupons available, paid no attention. That one exception -- a bespectacled divorcee with long, frazzled, black hair and ruddy cheeks -- glanced at Camille, gave her a toothless smile, nodded. She then continued observing her friends.

Camille took as many plates as she could carry with both arms. She gazed around the half-vacant room and tried to make eye contact with one of the bus boys to no avail as she staggered through the narrow hall by the manager's office. She deposited the plates in a black bus tub. When she'd turned around and began striding back to the booth, she noticed that her busser -- a beefy, Mexican man with a bushy goatee named Juan Antonio -- was already clearing the rest of the table. She went back to the kitchen window.

Another one of her co-workers, Heather, was now standing where Rodrigo had been, in almost the exact same pose. Cam edged up beside her and put one of her palms on the tabletop, the other on her hip.

"I have a question," Camille said. "There's this guy . . ."

"Ooh," Heather said. "Sounds good."

Camille blushed and glanced at the ground. Looked back at Heather. "I'm going on a date tomorrow. What should I wear?"

"First date? Second date?"

"First."

"You wanna' fuck him?"

Camille rolled her eyes and looked away.

"Wear something conservative, but slightly revealing. Check out Forever 21." Heather pushed herself forward and fiddled with one of the tickets on the window. She grasped two plates that had just come up, turned with the dishes and made her way out into the main dining room, saying "Can you toss that ticket for me, hon?" to Camille on her way.

Camille sighed as she plucked the ticket, crumpled it, tossed it into a large garbage can. *Why would she say that?* Camille was glimpsing at herself through Heather's eyes now, seeing herself as a weird, asexual, hermit-chick people wanted to avoid, shake their heads at. Heather had wrested her from her own subjective self-understanding, naked, shivering. She was split in two now, one half laid out on a cot at the center of a quiet, crowded operating theater called Tilli's Restaurant while the other half had to watch in silence, from a distance, as all the ugliness was exposed.

Camille was suddenly reminded that she still had that one remaining table, probably wanting their check, when she noticed that Angel, one of the three chefs, the short one with a black-ink tattoo of a cobra on the left side of his distended neck, was gazing at her, saying: "Jew gonna' take this, azucar?" He tapped his long, silver tongs against a steaming bowl of penne rose.

"Shit," she muttered, ignoring him, walking to one of the computer screens along the restaurant's front counter. She printed out the check for table sixty, fixed it in a black booklet and headed to the booth. As she neared her table, she caught eyes with Heather, who was now on her way back to the kitchen window. Heather grinning at her. Camille smiled back, but Camille's facial expression then soured into a look of anxious confusion after Heather had passed.

"Anything else I can get for you ladies?" Camille said to the women at her table, who were still wrapped up in conversation -- now a collective meditation on the latest episode of *Top Chef* -- and not paying attention, even though their table had been completely cleared, wiped down and appeared as though it belonged to a museum commemorating humanity in a post-mortal world.

Camille continued to stand in front of the ladies, swaying left, right. She dropped the check at the center of the table. "Take this whenever you're ready." She noticed one of the women was glancing at her, nodding, smiling. Camille found herself mirroring the gesture. She then turned and paced back to the kitchen window. Again she disregarded vaporous plates modeling themselves beneath hot lamps. She drummed her fingertips on the restaurant's front counter and gazed at Heather, who was standing in front of a metal table with wheels. Heather batting a hunk of turkey meatloaf from a mucky plate into a plastic container with a fork.

"What did you mean when you said I should dress

conservative, but revealing?" Camille said, strolling up to Heather.

Heather snapped her plastic box shut and smirked. She ducked down and dumped her empty plate into a bus tub. "You're kind of a babe in the woods." She stood back up, glanced at Camille. "I can tell. It's cute. *He'll* think it's cute -- but you gotta' be careful not to come across as a plain-Jane. Conservative, but revealing." She winked. Tossed the plastic box into a wrinkled, two-handled bag.

"I'm not a plain-Jane," Camille said, raising her voice.

Heather lifted a threadlike brow. "Okay." She swept past Camille with the to-go bag.

Cam turned, following her, cheeks now inflamed. She was stopped by a tapping on her shoulder. Turned to find Richie standing right behind her, shaking his head.

"Didn't we just talk about this?" Richie said. "Why aren't you running those items in the window?"

"You're right," she said, putting her head down and marching back to where she'd come from. She breezed past Richie again with arms now full of weighty plates. After placing the dishes on a high-top alongside a window, where two brawny guys in dark baseball caps and a zaftig, young girl with long, chocolate hair sat slurping cocktails, Camille walked to a tiny corridor by the manager's office and pretended to busy herself by opening cabinets and looking at condiments.

She stood on her tiptoes and aligned disarrayed, splotched bottles of A1. *Now everyone's going to think I'm a psychopath.* She slid a bottle against the back of the cabinet a little too hard. The A1 made a booming smack and toppled. *Whatever*, she thought, coming back down

49

on her feet, letting the bottle lay. *If I took advice from people like Heather for the next ten years, I'd end up sucking dick for coke.* She stopped moving and her eyes fell to the floor. *That was really mean.* She wanted to go find Heather now, apologize. Maybe they'd have a tête-à-tête on the sly, when Richie wasn't looking, and then she would let out all of her intimacy issues. She'd talk to Heather about her struggles to navigate her way through this dark and chaotic world with only a fragile, sensitive, poetic spirit as a beacon. Heather would listen and touch her tenderly and they'd become best friends, over time. This important day would mark the beginning of a new way of living. Henceforth she'd be honest with everyone about everything and damn the consequences.

"Camille," Richie was saying behind her. She twirled around. He was posing by his office door, arms akimbo, fingertips pressed into the sides of his paunchy stomach.

"*What* are you doing?" he said.

"Dylan asked me to do this when I came in today. I just thought . . ."

"No," he said, shaking his head. "Go back to the window. I'm writing you up."

Her eyes dropped. Heart tolled a requiem in the steeple of her chest as she moved past him. Heather and Rodrigo now standing by the window, chatting. She stood beside them, giving Heather a quick half-smile but then staring at the window without saying anything else.

January 7, 1978

"Sorry, sir?" their waiter said.

"Moet," Martin said. "We'll have the Moet."

The waiter smiled, nodded, disappeared.

"This is truly lovely," Ellen said, sitting back in her wide chair and glancing around the restaurant with a grin.

Martin reached across the table and took her hands. "I love you, Elle. I'm really in love with you. Have you been here before?"

She shook her head like a four-year-old demonstrating knowledge of right and wrong. "No. It's so beautiful, though." She looked down at the table, then back at Martin with a smile. Wasn't going to tell him that her ex-husband Stephen had taken her here four years ago. Wasn't going to talk about how Stephen and she couldn't even get through the Oysters Rockefeller, because she was so miserable about being married she couldn't appreciate Stephen's kind demeanor, was insulting and condescending to Stephen about his working too much, even though she verily appreciated how Stephen's income had been supporting the both of them. She just wasn't going to talk about it; wasn't that person anymore. She was mature now, and ready to be in a loving relationship with a man.

"You're sure you like it?" he said.

"Yes, Martin. Yes. Why are you so nervous?"

The waiter returned with a bronze stand and bucket filled with ice. He disappeared again.

"I'm not nervous," he said, leaning back, folding his brows. "I . . . Ah, fuck it. Never been good at shit like this anyway."

"What are you talking about?"

"You've really shown me the beauty of stability

over these last two years, Elle," he said. "How important it is to have a strong foundation, a household, a family. Spent most of my life running around with people who always seemed to put their love into what they had going for themselves, not those around them. You start to feel like a forlorn island when you're around cats like that, but at the same time you're so busy you don't really take note. It's just this horrible wailing that sits in your heart at night and gets muffled by the buzz of your thoughts. Hear what I'm saying? I know this is kinda' esoteric."

She stared at him, wide-eyed.

"You, sweet sunshine, are the opposite of just about anyone I've ever known. You've completely pledged allegiance to the pursuit of sharing your life with another person. Because you are who you are, I'm beginning to understand how good it feels to know you truly have someone in your corner every day, how special it is to be able to recall all the foibles and idiosyncrasies about the one you love some random moment throughout the day, to be that close. I'm so happy." His eyes shifted toward a self-conceived vacuum he'd effectuated just beside Ellen's head. He squinted at the void. "I was always too ambitious. I thought that's where someone found true fulfillment in life and I felt bad for all those people who'd saddled themselves with marriages. But that's not the case. You need the foundation in order to achieve your goals." Eyes turned back to Ellen. "You've shown me that. *You*. I'm ready to do something different and I'm ready to do it with you." He stood while still holding her hands and knelt beside her. "Will you marry me?"

Her eyes filled up with tears. "Yes. Yes."

He grabbed her arms and leaned upward, pressing

his lips to hers. She put her hands around his nape. In a violent fit of touching and caressing, their tongues just couldn't seem to express enough ardor. After both became tired, Martin edged back, looked her into the eyes, smiled, then returned to his seat.

The waiter came up with a bottle of Moet White Star in one hand and two champagne flutes in the other. "Congratulations," he said, putting a flute in front of each of them, popping the bubbly.

"Thank you." They looked at each other and gripped glasses, clinking.

"I can't begin to tell you how happy this makes me," she said, shaking her head, eyes dampening again. "I have to call Mom, Paula . . ." She looked around for a pay phone.

"Now?"

She smirked and looked down at her glass, sipped. "No. Of course not. I'm just excited."

"Me too, sunshine," he said, leaning back. "Me too." He sipped his drink, looked off at the lobby. "Yep. There it is."

July 13, 2011

Taken Camille nearly three hours to get ready. She tried on seventy-five percent of the clothes in her closet, posing in front of her long mirror, telling herself she was too dressed, too obvious, too plain, too skanky, too everything. Now she stepped out of the cab as it pulled alongside a curb on Broadway in a white, one-piece, muslin dress with blue flower design, which she still felt too "hippie." Fidgeted with the dress bottom as she walked toward the front patio of Wilde.

She could see Jake standing by the doorway, half his face obscured by the darkening eve and the other illumined by fire from one of the restaurant's tiki torches. As though he'd shifted from human in her life to symbol about her life, a pictured statement dealing with revelation and secrecy. She thought about walking the other way with her head down, but Jake had already caught glimpse of her and was smiling. *Warm, fatherly, irresistible smile.*

"Good to see you again, cute one," he said, stepping forward to give her a hug.

She tried to hug back, froze. *Why is he so confident?*

"Outside? In?"

She shrugged. "Doesn't matter. Inside -- unless you wanna' sit outside ..."

He waved his hand and tilted his head, motioning them in. She followed behind as he began talking to a host. Her eyes darted around the restaurant. It was long, wide, half-full, resounding with the song "Sky Pilot" by Eric Burdon & the Animals. Had the feel of an early twentieth century saloon between its walnut wood and framed paintings and dim chandeliers.
She followed Jake and the host now, single-file, deeper

within.

Cam caught eyes with a table of girls just below an extended railing on her way. Two of those girls looking right at her, not because they were appraising her, but because they'd reached a strange pause in conversation and found it pleasant to rest their wandering eyes upon the willowy young thing who'd just come in.

She looked down. *The fuck do they think they are, looking at me like that, judging me?* Looked back up. The host, a shapely, olive-skinned college kid who'd kept looking off into space as though approaching a pyramid in Egypt, was now pointing to an empty table for four with wing chairs. The table beside an antique bookshelf packed with ragged books. The host continued to maintain her meretricious grin as she waited for Jake and Camille to sit. Placed two heavy, black menus in front of them, said: "Have a great night. Oops, I mean: You server'll be right with you." She giggled. "Thanks."

"I requested this table for us," he said, nodding at the bookshelf. "Figured you wouldn't mind being close to the written word." He leaned toward her, put a hand over his mouth to screen what he was saying: "These books are horrible, though, if you look close. Nora Roberts and the like."

She'd already opened her menu, was studying it. "Good call."

He opened his. "What do you like to eat? I hope this place is alright."

"I'm picky," she said, staring at the menu with more intensity.

"Vegetarian?"

She looked up, eyes grave: "Why would you ask that? Do I look emaciated?"

"Easy, Havisham. Just seemed like you might've been."

"Ever compare me to Miss Havisham again, that'll be the last time we talk."

He looked back down at his menu, took a long breath. Flipped a page, trying to decide what he wanted. *Why would she text me if she's going to act like this? She's so beautiful, though.* He visualized her dimpled, rose-red lips, Mediterranean eyes, that sexy jaw line as he continued to peruse, finally choosing the cobb salad. *There's a whole poetry to the way she's put together.*

"How do you know Meredith?" he said, looking back up.

"Met her after college," Camille began to say, but was then cut off by the presence of a blond-haired waitress now hovering over a corner of the table, smiling at them. "Can I get you anything to drink?" the waitress said, putting down tall cups of ice water.

Jake glanced at Camille, back at the waitress. "Goose and soda, splash of cran."

"You're a server, aren't you?" the waitress said to Jake.

"Bartender."

"Do you work at Lion's Head Pub?" She was pointing her finger at him, tilting her head. "I've seen you …"

Jake, shrugging: "I see a lot of people."

The waitress paddled her hand. "No worries, I was *super*-wasted that night anyway."

He pointed back at her. "Wait a minute. Were you guys daring each other to snort salt?"

The waitress scrunched her lips, looked away. "So embarrassed."

"It was hilarious," he said. "You a DePaul kid?"

"Because I was at Lion's Head? No, just ended up there. Stupid, I know."

"Stop apologizing for yourself."

Waitress gave him a buoyant giggle.

Camille, meanwhile, tried not to watch them but found herself doing it anyway. She mimicked the waitress's laugh under her breath. *Vapid, little make-up monster,* she thought. *You and your legion of Google-drunk trolls, pissing all over the twenty-first century.* She gawked at the table. *Why are you acting like this tonight, Camille? Why are you so unhappy?* She considered getting up and walking out -- perhaps leaving them both with a sharp invective on her way: something that could cut both their hurtful hearts: two birds, one stone. Just as she was convincing herself to do this, just as she'd reached that point where her dark vision of what was happening between Jake and their waitress had become the ultimate reality for her, Jake and the waitress came to a sudden pause in their badinage. Jake flashed his eyes at Camille, as if snapped from hypnosis. He tried to smile but quickly looked down at the table. The waitress strode off, then returned.

"So sorry," the waitress said, now grinning at Camille. "Don't know where my head's at today. Late one last night. Can I get you anything to drink?"

Camille, glaring at her. "Coke."

"Where'd you go to school?" Jake said to Camille after the waitress left.

"Florida State."

"Gainesville?"

"Tallahassee."

"You from Florida, originally?"

"Can you stop asking so many questions? I don't even know you."

"That's the point of a date. You get to know each other."

"Don't lecture me."

Jake threw up his hands. "Alright, alright, I surrender. New subject. No more questions." He took a sip of ice water and waited for the waitress to come back. The sound their drinks hitting the table echoed over the silence like a medieval dirge.

"You ready to order?" the waitress said.

He looked across the table and gave Camille a stern nod, stuck out his palm, pointed it at her.

"Turkey burger," she said. "Fries."

Jake ordered his salad, waited for the waitress to leave, then said: "You seem angry, Camille. Are you upset about something? Someone do something to you? Did I?"

"What the hell are you talking about?" she said, her nose scrunched. "Who the hell are you to pry into my life like that? I've known you all of twenty minutes, Jake. This is pretty audacious." She wasn't quite yelling, but was speaking loudly enough for the girls eating beside them to have stopped what they were doing and glanced at the table.

"Calm down. Why are you so mad? I'm that fun, cool, overwhelmingly handsome guy you met at the bar a couple weeks ago. Remember? Why are you attacking me?"

She fought to subdue a smile, lost. Forced her lips back into a tough pout, sipped the Coke. "I've had a lot of bad experiences."

"So it seems. Like what?"

Her condemnatory eyes; her features still as an open-casket corpse.

Jake, thrusting his hands back up: "Sorry. No more questions. If it makes you feel any better, I just got out of a wretched relationship with this centaur named Cassie. That thing dragged on for over three years. Mostly my fault. I should have cut her loose after two, after that time she came over and punched me in the stomach for not calling her when I was supposed to."

"She *what*? She punched you?"

"That was only the beginning."

Cam took a long slurp of Coke. "I can't believe that."

"Learning experience," he said, waving it away. "There was a reason I kept myself in that situation. I was addicted to her affection." His eyes wandered around the restaurant. "This is probably the worst thing I could be talking about on our first date, right?"

She stayed quiet, now gawking at the table.

"Sure you don't want to do this another time, Cam? When you're feeling better?"

She started shaking her head. Eyes narrowed. "Do you have any idea how inconsiderate you're being right now? Do you care?"

"Okay, who are you talking to right now, Camille? It's certainly not me."

More head shaking. "I knew it," she said under her breath. "Of course this would happen. Perfect." She began to look around at the surrounding tables with exaggerated gestures.

"What are you doing?"

"Trying to help you out, man. Trying to find that sagacious server of ours. I'm just sure she'll have more to

61

offer than me, and I just know how enthralled she'd be to give you a little more of that service."

He closed his eyes, whispered the Serenity Prayer. When he opened them back up, he pulled out his wallet and placed sixty dollars on the table. "I'm sorry, but I don't think I can do this tonight. Best of luck, Camille. I truly hope everything works out for you."

She sat stiff in her chair, glaring at him, but then not allowing herself to watch as he walked out of the restaurant. She looked down at the table instead. Sat there for some time, an old sculpture. It seemed every single muscle in her body was bursting with tension. She was so physically uncomfortable, in fact, she couldn't even consider what had just happened or that the waitress was now standing behind her, trying to figure out whether or not to say something.

"Food'll be ready in about five minutes. Still want it?" the waitress said, creeping up.

Camille looked at the money on the table and then the waitress and stood. She strode out. Nothing had happened in her mind. She was out on the evening streets now and hailing a cab and it was as if Jake had never existed. Lit up a Camel Light in the back seat of the Royal Taxi that picked her up and gazed at the seat in front of her with dopey, blank eyes. She could now start to sense a faint hint of the public disgrace that had just been, haunting the outskirts of recent memory. This notion of having all her secret sufferings uncovered by Jake, exposed to him, the mockery she was, the embarrassment of Meredith hearing about her weirdness -- it was overwhelming. She closed her eyes.

"Right here?" she heard her cabbie say.

Cam opened her eyes, glancing at her window, at

the old apartment building she lived in which looked like it was sleeping deep in the night's emergent darkness. She said nothing to the driver, paid, stepped out.

September 14, 1988

The cloudless fall sky and its omnipresent pillows of cold, gusting air so that Camille couldn't tell if life was more rejuvenating in this American, Midwestern corner of the world or if it was just the sublime nature of her childlike senses. The pale, jagged bricks of Braeside School, in front of her, like some majestic castle. Ecstatic screaming from children, untrammeled voices calling out into the still morning from every direction. In the near distance, along the periphery of her vision, images of web-like treetops – two hundred year-old Native American ghosts bivouacking in their midst – that seemed so distant beyond the school fences, a mystery from Eternity, ever-expanding before the incipient mind, always revealing itself.

Camille looked up and watched the rubber kickball as it sailed through the air, lost its motion, began to descend. Came into her firm embrace. A high-pitched sally erupted from third base -- "You're out, Weinberg! -- and broke the breathy tension that had surrounded the field. Her little body sprinting toward infield, little lungs and mouth giving out laughter, long, stringy, red hair flopping against her shoulders. Running toward Michael Parker who was sitting on a concrete partition between the field and pavement, kicking his gym shoes against it.

"Why aren't you playing?" she said, stopping beside him as though it were just a brief pause in a series of leaps, lips forming a sarcastic smile that tried to make sense of the unfamiliar excitement in her breast, hands gripping the ball.

"Kickball's boring," Michael said, gaping at his propelling shoes.

"You're so silly."

"Give us the ball!" a squeaky voice rang out. She

turned and threw the kickball at Aaron Reznik, a short, skinny, curly-haired kid standing center of the newly formed outfielders, glaring at her. Turned back to Michael, ran up to him and flicked his nose. She let out a slaphappy laugh and then sprinted the other way.

Michael rubbed his face and shook his head, smiled as he watched her move away.

Cam's best friend Ali -- dainty, vivacious, blue eyes, skin like a china-doll -- had been standing by the back edge of the field, watching them. "Why are you talking to Michael Parker again, Cammy?" Ali said, swatting Cam's arm when she approached. "He's *so* weird."

"Shut up," Camille said. "You're weird." She whipped her head back toward Michael in the distance. He was still playing with his shoes. He was little, radiant, purposeful, like that boy in *The Giving Tree* -- already aware of what was going to happen when he'd grow too old to play. She wanted to run back and hug him. She giggled, turned to watch Derek Segal now as he walked up to home plate, closed her eyes, took in a deep breath.

The howling around them had become a collective blessing to the earth for giving the gravity they needed to play kickball. They were all living, breathing, laughing, sneezing, coughing, smiling statements about people who had produced them and those that had produced their progenitors, so on. They were the moving accounts of previous circumstance, love and hate, coming together, preservation.

July 17, 2011

Camille thought she could hear Mom's voice, but was far too engrossed in Facebook to care. "So rude," she was messaging to Meredith. "He made me feel like I was under interrogation. Sorry it didn't go well -- I know he's your friend. Call me soon. Love you."

She didn't know what words had already been exchanged between Jake and Meredith. Despised herself for not having called Meredith as soon as the date was over -- pre-empting Jake's complaints about her with her own about him, fighting with all her mental skill to protect her reputation and preserve Mere's good opinion of her.

Ellen's voice fading in: "Cam, lunch!"

Camille stood up and shut down her mom's iMac, making her way along a narrow, wood-floored corridor and into the dining room.

Ellen Garner was sitting in a tall chair at a corner of her wide, mahogany table -- the same seat she sat at every time she ate there. Camille's brother Joseph sat to her left with his girlfriend Kelly. Two of the three chairs across from them taken by Camille's aunt Paula and her husband Gregory, who'd been in town from San Diego for the last three days. They were all surrounded by a winding fence of elevated windows that gave view to a northeastern corner of the city from 560 feet, the skyscrapers around them like dark, metallic kings brooding over how to deal with the populace, the smoky fog that sat just above North Avenue beach, to the left, like a portent from a Roman god. Every now and again a commercial airplane would float past on its descent into O'Hare as though coming by just to say hello. The dining area was abutted by an open living room with long, curvilinear lamps, potted plants, cushion-heavy furnishing, everything evenly spaced.

Ellen gave Camille a big smile that made her eyes crinkle. Joseph a quick glance before returning to his conversation. Kelly said "Hey, Cam!" in a way that made all those at table who'd met Camille's presence with seriousness question whether or not that seriousness was silly and trivial. The spirit of Kelly's joyous voice lingered around the room, in fact, turned up the air conditioning, decorated everything with early Christmas lights and reminded everyone they were once children without scorn and assertions.

Cam gave Kelly a quick, involuntary wave.

Hard to decipher Gregory, Paula's second husband -- hard decipher his intentions through his speech and hard to understand his facial expressions. When he looked at Camille, a smirk moved along his lips: a gesture quite out of character with his gray-browed face. His thoughts toward her could have been anything from condescending to sympathetic. Paula's bespectacled eyes flashed around the room, taking in all and sundry in a moment and then returning to their restful place center of the table.

"Grab a seat, hon," Ellen said, gesturing to an open chair beside her.

Cam began shuffling, head down, sat. Looked at her Mom. "Where's David?"

"Still at Idlewild," Ellen said, looking at everyone else. "Golfing with his high school buddies. Let me call." She picked up her iPhone, gazed at it, squinted, tapped. "No, everyone's here, David," she said after another minute, phone to ear. "Bye." Phone back down, she looked around at everyone again. "He's on his way."

Paula, turning to Camille: "What's shakin', baby

69

girl?"

Everyone quieted and looked at Camille. Ellen the only one pre-occupied with grabbing a large, ceramic bowl of pasta salad and placing it in front of Camille's empty plate.

"Just working," Camille said.

"Still at that one restaurant in Lincoln Park?" Paula said.

"Yeah," Camille said, picking a few noodles, putting them in her mouth, chewing, swallowing, giving a feeble smile. "It's good for right now. Still looking for something better."

"What's the name of that place?" Paula said.

Cam looked up without looking at anyone, back down at her food. "Tilli's."

"Tilli's," Paula said. "Tilli's." She looked at her husband, then Ellen. "That the little place over by Boston Blackies? Didn't you and I have drinks there a hundred years ago, Elle?"

Ellen nodded, smiled.

Paula, turning back to Camille. "Has it been open a long time?"

"I don't know," Camille said, almost inaudibly, staring at her food.

"I was there," Joseph said. He turned to his girlfriend. "Brian's engagement party."

Kelly nodded at him eagerly.

"I heard you and Kelly are planning a trip to Europe," Camille said, smiling at her brother now.

Joseph leaned back, nodded, patted his stomach.

"Thanks," Camille said. "A very detailed response. Seriously, are you going?"

Kelly gave Joseph a light, back-handed swat. She

looked at Camille. "We're going to start in Barcelona and see where we go from there."

"Ah, to be young and carefree," Gregory said, turning to Paula.

"How did this come about? Where you gonna' stay? What about work?" Camille said, still gazing at Joseph and Kelly.

"What's with the twenty questions?" Joseph said. He smirked, looked down at the table.

Cam went back to her food, cheeks now hot, rosy. *He's right. What the hell do I care? Not like we ever hang out. Not like I want to. That's rude. I take it back. He's my brother.*

"We're just gonna' go there, try to find jobs and see where it goes," Kelly said with a shrug. "It's supposed to be really easy for Americans to get jobs in bars or restaurants." She was glancing around the table, beaming. "We figure we could just buy a plane ticket and come back home if it doesn't work. We can always work for my dad."

Her youthful plea inspired an inharmonious chorus of approbation and personal anecdotes from the elders at table. When Camille looked back up, Kelly was smiling at her and Joseph transfixed by his iPhone. She could discern Joseph's insecurity on the whole matter. Looked back down at the food. To watch Joseph was to watch herself eight years ago, shake her head at that pitiable, bygone Camille with her little mind inextricably steeped the Hollywood fantasy about what life would become. She knew it was exciting for her brother *now*. Knew how little Joseph realized his future was lurking right there in the near distance, just waiting to teach him cruel lessons in practicality and adulthood. She ate, tried

71

to feel happy for the both of them.

Now she couldn't help but remember the moment she'd first stepped off the London Underground at Baron's Court. She was twenty-three. The cool, murky, raininess; the way it cloaked the lines of small shops. That peculiar, heavy smell of dank air, unlike any climate she'd experienced before. It was as if the weather in that part of the world had been sitting over the land for hundreds of millions of years and grown lazy, complacent, fat and groggy. Wasn't going to budge. Remembered the feel of the big, stuffy, military duffle bag slung over her right shoulder, filled up with all the possessions she'd wanted to keep, among which five hundred quid to her name and a temporary visa to work abroad she'd applied for, on a whim, while still in college. That mammoth bag of hers had been relentlessly determined to bring her skeletal body to the ground and it was her sheer will alone keeping her in forward motion: that shimmering need to put an ocean in front of all that which had been causing her so much pain:

The promising, entry-level career at BBDO that she'd left on the other side of the water, for one, the graduation present via nepotism from her older stepbrother's boarding school friend who'd been working at the company for years. That world of inceptive 401(k)s she'd left on the other side of the water, the recurrent cautioning about big life decisions from Mom and David in the privacy of leather-cushioned car rides. Dirty martini sipping at the same posh, downtown lounges every weekend, which, without fail, marked by an insufferable absence of conversation on account that the next twenty-five years had already been worked out for all of them by their companies and by the influence of their parents. The bi-weekly, direct-deposit-paycheck prescription she'd been using to numb up a suppressed ever-wailing of her honest feelings and thoughts.

Camille continued to chew, silently, her head down.

But her shame had then begun when the glow of the European jaunt had faded to dark, when she'd tired of living off fifty pounds a week and microwavable dinners as a front desk attendant at a youth hostel in Russell Square, when the international vagabond's loneliness, a strain particularly invasive and ubiquitous, had set into her heart -- myriad words from myriad, nameless travelers to her like screaming echoes from the living to the dead, words expressed with passion but unheard, unfelt -- and she'd had to return home. Home to Mom and David's sterile condo on the Gold Coast where the loud and quizzical voices of adolescence had long since ceased and in their stead, beneath a small arsenal of framed family photos, crept the thick silence of the inevitable future come present -- all the kids four steps closer to parenthood and the two parents further along in their shuffle toward death. She'd had no place living in that condo at the age of twenty-four, but there she was, sleeping on an air mattress in Mom's small office by night and trying her damnedest to avoid the awkward conversations with her parents by day.

"Have some chicken, honey," Ellen said, passing another ceramic plate.

"Really not that hungry, Mom."

"Are you sure?"

"I'm 31. I know when I'm hungry and when I'm not."

Ellen puffed her lower lip, looked away.

Just my anxiety, Mom. I don't mean it. I'm not trying to hurt you. Don't you get that?

Paula began talking about another trip to Italy she was going to take with Gregory, about Camille's little second cousins. They were getting so "big."

Now Camille started to muse about how much one had to engage the mind in her family. Thought about how different it was in other households she'd visited. *Some families just live in a sloth-like state*, she thought, remembering the small dining room tables of the American Bible-Belt homes she'd gone to with friends from Florida State during holiday breaks. Modest family structures where the television did all the talking. *Some families are just so concerned with one another's emotions*, she thought, now thinking about her buxom, Aussie friend Rebecca: her cheery co-worker at the hostel in Russell Square and fellow drugged-up clubber in the London witching hours. Remembering Rebecca's pastoral, wooden two-story home in the bosom of Newcastle, Australia. She'd stayed in touch with Rebecca through the occasional my-life-is-just-too-amazing-to-even-begin-to-describe e-mail and then actually decided to go visit one summer. "Good onya, Camille. We're so glad you came to Newy! You and Becks are great mates!" and "Sure you don't want any more lasagna? There's heaps here" and "Make sure to get yourself some brekkie, 'fore you go out, dear." Rebecca's parents would exclaim over a small dinner table, again and again and again, as though their pleasantries were a continuous stream of beach air coming in through the open window.

Camille stood up, excused herself.

She knew Ellen was giving her a subtle yet nettled gaze without even looking, but didn't care. Didn't want to keep fending off their conversation -- her head hurt. There was a mountainous void inside her about what had happened with Jake. She'd embarrassed herself. It was now apparent to others there was something *wrong* with her.

October 31, 1990

Camille and Joseph sat on tall stools against an elongated kitchen countertop. Camille wearing a long, ratty, black wig and gold glasses with peace signs printed on the lenses. She had on a long, red, tie-dye shirt and tight, blue bell-bottoms. Joseph's small face smeared with cream paint. His black hair slicked back so that his little widow's peak was the most prominent feature on his forehead. His eyes were painted midnight and lips blood red with three little drops of paint trickling down from the corner of his mouth. He wore a plastic set of teeth with fangs, kept grinning to show them off.

"What are you, sweetheart?" Martin said, pointing his camcorder at Camille. "Are you a hippie? Just coming from Woodstock? Pretty cool, man."

Camille threw up a peace sign.

"And you?" Martin said, turning to Joseph. "Are you Dracula? Out for blood?"

Joseph grinned, hissed. He took a corner of his black cape and tossed it in front of his face.

Martin pointed his camera at Ellen. "How about you, Mom? What are you?"

Ellen glanced at him as she strode to the staircase beyond the kitchen. She stopped for a moment, smirking. "Just a mom." Continued on her way.

Martin turned and pointed the camera at Joseph and Camille. "What are we doing today? What's happening here on October 31st, 1990 in Highland Park?"

"I'm going to Woodstock, man," Camille said. "I'm going to see Janis Joplin."

"No!" Joseph said. "We're going to the Halloween parade at Braeside."

Camille stared at her brother, rolled her eyes. "Why don't you be in character?"

"You're so stupid." Joseph said, shaking his head.

"Guys, guys," Martin said, still filming. "Who's coming over? Who are we going with?"

The doorbell gave out a pinging chime.

"Speak of the devil," Martin said. He turned and started heading for the front door with camera against his eye.

Joseph and Camille were bolting past him, now waiting at the door.

"Who could this be?" Martin said.

"Martin," Ellen said, standing at the top of the living room staircase. "Put the camera down."

When Martin opened the door, he was pointing his camera at a young couple and their two daughters. The man, with short brown hair, rectangular glasses and a handlebar mustache, smirked and stuck up his palm. "No pictures today. Please." He chuckled. The woman beside him -- a striking redhead with small, plump lips and piercing blue eyes -- tilted her head and smiled, blushed. "Hi, Martin," she said, waving. Their two girls, both of whom dressed like butterflies with gossamer wings protruding from their sides, ran ahead and began chasing each other around the living room. "Arabella!" the woman at the doorway said, watching her two girls, "Shannon! Get back here right now."

"That's okay," Martin said, turning, filming the girls. "What are you two today? Are you birds?"

The girls stopped, looked at each other, laughed. "No!" they said in unison as they stared at Martin. "Butterflies!"

"I wouldn't have guessed that," Martin said.

The girls looked at each other again, giggled.

"Martin," Ellen said. She was walking to the

doorway now. "Stop filming." She looked at the couple. "Come on in. Want something to drink?"

"We're fine," Ryan said, guiding his wife inside, shutting the door. "Big lunch."

Alice bent down to look at Camille and Joseph. "My-my. Look at your costumes. Let me guess: Dracula and …"

"I'm a hippie," Camille said. "Peace."

Alice giggled, stood up, smiled at Martin. "I can tell she's *your* daughter."

Martin, filming Alice: "Where's your costume, darling?"

"You know I'm too old for that, Martin."

Martin gave an incredulous sigh and put his camera down. "Never. Always a kid at heart, doll."

Ellen grasped her husband's arm. "Come in, come in," she said, waving to the guests.

The foursome made their way to the kitchen and the kids stayed behind. The three girls gathered by a long, white couch with black, frond embroidery at the far end of the living room. Joseph lingering by the staircase and fiddling with his cape.

"You look weird, Cammy," Arabella was saying. She giggled and jumped on the couch.

"Shut up," Camille said. "I'm cool."

"Don't say shut up," Shannon chimed.

"I can say whatever I want to say," Camille said.

"I'm telling," Shannon said. She ran off to the kitchen.

"What'd you do?" Joseph said, shambling up to the two girls, gazing at Camille.

"Nothing, Joseph," Camille said. "Go away."

"No," Arabella said. "You can stay."

Shannon came sprinting back to the couch. "Mommy said you have to be nice, Camille." She sat on the end of the couch and began to play with one of her wings.

***

The Braeside Halloween parade took place in front of the school. All the kids -- grades one through five -- were taking laps around a circular sidewalk to show off costumes. First graders walking with other first, second with second, so on. Camille and Arabella had now paired up with their fellow fifth graders, Joseph and Shannon their fellow second. Parents lingered on the outskirts, on a wide, grassy patch adjacent the school's front playground where they were filming the kids, mingling.

Mothers stood beside mothers, speaking loudly, hyperbolically, about how great this person, that, how terrible this restaurant, how transcendent that salon. Some moms hovered by their spouses in quiet poses of erotic vulnerability, looking around at other husbands they knew, didn't know, with furtive eyes, offering clandestine invitations into the plush and perfumed bedrooms of their homes during weekday business hours. Fathers teetered back and forth in semi-circles of other fathers -- all of whom old high school and/or college friends in many cases. They gazed at the ground, rubbed their paunchy stomachs, fired off cynical comments about the Bears' fate in the absence of Jim McMahon.

Camille had long since ignored Arabella and her other friends and was walking beside Michael Parker, who was dressed as Abraham Lincoln.

"I still don't understand why you wore that?" she was saying.

"He's important," Michael said, adjusting his top hat.

"How?"

"He ended slaves."

"What do you mean?"

"Nevermind."

"I want to know."

Marcus Levy, a less popular kid from their grade who was dressed like Freddy Kruger, turned and began walking backward so he could be in front of them. He brandished his plastic knife claw. "Mikey and Camille sitting in a tree," he began to sing, interrupting their conversation.

"You're retarded," Camille said. "Go away."

Marcus laughed and turned around.

"Can't wait for junior high," Camille said after a minute or two of quiet walking. "What do you mean slaves, Michael?"

They passed the front steps of the school -- long, concrete slabs adorned on both sides by siding with stone bricolage. The school's principal standing at the bottom step, smiling like a robotic animal at Chuckie Cheese. She waved her right hand at the students. When she saw Camille passing, she feigned a gasp of surprise and astonishment at Camille's costume. Camille, seeing this, rolled her eyes.

"Black people were slaves," Michael responded to Camille. "They're from Africa, but we brought them here and made them work. Lincoln made them free."

She let his voice coast into her ears. She wanted to hold him, absorb him, suck him into her. Wanted to run away with him, create a world together, have adventures like in a Disney movie. She stared at the school's backyard as they rounded a corner of the sidewalk.

"Come with me," she said, taking his hand.

"Where?"

She nodded at the backyard. "Over *there*."

"You're crazy," he said, letting go her hand. "You always want to get into trouble."

They began to pass that grassy patch where the parents congregated. Martin, Ellen, Ryan and Alice had now come up to the edge of the sidewalk. Martin held his camera, waved. Ryan held a similar camera, did the same.

When Camille and Michael looped past the front of the school again, Camille squeezed Michael's hand and tugged him out of line. She pulled him past a corner where the concrete walkways became a long, rectangular strip of blacktop. They could hear students behind them screaming, trying to incriminate them, but Camille knew they were moving too fast to be identified. At one point Michael's top hat almost fell from his head, as did Camille's long, black-haired wig. They were holding their heads as they jumped over a three foot concrete rail that separated the blacktop from the school's athletic field. Hit the ground and began rolling in the tall grass, pieces of their costumes falling off. Camille laughing, Michael gasping. When they finally stopped and lay sprawled out, Michael, defeated, tried to admonish Camille but found himself out of breath and incapable. His exhaustion made him giggle.

They remained silent awhile, looking up at that afternoon sky, now nearly sapphire with scattered, dissipated clouds -- still a bit nostalgic for its summer tones of pale blue and orange but preparing for the dismal hues of winter.

"Let's stay like this," she said. "They're gonna'

come looking."

"See why I never played kickball?"

She rolled over and propped up her head with one hand, staring at his Lincoln beard, his eyes. "No. Why?"

"'Cause it's cool to be quiet and just look around. Let's pretend we're two deer, you're the mama, I'm the daddy. Ooh, wait." He pointed up and to the right. "Look at that cloud. Looks like a flag."

She gazed at the faded, craggy, rectangular shape high above a small convenience store to the north. "Looks like it's waving at us," she said, laughing. She rolled over, got on top of him and began tickling his sides. Gave him a look of curiosity, excitement and disgust. She breathed quickly and deeply, as though expecting something.

Michael's eyes widened in terror.

She rolled off and shook her head.

They went into the type of silence where one forgets whether or not they're in the company of someone else, but the strange meditations were quickly broken by shuffling footsteps across the blacktop.

Camille slapped her open palm against Michael's chest and accidentally knocked down his Lincoln beard with the tip of her pinkie. "Shh."

"That hurt!" he said, glaring at her, shocked, lips parted.

"Shh!"

Kathryn Carver, the school's principal, and Melissa Goldman, the first grade teacher, were now standing atop the concrete rail and staring down at them like wrathful angels. Melissa shaking her head, tsk-tsking. Kathryn Carver's knuckles pressed to her hips.

"Get up and come with us right now, Buster

Brown, Lady Jane," Kathryn said. "You're both in very big trouble."

"We're sorry!" Michael said. "It was an accident. I wanted to . . . she . . ." His voice choked up.

"Sorry's not going to cut it, mister," Kathryn said. "You shouldn't have left the parade."

Melissa continued to shake her head, tsk-tsk.

"Let's go," Kathryn said. "Up." She motioned for them with her index finger.

Michael and Cam stood like machines, limbs commanding them as opposed to the reverse. Michael stared at the ground. Camille looked directly at the teachers with blank eyes. They were instructed to separate: Camille now walking beside Kathryn and Michael, Melissa.

"Where we going?" Michael blurted out.

"To find your parents," Kathryn said, not looking at him.

They stopped in front of a narrow door alongside the school -- a quaint, latticed affair with clear window panes and sharp, brown paint. Kathryn reached into the right pocket of her olive slacks and pulled out a set of keys, jiggling, picking out the right one. She opened the door and they filed into a vast, darkened gymnasium. Kathryn turned a switch and the gym became illumined with bright, white lights that buzzed steadily. The space polished, pristine with the exception of a few motley, timeworn Nerf balls and Hula Hoops sprawled out in a corner.

"Come on," Kathryn said, motioning them with her index finger. "Let's go."

They strode single-file across the gym and then into a dark hallway. Kathryn hit another switch and the hall brightened up with the same white lights as were in the gym, but these didn't buzz. A bland, gray carpet at the hall's center, carpet surrounded on both sides by little, red lockers. There were drawings scotch taped to the egg-white walls that reflected academic lessons for different grades: crayoned pictures of dinosaurs from the Triassic and Jurassic periods, pencil sketches of weather conditions from all four seasons. Michael began walking beside Melissa and Camille, Kathryn.

They came to the waiting area at the front of the school. A pair of vacant, cushioned benches sitting across from one another on both sides of the room. The flock of people parading around outside could now be seen through a set of glass doors that led to the school's front steps.

Kathryn took Camille and Michael's hands and guided them out the doors. She glanced at Melissa. "You can go back to your class now, Mrs. Goldman. Thank you."

A vast majority of students -- even most teachers -- within the vicinity of Michael, Camille and Kathryn, stopped to gawk at them. People were bumping into one another. The presence of Camille, Michael and Kathryn outside the parade -- what it symbolized in terms of scandal and discipline -- was now causing students to hiss and gasp and catcall. Teachers had to calm them, re-focus their attention on walking, displaying costumes. Camille put her head down and tried to brush her black wig in front of her face. She continued to stare at the ground until Kathryn said "Camille Carlyle ..." and gave her hand a jerk. When Cam looked up, she saw they were standing in front of Martin, Ellen, Alice, Ryan.

"Mr. and Mrs. Carlyle?" Katherine said, shifting

eyes back and forth between Martin and Ellen.

Neither said a word, but both seemed to say "Yes? What? What is it?" in their rattled stillness.

"I found these two lying down in the athletic field when they should have been at the parade. Unfortunately, we won't be able to have Camille at the parade this year. Please understand that this type of behavior is a liability for us. I'll leave her with you. I'll need to go find Michael's parents now."

"We're very sorry," Ellen said, nodding, closing her eyes as she did so. She took Camille's hand and pulled Camille beside her. Looked down at Camille and said: "You stand right here and be quiet." Then glared at Martin.

"Why don't you go take her home?" Martin said. "We'll figure out the ride situation."

"We can give you and Joseph a ride later," Alice chimed in, looking at Martin.

Ellen flashed her eyes at Alice.

"If you guys need, of course . . ." Alice said. She turned back to the parade.

Martin looked at Alice, back at his wife. "Why don't you just take her home? Joseph and I will come after the parade."

Ellen adjusted her purse and seized Camille's hand. They began striding off, toward Brownville Road. Camille turned behind her and searched through the cluster of parents for Michael, to no avail. The large bodies in front of her appeared like loitering strangers, bloated ants with covers of flesh who were hissing about aimlessly, sucking up space, getting in the way of her and Michael on purpose. She turned again when she felt another tug. This gesture forced Camille to focus on being alone with and in the reign of her mom -- being enslaved to the state of her mom's whim. She felt like she was stuck inside a tight and uncomfortable space. She'd been here before.

Ellen let go Camille's hand as they approached Ellen's royal-blue Ford Explorer, parked along the street curb. Ellen made her way around the front of the car and let Camille wait by the passenger door until she got in and unlocked. The jail-cell silence between them continued as they situated themselves within. Ellen turning the ignition and tugging the gear shift, backing up, moving forward, back, forward, back, forward, even though they were at least ten feet from another parked car. Ellen then took her left onto Lincolnwood.

"I was just trying--" Camille said after they'd been listening to the soft, mundane, whooshing sound of twenty-miles-an-hour-with-windows-up-on-Highland-Park-back-roads.

"No," Ellen said, cutting her off. She stuck a finger in the air. "Not one word. Nothing."

Cam stared at her seat. Wondered if her mother would ever forgive her. Wondered why Mom wouldn't just try to understand. Thought Mom hated her, plain and simple. She imagined there was some great force delivering her a bad fate, bad life. Made her more depressed.

Now passing three-story homes on Saint Johns Avenue, white and brown buildings cloaked by tall trees, small shrubs and divers Halloween garnishments. Camille noticed that the silence between her mother and her had thickened, like they were now existing in a giant vat of hot tar, Camille the vat's writhing occupant and Ellen the evil steward stirring the scorching liquid with a large, metal ladle.

"I'm really disappointed," Ellen said, shaking her head. "Really disappointed."

Camille remained quiet.

Ellen took a left onto Lake Cook. "Out of all those kids at Braeside, you're the only one who has to be sent home from the parade. Unbelievable." She suddenly smashed her palm against the top of the wheel. "Why can't anything in my fucking life go right? It's all my fault. Got yourself into another perfect situation, Ellen. Just fucking perfect. Perfect. Perfect!"

"Michael got kicked out of the parade, too," Camille mumbled. "Not just me."

"What?" Ellen said. "What did you say?"

They were coasting onto Rambler Lane. Plastic goblins sat at the ends of peoples' lawns, cardboard cut-outs posted to front doors, torn cobwebs shrouding shrubbery.

"I think we're just going to put you into a special school," Ellen said, nodding. "Yep." She pulled into their circular drive.

"Special school?" Camille said. "Mom, no!"

Ellen turned off the car and kept her hand on the door handle as she looked at her daughter. "Get out. Now."

Tears were falling along Camille's cheeks, her lips quivering. She opened the passenger door and began sprinting to the house.

"Camille!" Ellen said, stepping out, slamming her door, striding around the back of the car. "Slow down! Stop! Now!"

Camille stood at the front door with her back turned to Ellen, hunched over.

"Don't you dare run away from me," Ellen said, grabbing her daughter and spinning her round. "What's wrong with you? What the hell is wrong with you?"

Cam cried more loudly.

"Stop it!" Ellen said. "Stop, right now!"

Their voices continued to escalate until Camille let out a prolonged shriek. Her sound cut through the breezy quiescence of trembling leaves, faint rustling of grass around them. Provided the realization to all those within hearing that as pacific as Highland Park appeared, it could never inspire disregard for the chaos inside each individual human being.

"You've got to get a hold of yourself!" Ellen was saying, grabbing Cam's arms, screeching almost as loudly as her. Ellen reached into her purse and unearthed a set of keys while still holding one of Camille's arms.

When they stepped inside, Camille wiggled free and ran up the living room staircase to her room, slamming the door.

July 19, 2011

"Said *what*?" Camille said. She sat back against a reclining lawn chair she'd brought out from her bedroom closet, rubbed her thighs, cradled a plastic cup half-filled with flat Coke. Stared at Meredith, wide-eyed.

Meredith, lying on the couch: "Nothing. Chill." She slid her knees to her chest and wiggled her bare toes. "Just that he wanted me to talk to you and make sure you were okay."

"Okay? He was the one who stormed out of the restaurant, throwing money at me like I was a whore. I know he's your friend, Mere, but I'd think twice about spending any more time with the dude." She slurped the Coke. "Coo-coo. Coo-coo."

Meredith continued to watch her toes. "I know him, Cam -- he's sweet. Maybe a little too girly, but a definite sweetie-pie. Super smart, like you. What happened?" She whipped her eyes at her friend. "Tell Doctor Meredith."

"We went to dinner at Wilde in Lakeview. His idea."

"Never heard of it."

"Just this fratty gastropub -- blond-haired college bitches talking about bullshit, burgers, beer, a hundred big-screen TVs. You know the scene."

"Wouldn't it have been weird if he took you somewhere like Blackbird?"

"You're right. It was cool. He got us a table right by a bookshelf, because he knew how much I loved to read."

"See?"

"Hold on. First of all, he started trying to pick up the waitress right in front of me."

"He *what*?"

"Yah. This mousy, little blond chick who was about ten." She mimicked the waitress, giving out a high, ditzy laugh: "'You're so funny, Jake. Where do you hang out?' And on, and on, like I wasn't even there."

"No way. I don't believe you."

"Believe it, it's true, but it gets better. He starts belaboring me with questions, like I'm now the centerpiece of a McCarthy trial: Where are you from? Where did you go to school? What about this? What about that? I don't even know this guy. Then he becomes my psychoanalyst. What do you think the source of your anger is, Camille? Blah-blah-blah. Starts going on about how bad his relationship with his ex-girlfriend was."

"Cassie. Psychopath."

"Whatever. Great way to start a first date. He was just so fucking audacious." She stared at her window, nodded. Her small mouth tightened and lips pursed. Pellucid-blue eyes two shimmering beacons for the Apocalypse. Her entire face battled to preserve a force concealed in her throat. She opened her mouth and began to titter, then looked down at the wood floor in silence. Sniveled, started to cry.

Meredith pushed herself up, knelt down in front of her friend, put her hands on Cam's arms. "What happened? Talk to me. I know Jake. He means well. He didn't want to hurt you."

Camille had now completely covered her face. Her narrow shoulders shook as she cried. Mere held her. In the chilled quiet of that embrace, the faint popping of drips could be heard from a kitchen sink, the steady thrumming from a vent. Intermittent processions of cars coasted back and forth beyond and below the half-open window.

Camille snuffled, wiped her face. "You're right. I can't keep lying to myself. I've become so good at vilifying people. He *is* sweet, sensitive, interesting and he loves literature and I like him a lot. There. I like him a lot. Fucking terrifies me." She looked up at her ceiling. "I was so nervous, Mere. Couldn't even look at him. I was such a bitch. He was just trying to get to know me." She stared at her friend, eyes motionless. "Scares me so much to open myself up to someone like this. I can't. I can't. I can't."

"Okay, relax, calm down. Let me call him. I'll explain. You two can try again."

"He probably doesn't want to talk to me," Camille said, shaking her head, staring at the window.

"He's a dude. Dudes are stupid."

Camille giggled.

"You can talk them into just about anything. Trust me. Especially Jake."

They were interrupted by a loud beep from the phone lying on Camille's old coffee table. They stared at each other. Camille leaned over, grabbed it. "Oh my god," she said after reading the incoming text, thrice. She showed Mere the phone:

It's Jake. A deep apology would do nothing to take away the impact of my wretched behavior. I know. No platitudes. Just want to let you know it really was wonderful meeting you. You seem like such a special person. Hope I get the chance to try again. Have a beautiful day.

"That doesn't even sound like him," Mere said, staring at the phone. "What does *platitudes* mean?"

"Something trivial." Camille hadn't moved, even when Mere tried to offer the phone back. "What should I say?"

Mere put the phone down. "You can't respond for at least two days."

"I don't know, he put a lot of thought into that."

Meredith shook her head. She wandered back to the couch, fell onto it. "Jake's a gem. I'm talking about a much bigger, feminist principle here. If you get back to a dude right away, in the beginning, he'll think your feelings are intense. Think he has the upper-hand. You want Jake to be on his best behavior, don't you? Enough men already get away with doing whatever the fuck they want. Wait two days."

"You fascinate me," Camille said, cackling. She reached for a pack of Camel Lights, took one out, fired it. Made a childlike face of disbelief as she sucked the Camel from a corner of her mouth.

"Serious," Mere said. "Two days -- then text him back. Do it for all women."

"What should I say?"

Mere rolled over and gazed out the window. "Something real short, like, 'Don't worry about it.' or 'We'll see what happens.'"

"That's something I *would* say, but really wouldn't want to say. You know what I'm saying?" Camille said, stubbing her cigarette in a ceramic ash tray. She blew smoke at Meredith and laughed. Stood up, walked to the kitchenette. "I'll figure it out. Let's not talk about it anymore." She plucked open the fridge and reached for a three-day-old box of cheese pizza, put two slices on a baking sheet. Set the oven and lingered by it a moment, closing her eyes -- the echo of Jake's written voice, the indelible tingle, it starts in the chest. *There's still a chance...* She drifted to the doorway and gazed at her friend. "Whatever happened to that one cute dude you met at MOCA? What's his name?"

"Douche bag."

"What? Why? Thought you said..."

Mere was gazing at her knees. Her face had gone from languid and silly to something dour, inert. "He never called me back."

"What do you mean?"

"I called him yesterday," Mere said. "Left a message. Told him I liked him -- that I was happy we were hanging out..."

"You never say that."

"He hasn't called back."

"Maybe he's just busy. Maybe out of town."

Mere hadn't moved. "We talked on the phone for hours. I fucked him. Twice."

Camille put her food in the oven and stared at the stove. She felt a profound sense of being shunned by people in Chicago -- being seen as worthless and insignificant when not too long ago she'd fancied herself a legend, object of veneration to all. She knew it was the same for Mere, and she could sense it was the same for so many others. What came out of her mouth wasn't quite a laugh, nor a sigh. She came back to the living room and curled up next to her friend. "Let's do something fun today. Forget about men and just have *fun.* Pretend we're sixteen."

Mere became animated, as if her all-consuming sadness was but a grunt one would utter out of discomfort or mild sneeze quickly forgotten. "Day-drinking!" she said. "Beach!"

***

They took the 151 bus toward North Avenue. Mere had borrowed Cam's purple, two-piece bathing suit. Both wearing summer dresses over their suits as they sat at the back of the bus, chatting loudly. Camille had a large, hemp beach bag on her lap, filled with lotion, towels, copy of *People* and *Love in the Time of Cholera*, her weed, bowl, cigarettes, headphones, the little things Mere didn't want to carry, their phones, retro sunglasses . . .

Bus was packed. At least four different languages being spoken, casually, softly, from different sections. People staring out the windows at old mid-rises and grassy fields that were passing. Staring at their cell phones and smiling or frowning or feigning looks of fierce concentration before punching on phone keypads. People with earphones jammed in their ears gazed at nothing, their minds enraptured by some private ether. People talked to their young children, or just listened as the children tried to sound out sentences that helped them make sense of their formative lives.

"Bet Jake has a big dick," Camille was saying.

"He does."

Camille gasped, became silent.

"Kidding," Meredith said, giving her friend a love-tap. "I don't know. I told you: we only kissed, once. We were drunk. You really like him, don't you?"

"I do," Camille said, staring at her purple sandals.

"We're not talking about this, remember? Let's get beer."

They stood and made their way to the bus exit as the bus pulled up just beyond the Lincoln Park Zoo. Mere dancing her way through the crush. Camille tiptoed behind, waiting for people to see her and move, then giving small shoves when they didn't notice she was waiting.

"Where we going to get beer over here?" Camille said. Her voice trailed off and got lost in a cacophony of growling cars, scattered voices, striding footsteps outside the bus. "I said where can we get beer over here, Mere?" she said as she scurried beside her friend.

"I know a place," Meredith said, moving north on Inner Lake Shore, her dusky hair whisking back and forth with random gusts of wind.

Cam became quiet. She now felt unhinged, going places she normally wouldn't, being around these nettlesome crowds of mindless young people, wasting her time. She was pissed off she'd been following Mere around. Then she got pissed off she was pissed off. *Live life all chained up.* "I think it's time to reconsider some of your friendships," she suddenly remembered Mom saying to her once, a long time ago. She was fifteen and sitting in the kitchen of their Riverwoods home. Sitting at a long, wood, dining room table in an uncomfortable silence as Mom stood in front of her, cooking, admonishing…

"You okay?" Mere was saying.

"What?" Camille looked around and noticed they were now on the beach boardwalk. Coming upon a giant, two-tiered building in the form of a cartoon boat. From all directions, the building's fulgent red, white and blue paints were splotched out over the architectural lines meant to confine them. A series of ship windows and little poles like stays freckled the bottom level where wet, sandy, half-naked people of all shape, size, age, nationality were coming back and forth to take advantage of the only two bathrooms for a mile or so. The second tier, the ship's deck, encased by blue rail, was an outdoor restaurant brimming with plastic tables and chairs, almost all of which full. Two mock smokestacks shot upward from the center of the space, a thin, high-reaching mast with a wavering American flag.

"Never been here before," Camille said. She adjusted her bag, took in the pungent odor of wet sun-tan lotion.

Meredith was already moving toward the building, walking like a Navy Seal with the curves of her muscular arms accentuated in a play of sun and shadow.

Camille hurrying behind, catching up, trying to take on Mere's gait.

They walked up a winding stairway of concrete steps dusted with sand. The lines of round, plastic tables and chairs around them being inhabited by white city-dwellers, originally from the suburbs, clad in checkered board shorts and low-cut bathing suits and Prada sunglasses, flirting with half-empty cups of Bloody Mary or vodka soda, forever unable to shake off the Midwestern culture of neurosis, allegiance to mediocrity and self-censure, notwithstanding the continuing plea of a burning sun to just relax and blend into nature. "Crazy" by Gnarls Barkley was jamming from speakers that couldn't be seen.

Mere continued to move past tables in an elated daze and Cam observed the way young men would look at her, leer at her. Camille assumed they were looking at her the same way, but deep down feared maybe they weren't. Deep down worried Mere was the attractive one, not her.

There were three shirtless men sitting at a table by a far corner, drinking Miller Lite, laughing as they stared at the lake. They were surrounded by open chairs. All watched Meredith as she came toward them with Camille trailing behind and all became silent.

"Can we sit with you?" Meredith said, standing in front of them.

Camille tried to smack Mere's arm, get her to stop, but too late:

"Course you can," said the guy center of the table. He motioned to the open chairs. "You ladies ready for a drink?"

"Yes!" Meredith said, sitting.

Camille beside her.

"Mark," the guy at the center said, sticking out his hand.

Mere gave a limp handshake.

Mark nodded to his right. "Kurt." Left. "Michael."

Camille stared at Michael with a bemused gaze. She studied his chopped, messy, brown hair, dark brows, chocolate eyes. Took in his scent of sweat and banana muffin. Imagined this is what her Michael might have become if... Still staring at him.

"What's your name?" Michael said, smirking at Camille.

"I'm Camille." She took his hand.

"Now that we're all friends..." Mark said, standing. "What are we drinking, ladies?"

"Bacardi and Coke," Meredith said. She looked at her friend. "Two Bacardi and Coke."

Mark disappeared and the four remaining played an awkward game of eye tennis. Mere looked at the lake, closed her eyes, smiled.

Camille, no longer fixated upon Michael, fumbled to keep a consistent facial expression as her eyes darted between the two guys and Meredith. She smiled; she took on a stern gaze; she kept her lips slightly pursed in a pose of cool detachment.

"Where you guys from?" Kurt said, finally. He was leaning back in his chair with bare, dirty feet propped up along a side of the table. His oily-blond hair glistened in the sun. Seemed like a West Coaster who'd ended up in the Midwest by accident, but was too easygoing to concern himself with getting back.

"Here," Camille responded.

"The beach? Shit -- where you been all my life?"

Both guys laughed and Mere chuckled.

Camille glanced at the table. Her cheeks flushed. *Stop! Leave me alone. All of you.* She thought about getting up and running away, fleeing to the shelter of her little apartment where she could lock herself in, turn off her phone, nestle up with the nutritive silence that was sensitive to her most intimate emotions.

"Relax," Kurt continued, leaning across the table and rubbing Camille's shoulder. "I'm teasing. I grew up in Schaumburg."

"Please don't touch me," Camille said.

All went back into silence. Michael scrunched his brows at Camille. Mere was still looking at the lake. Kurt chuckled.

"The fuck's your problem?" Kurt said to Camille.

"*What*?" Camille said.

Kurt leaned toward her. "I said what the fuck is your problem? Why are you being such an uptight bitch?"

Michael trying to pat Kurt's arm, get him to stop.

Camille grinned. She looked at Meredith and stood up. "That's it, Mere. I'm leaving. These guys are a bunch of fucking losers."

"What was that?" Kurt said, standing.

"Sit down," Michael said, grabbing Kurt's arm. "Just let them go."

Neither Cam nor Kurt said anything. Both continued to glare.

"Pssh," Kurt said, waving his hand at her, looking away, sitting back down.

"No -- what?" Camille said. "What do you have to say? Say it!" She was about to walk around the table, yank his hair, punch him in the face.

"Come on, bitch," Meredith said, standing with Cam's beach bag, grabbing her.

"No!" Camille said, but was cut off when her friend spun her round and they began striding off.

Guys behind them shouting something that faded away beneath the music as Mere and Cam moved toward the restaurant's staircase. "Fucking asshole," Camille muttering.

"We gotta' talk," Meredith said when they'd gotten back out onto the boardwalk. "What's the deal? First Jake, now this guy... out of nowhere..."

"He was a callous prick! You heard what he said..."

"Calm down." Mere put her hands on her friend's shoulders. "Just talk to me."

Cam scowled at the concrete. Took sharp breaths. Her breathing began to ease and she started shaking her head. "I'm so embarrassed. I'm sorry." She sniveled and stopped tears.

They began walking on the sand, Cam still sniffling, wiping her face and trying to smile.

People around them sprawled out on towels or sitting in folding chairs. So many people at the beach that

Cam and Mere had to tiptoe and look down as they moved so as not to step on anyone. Some people listening to music on the little iPod set-ups they'd brought. Some reading books. Some just laying and letting the sun make love to their skin. Some cuddled with lovers. The sound of swishing water in the near distance commingled with cries of excitement and hearty laughter.

They found a spot close to the water -- close enough to get their feet wet if the wind were to pick up and hit the lake hard enough. After they'd flung off their dresses, Mere plopped down on the sand and Camille bent over to dig through her bag for towels.

"Ready to talk to me?" Mere said, looking at the water.

Camille now hung over her friend, dangling a cream beach towel that she'd snatched from her mom's condo. "Get up, Mere." She laid the towel down and then began to brush her friend's legs when Mere stood.

Mere staring at the water like nothing was happening to her. Camille had to tell her to sit before she was able to snap out of her gazing and lay.

"We need to put some lotion on," Camille said.

"Stop avoiding the issue. Tell me what's going on with you."

Camille, now supine, shut her eyes from behind her tinted sunglasses. The anger she'd felt toward Kurt for being so rude, Jake for being so invasive, the world for not giving her what she felt she needed had now become a discomfort in her chest that was identifiable, manageable, abating. She felt soothing calm come over her body -- as though her veins flowed with summer breeze as opposed to rushing blood. Rather than racing with thoughts, her mind turned its attention to her warm breath and her expanding, contracting chest. "I'm just a weird person, Mere. People don't want to know me. They're programmed to judge me and tear me down. I'm not going to let them." She rolled her head toward her friend but kept her eyes closed.

"Nobody's judging you. You convince yourself people are a certain way instead of giving yourself the chance to get to know them. That's why you get all riled up. People are varied."

"I know that, theoretically, but we're dealing with issues of subconscious. I don't think about why I do what I do when it's happening. I'm just being me."

"That's extreme. You're making yourself a victim without any... Without any real basis. Part of being human is the ability to check yourself before you do things that could be harmful. Animals just react. That's all they can do. That's why they live and die without rhyme or reason."

Cam rolled supine again, surrendering herself to the sun's hot, omnipresent, benevolent force. "Humans aren't in control of their fate ultimately, Mere. Our ability to think is not that powerful. We're born and we die without rhyme or reason just like animals. But I get what you're saying. I know. All I can do is move forward and hope tomorrow is better."

"Hope?"

Cam chuckled. "You're right. 'Work' on being wiser tomorrow than I was today."

"Start with Jake."

"I'm going to text him back." She grinned. "In two days."

"Good. I think you're going to be happy. I have a good feeling about you two."

They sank into docile quiet amidst the white noise of waves, gleeful shrieks, distant music, buzzing from aerial advertising planes. Words exchanged now just two corporal reminders of energy once expended, energy spawned from a community of meanings that were already forgotten. Mere fell into an abysmal sleep. Cam rolled over and reached for her dog-eared book.

April 18, 1991

Martin tore down Rambler Lane in his black Mercury Cougar convertible. Swung a left into the roundabout driveway of his green and white two-story on the outskirts of Ravinia. He turned off the car and grabbed his attaché from the passenger seat, hopping out, slamming the door behind him without looking at what he was doing. Strode to the small walkway at the front of the house. When he opened the front door and shuffled in, Camille came running at him.

She fake-punched him in the gut and said: "Boom!"

"Ohhh," Martin said, hunching forward and rubbing his stomach. "K.O." He stood back up, brushed her chin, said: "How are ya', kiddo?"

That same moment, Ellen stepped out of the kitchen and into the living room. Her long, brown hair frizzled and eyes puffy. She gave Martin a ireful stare.

Martin continued to look at his daughter. "How was school, kiddo?"

Camille shrugged.

"You don't know?" Martin said, tickling her. "*You don't know*?"

She let out a giddy laugh and began running to the kitchen.

"Slow down," Ellen said. "Slow down!" She grabbed Camille by the arm, stopping her. Cam's excited panting and noises ceased. "Go to your room," Ellen said. "Now."

Cam turned with head down and raced up a set of carpeted stairs, across a landing, into her bedroom, shutting herself in. She sat crossed-legged with her ear to the door, trying to listen to her parents down below.

"The fuck is it now, Ellen?" Martin said as he

brushed past her and into the kitchen. He tossed his bag onto one of the couches in the adjoining den. Walked past Ellen again, without looking at her, and plucked opened the fridge. Grabbed a Stella, then leaned back against a kitchen counter corner, one palm pressed to the countertop. Stared at his wife.

"What's going on between you and Alice," she said. "Tell me, now."

"You've got to be kidding me."

"I smelt her perfume on you last night. Stop lying to me!"

The sound of Ellen's muffled voice could be heard by Camille through her closed door. She knew Mom and Dad were upset. Knew it wasn't good. She began to breathe heavily. *Just stop,* she thought. *Stop.*

Martin, staring at the floor, swigging his beer. "Why didn't you say anything when I'd gotten home?"

"How long, Martin? How long? You think I'm stupid? Course you do."

"You don't understand, Elle. Let me explain…"

"Don't lie to me!"

Martin shook his head, began to glower. "You're completely psychotic, aren't you?" His voice lingering on the verge of a grainy scream. "This is un-fucking-believable. What a mistake." He sat down on one of the couches in the den and kept sipping his beer. "All you do all day is lah-di-dah around the house and around town in your brand new SUV, like all the other pretentious succubi in this God-forsaken excuse for a town. All the time in the world to bandy about bullshit with your phony friends, isn't there? Get these elaborate notions I'm cheating into your head, huh?" He picked up a small, boxy remote lying beside him and clicked on the TV, then flashed his eyes at his wife. Theme song from *The Wonder Years* could now be heard. "I *was* with Alice last night. Because Ryan hit her again and just left and she needed someone to talk to, okay? She's too ashamed to tell anyone. I suppose something like that couldn't possibly occur to you, though. Because you can't be victimized in a scenario like that. Can't blame everything and everyone else for your own petty fucking problems. Get one thing straight: I don't ever have to tell you where I go or what I do or why I do it." He sneered. Eyes drifted back to the television and he gazed at it as though nothing had been said at all.

"What the hell kind of husband are you?" She stormed over to him, planting herself in front of the TV. "I won't take any of this from you anymore! Everything about you makes me miserable!" She clasped the remote and threw it against the wall. "Who the fuck do you think you are, treating me like this?" she was screaming as the remote made its final, cracking thud.

He stood up. "Calm down. You're acting crazy! Nothing ever happened between me and Alice. Nothing. She's a nice person in a bad situation. That's it. C'mon now, calm down. Camille's upstairs. Joseph'll be home--"

"Don't even pretend like you give a shit about anyone but yourself, Martin," she said, glaring at him, the eyes brown sorbets of glass, "or ever did."

"Elle," he said. He put his arms on her shoulders, but she shoved them off. "Relax."

"I won't relax and I won't do this anymore. You're a terrible husband and a terrible father. I want a divorce."

Her noise had been so loud and consistent that Camille, upstairs, creaked open her door and tiptoed out.

She tottered her way down the staircase and began to cry as she moved. Ellen heard her in the near distance and began striding in that direction.

Camille recoiled when she saw Mom appear from around the corner.

"What did I tell you?" Ellen said.

Martin paced over and picked up his daughter, now in hysterics. They journeyed up to Camille's room, shutting the door behind them.

"Shh," Martin was saying as he put her down on her train bed and began to stroke her damp cheek. "Mom's just a little upset, sweetheart. Remember when you get upset? Everyone has bad days…"

She nodded, sniveled.

He dropped to his knees and tickled her flanks. "Come on now," he said, letting out an excited gasp. "Isn't it Thursday night tonight? Isn't *Beverly Hills, 90210* on tonight? You love *Beverly Hills, 90210*."

She looked at her legs, nodded.

"Don't be so glum, chum. This is… nothing. People get mad sometimes. We can't always be happy. It's okay. Everything comes back to the way it was."

Cam, still staring at her legs, began to give out scissor kicks.

"Ace," Martin said, touching her chin, lifting her head. "Listen." His eyes flipped left and right. "There are a lot of weak people in this world. Only a few strong ones, and the strong have to lead the weak. You're one of those leaders, kid. *You*. I know. I see it in you. You're from me. You're going to be just fine. Doesn't even matter if I'm here or not."

Cam's eyes widened. "Where ya' going, Dad?"

"Nowhere," he said. "Nowhere. Just relax, baby.

109

Just trying tell you how special you are, and that you should know it. That you're your own, strong person and you don't have to worry about Mom or me. I'm going to go out for a little while. I want you to be a big girl now. Can you be a big girl for me?" He continued to stare at her and tapped the corner of his left eye.

She tapped her left eye, too.

"That's my girl," he said, standing, grinning.

When he turned and began to walk to the door, she jumped up and ran after him. Squeezed his waist and pressed the side of her face to his stomach. That familiar and fortifying coziness of his big body. The sharp, clean scent of his cotton shirts that reminded her of home. "Take me with you, Dad. Please! I don't want to stay. Take me, take me, take me."

"Camille," he said. "Stop." He put his hand on her shoulder and edged her off, gently. "Go back to your bed."

She flung back to him and clung to his waist. "No, Dad! Please take me with you. No, Dad. Don't go. Please take me with you. Please."

He looked up at the ceiling. "Goddamnit." Bent down, uprooting Cam's grip, touched her arms, stared at her. "I'll stay just a little while longer, but then you're gonna' be a good girl, right? You're gonna' let me go?" He pointed his index finger.

She nodded, tight-lipped, anxious.

They made their way back toward the bed.

July 24, 2011

Camille gazed at the yellow notepad on her wood dining table. Her eyes pulsed. She leaned forward, half-used pencil in hand, continued to write:

The present is sick
Swollen
Sullen
She's bedridden
Bedposts affixed to
the bounds of perception
She's coughing up bygone bile

She was halted by the ring tone on her phone: Mazzy Star chanting "Fade Into You." She looked at the caller ID: "Martin." Grabbed the phone, stood up, pressed talk and began to meander around her apartment.

"Dad," she said, phone to ear.

"Been awhile."

"How are you?" She stood by her half-open window, looking down at east and westbound cars, stopped and honking, backed up from nearby intersections. Beachgoers, clad in sundresses and cargo shorts, as they strolled along the sidewalks toting their distended backpacks and carrying folding chairs in route to the lake. That Korean-run dry cleaners at the bottom of the red-brick mid-rise across the street, now closed, darkened, looking vacuous amidst the life flourishing around it.

"Good, kid, good," Martin said. He took a slurp of coffee. "Ocean's angry today."

"Don't make me jealous."

"My home's your home. You know that. You're always welcome. Why don't you come down here?"

Her eyes dropped. "Gotta' to save money."

"Still doing that restaurant gig?"

She began to pace, gave a baleful laugh. "Yeah. It's good for now…"

"How many more years you going to do that, kid? What about grad school?"

"Fuck that," she said, shaking her head. "I make my own way, Dad. Still not ready to cash in the last of my ideals for another diploma, nine-to-five, commuter trains and a house in the 'burbs." Her voice soared off into a magnetic silence that sent the words right back to her so that she had to abide her own pretensions. She sighed, her shoulders heaved. "You're really starting to piss me off. Why are you giving me the third-degree?"

"Easy, kid. Just curious. I don't see you that much. All I get are these slivers of your life. Want to catch up is all."

She stopped. Her teeth clenched. "What's going on with you?"

"Me…? Well, just finished shooting *Melee*. My other film picked up two awards for best actor and actress at the Jacksonville Film Festival. That's pretty good."

"Wow."

No noise from the other end.

"Dad? Hello?"

"I'm here."

"Why do you get so quiet? You get really quiet."

"Just thinking."

Fucking talk, she thought, sitting on her couch. She reached for a cigarette atop her coffee table, put it in her mouth, lit up. "What are you reading these days?"

"Just finished *Wild Fire* by Nelson DeMille. What a waste of paper. He used to be so fucking good and now he's just doing the same thing over and over. Haven't picked anything up since that one."

"Hate to break it to you, but writers like DeMille always were and will be doing the same thing."

"Not sure I follow you, kiddo."

She rolled her eyes, puffed. "We're talking about *New York Times* best-selling authors -- entertainment whores, monkeys for the mass market. They write in formulas, same thing over and over. I don't know why you spend your time reading that garbage."

"I don't know, kid, I thought *The General's Daughter* was pretty fucking good." He chuckled. "You're becoming more interesting." His voice got muffled as he put his hand over the phone and yelled at his girlfriend. "It's in the Bedlam Productions folder!" Camille could hear him saying. "Go look for it!" His full voice came back: "Sorry about that. Dating anyone now?"

"*Dating*? What do you mean? Am I hanging out with people? Sure. Is there someone I'm seeing consistently? No." She stubbed her cigarette, wondering why she'd said that. She leaned forward, crossed her legs. "It's frustrating." Her eyes began to wander to a far corner of the apartment where they dwelled but absorbed no detail. "There is this one guy. Jake…" Her eyes flew back to the floor. "It's new. Probably nothing. Look, I don't have time to dillydally through the day like some love-hungry middle-schooler just because a cute guy shows me attention. Fuck dating. More important things to worry about in life."

Another silence came to pass. This silence seemed to Camille as though it was populated by transparent agents for some empyrean bureau of honesty: ministers who were taking apart her syntax for her father like it was a flimsy ribbon, laying bare her basic emotions, her fear of admitting she was lonely. She hated her father for letting her be so exposed by his being so wordless. "Dad," she said. "*Why* do you keep getting quiet?"

"Just taking it in."

She lay supine on the couch, bending her knees, wiggling her azure-polished toes. Clicked the phone onto speaker and put it on her chest. "I have a lot of things to do. Can we talk next week?"

"Sure, kid, sure. Miss you…"

"Bye."

December 1, 1991

Camille had hardly slept. She'd tossed and turned and sweated in the dank humidity of Martin's spare bedroom, in the darkness. Lost here in North Miami. Her mind couldn't comprehend such a great distance from Chicago. *Chicago*. That name, that entire land now just a dissolving idea about suburban life from where she was lying. Her former territorial claim that still had attached to it a vacillating collage of past experiences, all of which she'd gladly turn her back on for these tropical new beginnings, to be with her father. Her 9am flight told her differently, her mother who'd governed all traveling arrangements. *Chicago*, the wasteland, necropolis, prison commanding her back into its elaborate cavern.

She understood a little about Mom and Dad's separation, when she thought hard, but just preferred to ignore it.

"I can do it myself; I wanna' do it myself," she remembered saying to Mom over a week ago now. She'd been kneeling down by her burgundy suitcase with a limp, folded t-shirt in her hands, looking up at Ellen.

"It's always good to pack as a team, Cam," Ellen said back to her.

Ellen walking to a series of wood cabinets in the bedroom Camille and Joseph were now sharing. She'd opened up a drawer and pulled out three pairs of ankle socks. Turned, looked at her daughter. "Did you remember socks?"

Camille finessed her stray t-shirt into the bulgy layer cake of packed clothes. "It's Florida, Mom. I just need sandals."

"What if it rains?"

She put her hands on both sides of the luggage. "You're so annoying. Go away."

Ellen, kneeling beside her, maneuvering the socks into the case. She glanced at Camille. "When you're an adult and you have your own house, you can do what you want. But this is my house and while you're living in my house, you'll follow my rules. Okay? Now, did you pack anything for the plane?"

"This isn't a house," Camille muttered. "It's an apartment."

At that same moment, Joseph shambled into the room, his ears covered up with bulky headphones from the charcoal Walkman in his left hand. Cam and Ellen watched him, in silence, with the same facial expression, as he made his way to the bottom bed of the bunk set-up he shared with his sister, plopped down, fully clothed, and rested his head on his palms. "You don't need socks. It's hot. No rain," he mumbled. His eyes were closed and he hadn't moved from his recumbent position. The muffled, musical buzz from his headphones trailing just below his high, slow voice.

Camille walked to her drawers and continued to survey clothes.

"What's Dad's neighborhood like?" Ellen said to her son.

"Fine," Joseph said. He rolled toward the wall.

Ellen's eyes sank. She put her hands on her haunches and hoisted herself upward.

"Can you just leave us alone, Mom?" Camille said, tossing a handful of hair bands into her luggage. "Please."

Ellen contracted her lips, looked at the floor, made her egress.

Camille reaching into a cupboard and pulling out a crumpled backpack. "She's so fucking annoying."

"No she's not," Joseph said, still looking at the wall. "Dad's the one who left."

Camille zipped up the suitcase. "Can you turn off your headphones? It's really irritating me. And Dad left because Mom pushed him away. Doesn't matter. We're gonna' move to Florida. He's only gone for a little while."

That had already been a week and a half ago now...

Camille sat up, now in Dad's guest bed, walked to a sliding window, twisted open the blinds and squinted as she looked down at the rippling Atlantic, which was being highlighted by the newborn, salmon sun. There was someone swimming by the shore: an elderly man with a round figure.

Why is he swimming, now, alone?

Again she felt that eerie feeling she'd picked up on this past week in the neighborhood Dad had moved into. This feeling which came from the way in which people of all ages, shapes, sizes sauntered around the sandy streets without looking at each other, as though they weren't going anywhere. Came from the way the ocean continued to hiss and hypnotize people into believing they had no past.

She turned and looked at her suitcase, all packed again and sitting center of the floor. She strode over to it, ripped open the zipper and grabbed clothes, throwing them in the air. *Nirvana* and *Jimi Hendrix* t-shirts began to dangle from the edge of the bed and form a messy pile below; little black and blue Gap jeans surrounded the closed door. She pulled open all the stuffed pockets of her backpack, which was sitting on a swivel chair by a desk. She threw her blue Walkman and it crashed into the wall

119

with a clunking thud.

Martin, who'd been passed out on his water bed across the hall, awoke. He waggled his way off, batting his eyes. Shimmied into a pair of faded Levis, snapped shut his Western belt and adorned his stout torso with a wrinkled button-down. He opened his door, then Camille's. "What are you doing?" he said, striding toward her, grabbing her arms, guiding her to the bed, sitting beside her.

"I don't wanna' go back!" she said. "I don't wanna' do this! I wanna' stay with you. Why can't I stay with you? Why won't anyone just listen to me?"

"We talked about this--"

"No!" She put her face in her palms. Her torso sank to her legs. She heaved and sobbed.

They sat in silence. Cam reached over and held onto him.

Martin gave a long sigh through his nose. He closed his eyes, opened them. "How would you like to get some breakfast before we go to the airport?" he said, trying unsuccessfully to nudge her off. He could feel her nodding against his chest. "We have to clean up and get you packed first. Okay?"

Camille let go her grasp. She began to pick up clothes.

"Let me help, honey," he said. He started folding the tousled shirts, slowly, stacking each one in her open luggage. He picked up the pieces of her broken Walkman, shook his head, chortled, looked at her. "Why would you do this to your brand new cassette player, ace? Now what are you going to do on the plane?"

She looked at the fractured device without expression, then continued to gather clothes.

"Hey, kid," he said, giving her a taunting smile, whistling like a steam locomotive.

She looked back up, stone-eyed.

"You're just like me." He tapped the side of his left eye.

Cam tapped her left eye, too.

She began to feel an overwhelming tightness as she reached for stray jeans. Dad wouldn't be around tomorrow -- he'd be so far away. She became immobile. "Why?" she said, sobbing again. "It's not fair! I'll do anything to stay with you! That's what I want! That's what I want! No one's listening to me!" She buried her face in her hands.

"Come here, sweetheart," he said, wedging his fingers underneath her armpits and helping her up, sticking out his hand for her to take. They walked through his white-walled hallway and into the living room, fell down on a puffy, black futon. Martin held her close as he reached for one of the remotes on his glass coffee table. They quieted before the glow and sounds of a *Saved by the Bell* re-run.

Camille fluttered her eyes, closed them. She began to snore.

Martin squirmed off the futon, guiding her into a lying pose. Went to the guest room and finished her packing. He took her bags and dropped them by the front door. Stood at a corner of the futon now with arms folded and began to watch *The Fresh Prince of Bel Air*, which had just come on. Looked at his daughter during a commercial break. *She'll be fine.* When the show came back on, he hovered over her, grinning. Leaned down and gave her a little poke.

Camille flapped open her eyes, gawked at the

tarnished, metal figure of a naked woman supplicating at the end of Martin's long, glass coffee table. The sweet, moist scent of South Florida filled her nostrils. These things made her remember where she was and her chest hurt again, heart beat fast, lips began to tremble. She sat up at the edge of the futon, her eyes lingering in the TV's periphery, then flickering with frustration. She pushed herself up and began walking to the guest room.

"Wrong way, kiddo," he said. "I packed you already."

She turned and saw her bags by the front door, then looked at her dad.

Martin put his hand at the center of her back. "This ain't so bad."

She traipsed away from him, waited by the front door.

He came toward her and bent down to be at eye-level. "Don't be so saturnine," he said, his face animate. "You'll go back to Chicago and be with Mom and then you'll be back here in no time."

Her eyes filled up with tears. She nodded.

Martin tapped the corner of his left eye.

She tapped her left eye, too, but then began to weep.

"Come on now," he said. He gripped the rolling frame of her luggage and began to wheel it out the door. He was pacing down his chilly hall. "What are you gonna' have for breakfast?"

"I don't know," she said, lingering behind to close the door, looking at the floor, shrugging, sniveling, adjusting her backpack. "Pancakes… french toast…"

They waited by the elevator door and Martin looked down at her, smirked.

"No eggs?" he said.

She was kicking her feet against the floor, watching them. "Nah."

When they got into the elevator, they kept glancing at their reflections in the mirrored walls. Continued to do this, in silence, like kids at a funhouse, until the lobby light lit up and the elevator chugged open. When outside, Camille stayed close to Martin. The wet-hot morning air, bushy palm trees with their curving trunks, the scattered, one-story houses with stripped paint appeared so different from Highland Park. It frightened her. She smelt stale cigarette smoke and sand as they situated themselves in Martin's used Nissan. Watched his pale, strawberry air freshener jiggle back and forth from a scuffed rearview as he flipped the car into reverse and they jolted backward.

After they'd been cruising on 95 awhile, Martin glanced at her and tapped her chin. He kept shifting gazes between the windshield and her crestfallen face. "You're going to be fine," he said. "I wouldn't have left till I knew you were old enough to take care of yourself." He stared at the windshield and his brows furrowed. "Your brother's a different story. I'm worried about him."

Camille tried to scrunch her brows like Dad. "But I'm *not* old enough."

Martin cleared his throat. He sniveled and fiddled with the tip of his nose. Glanced at the odometer. Gave the car a jerk and they began veering onto Broward Boulevard. The sudden change of motion made their bodies shake, gave their eyes dawn-imbued art deco buildings to look at, took their minds from trying to figure out how to relate to each other. That conversation of theirs now a vague and troublesome memory as they listened to the forty-mile-an-hour wind whishing against the car.

"Lester's Diner" appeared in tall, red, cursive writing -- a neon sign just above a series of long windows. They pulled into the lot.

When Martin and Camille had finally ambled out of the Nissan, walked in and gotten sat, they were approached by a scowling waitress. This lady standing stock-still in front of them without introducing herself, her wrinkly, lidded eyes fixed on Camille with irritated lassitude. She had a worn Bic pen in one hand and tiny notepad in the other, both of which she held directly in front of her.

Camille stared at Dad, her eyes wide, lips pursed.

"Give us a few minutes, doll," Martin said, tapping his menu.

"Anything to drink?" the waitress said back, shifting her gaze to Martin, but otherwise remaining motionless.

"Chocolate milk," Camille said.

The waitress scribbled on her notepad, glanced at it a second, then looked back at Martin.

Martin shook his head.

Few minutes later, Camille ordered chocolate chip pancakes, because Mom always made her choose either chocolate milk or chocolate pancakes when they went out to breakfast back home. She indulged in the thick, soft, viscous sweetness around her mouth as she chewed. The cool cocoa of her drink washed it away. Then the pancakes turned to sprinkles of crumbles floating in pools of maple syrup on her plate. The glass in front of her was empty and splotched with brown residue. She leaned back against the stiff booth and rubbed her tiny stomach.

Belched. She stared at her father, who was now wolfing down the last of his scrambled eggs. She yearned for him to remain hungry so they'd have to stay.

Martin made eye contact with the waitress, motioned for the check.

Cam stayed quiet while he pulled out his tarnished, argentine money clip stuffed with timeworn cards and crumpled cash and paid. She didn't even look at him. When they got back into the car and took off and she began to see planes roaring upward in the brightening sky, she wondered whether or not she'd ever utter a word again. For a few moments it just seemed more reasonable to keep her head down and let life continue erupting with its circus of unpleasant sounds: the wailing cries of ascending planes, pestering whistle of wind against the car, her father's cheery non-sequiturs.

There wasn't much said as they parked in the airport's garage complex, checked in at a Delta counter and made their way through security lines.

"I know you're sad," Martin said, finally. He was staring at her as she sat across from him on a firm seat in the waiting area for flight 1287.

She didn't look back, stared at her backpack, played with the zippers.

"Hey, kiddo," he said, leaning forward.

She looked up.

"Don't sweat the small stuff. Really."

His relaxed posture, cool brevity made her more distraught. There was no one like him in Highland Park. His uniqueness gave the town its warmth. "I know," she responded with a whisper. Put her head back down.

"We'd like to begin boarding for flight 1287 to Chicago O'Hare International Airport," a woman's voice announced over the intercom.

Cam's eyes flipped around the waiting area. She breathed heavily.

"We have time," Martin said, choking up when he said "time."

Cam's eyes became heavy with tears as she stared at him.

"Now boarding all passengers seated in rows one through seventeen," came the announcement again.

They remained quiet. Passengers shuffled around them -- purses rustling, bags scraping the carpeted floor. Neither took notice. They looked at each other and then the ground, or out the wide windows where the tail of Camille's 737 could be seen beyond the jetway. What they did notice is how the crowd of restless passengers around them began to dwindle, until there were only a handful left. The announcements, which had been continuing as background noise, now made perfect sense:

"Final boarding call for all passengers on flight 1287 to Chicago O'Hare International Airport."

Camille stood up. Her body trembled. It was hard to breathe. She began shuffling to the check-in stand, crying.

Martin moving behind her. "Ace."

She spun round, looking at her father as though for the first time -- five foot nine with short, curly brown hair. Wearing a cloudy-blue button-down, half-open, and a pair of tight jeans. An angel sent down to live amidst the hundreds of non-descript people walking around him.

He tapped the corner of his left eye, smiled.

She touched her left eye but her finger shook and she became more sorrowful. She noticed her father's eyes were now glassy and she felt sudden calm. She felt, finally, he was sharing in her grief. She took a long breath. "Bye, Dad," she said, turning again.

July 27, 2011

Camille and Jake sat across from each other on a pair of brown, suede chairs at the back of Starbucks in Lakeview. They were cradling the Caramel Macchiatos Jake had bought them.

"I'm really happy you texted back," he said. His eyes shifted to the floor and he flashed a grin that gave him an air of maddened cogitation. "Still can't believe things went the way they did."

She said nothing, stared at him, squirmed.

"Bottom line is I had no right to walk out on you like that. It was completely overdramatic, unnecessary, rude." He put his hand to his heart. "You seem like a really cool girl. You're obviously very smart, pretty, put-together... You even smell good."

"Stop," she said, looking at the window, blushing.

"But there are tons of cute, smart girls. Well, maybe less and less these days... My point is that I'm really glad I'm getting the chance to come here and talk to you. There was this realization forming in my mind that night after our date, something that appeared while I was tossing around in my bed, lying there all torn up with conflicting emotions -- emotions I haven't paid attention to for a long time (almost pushed away completely). You might think I'm a total weirdo. Might talk shit to Mere. May never even want to hang out with me again. That's fine. Long as I get this off my chest.

"You're a very special person, Camille. It's this energy or spirit or soul you have about you. Whatever you want to call it. This sublime, primordial beauty that might not be perceptible to most people, but is readily apparent to me, just by looking at your eyes -- those big, crystalline oracles. I've never met anyone like you before."

"Very flattering," she said, "but you don't even know me. Don't you think you're being a bit crazy?"

"'All thoughts, all passions, all delights, / Whatever stirs this mortal frame, / All are but ministers of Love, / And feed his sacred flame.' That's Coleridge. *Love.* I know I sound strange. Honestly, I don't spend my time going around like some latter-day troubadour, cooing over every pretty girl I see. I actually spend most days watching the Cubs lose. It's just that when a rare opportunity like this one comes along, when you just know you have the potential to connect with someone in such a deep way (even if it's friendship), you can't let it pass you by, especially not in today's world where everyone is so excessively self-focused, in this generation of mass alienation.

"I truly believe you have a difficult time in life not because you're malicious, Camille, but because you're too sensitive for the rawness and chaos of all things. You feel profoundly, all the time, and it pains you. It renders you laconic, hermetic, combative. Whereas most people ramble through their limited days half-asleep, like zombies being kept alive only by the musical hiss from their headphones, missing about ninety-five percent of what's happening around them
-- all those wonderful nuances --, your eyes are wide open. You miss nothing. I know it. You probably think this quality is a giant cross to bear. Probably think it's the reason for your overall estrangement, but it doesn't have to be." He took a furious sip, continued:

"I *don't* know you. You're right. But I'm willing to bet the farm there were two Camille's who came to dinner with me a couple weeks ago, the one who was on auto-pilot, the machine you've constructed to fend off all those inevitable travails that come your way, your jaded speaker-of-the-house who was so quick to rebuke me for being callous and insensitive without another thought on the matter. Then that other Camille, the pensive one, the one almost no one sees, the one who was conscious not only of her total self, her erratic moods, her conduct, the cause of her conduct, but who was also highly sensitive to me and what my true intentions were. Hence you knew I was a good person, knew I liked you, knew that I was *not* in any way flirting with that stupid-ass server but instead that I'm just a diplomatic guy, somewhat lighthearted, that I'm still probably healing from my previous relationship. I know it brought you sadness knowing where I was coming from, but still not allowing yourself to disassemble that defense machine and give me a chance. The potential for hurt was too great. Still is.

"Thing is I'm exactly like you, Camille. Maybe not as artistic, but I've always been freighted with the same costly brand of sensitivity. I opened myself up to Cassie, my ex. Gave her everything inside of me and I was pillaged like an indigenous village. I don't blame her. She is who she is, and is capable of only what she's capable of. I've always felt out of place, just like you, ever since I was kid. Maybe that's why I always have my head between the pages of a book. It's the only place safe enough for me to give free rein to my innermost self. Guess I've just learned to be really good at bullshitting. That's probably part of the small-town, Protestant upbringing. The shallow part. I'm rambling. Hope some of this makes sense. Hope you're not too freaked out." He took a deep breath and leaned back.

She continued to gaze at him long after he'd finished. Started to shake her head. She let out a loud cackle that made her shoulders shake. "Wow. Did you rehearse that? Part of me is totally captivated right now. Another part wants to go home and see how long it's going to take for you to appear as the new killer on *CSI*. Is that me or is it my 'machine' speaking now?" She leaned forward and tapped his knee, smiled. "Honestly, I don't know what to say. Thank you? I'm happy you've put this much thought into me. You're right. I *am* super-sensitive. I'm poetic, and, admittedly, probably way too melancholy. I've been through a lot of shit..." She looked to the windows, staring out at the swift-footed passerby like the images they were creating came from the center of a riveting Paul Thomas Anderson film. "This is just a bit too intense for now. How about we forge our new beginnings with something approximately ten to twenty degrees lighter?" She looked at him, raised her sharp, black brows, smirked. "Sorry I was such a bitch. I know I was."

"You don't need to apologize, Camille. I'm glad you're allowing yourself to feel contrition. Means you're embracing your humanity."

"Alright, Father Jake." She was grinning, cocking her head to the side. "Can you please step out of your cathedral a moment?" She continued to smirk as his eyes dropped with the sudden realization he was being way too baroque. "What'd you do today, Jake?"

"Just woke up about two hours ago." He lifted his cup. "Colombian breakfast."

"You find the fact that you woke up at noon embarrassing?"

"Kinda'."

"I'm a big sleeper, too. It's part of the reason I actually like being a server, like the easy hours. I definitely hate where I'm at now, but serving allows me to enjoy my life without having this rigorous, 40-hour-a-week work schedule imposed on me."

"What's the other part?"

"The what?"

"The other reason you like working as a server?"

She chuckled and looked away. "You pay a lot of attention, don't you? Nevermind, it's stupid…"

"No, really, I'm interested. Tell me."

"The intellectual freedom," she said. "I don't have to use my mind. Plenty of time to…" Her cheeks flushed. "I have these dreams of being a famous poet one day."

"*Dreams?* You can make them your reality."

She shook her head, sipped.

"Serious, I told you: I didn't come here to sharpen my ability at charm. I really believe there's something unique about you."

"So what do you do outside of work, Jake? Apart from paying homage to Chicago's feckless baseball team?"

He could have been an antediluvian cherub in a basilica fresco with the afternoon light kindling his stubbly face, pouched eyes, dimpled cheeks as he looked at the windows and smiled. "I'm going to let you get away with calling the Cubs 'feckless' only because you live on the North Side. Had you lived anywhere south of the Loop and said that we might have had to duke it out." His kinetic expression then vanished, features stilled. "I don't really do anything 'noteworthy.' Just reading. I'm more of an adventurer. I like meeting people, learning, asking questions, taking risks, accumulating life experience…"

"That's inspiring."

"Isn't it the opposite?"

"Contrary to popular belief... Where I come from, you were always expected to be doing something else. When I was a kid it was all those 'extracurricular activities' our parents raced to sign us up for: swimming, chorus, martial arts... Come high school, you better have been an honors student taking the practice SAT every night, better have been on the debate team, the student council, the yearbook committee. If you gave yourself time to breathe, you were lazy and destined for trouble. One of *those* kids." She mused, chuckled. "Flash forward, ten years later. If you're not a doctor, lawyer or financial analyst, there's a serious issue with you. Least according to the circle I came from.

"I've always been in your camp, though. Life's not meant to be kicked around and subdued for the sake of calming our anxiety. It's meant to be experienced on its own terms. I never really had the courage to take on that belief fully. There was always too much opposition. I started to feel like Edna in *The Awakening*, like I was drifting toward my own private, self-aggrandizing suicide."

That last word fled from the custody of her Internal Censorship Board. She watched in terror as the word whirled around the room, lingered by Jake's ear, prepared itself to jump inside his brain and corrupt. She put her head down, frowned, stared at the floor.

"You okay?"

Her eyes still enchained downward, wriggling to and fro. "Fine-fine. Just had a shooting pain in my stomach."

He smirked. "A chicken and an egg are lying in bed."

"A what?"

"Chicken's smoking a cigarette with a big grin on its face. The egg frowning and pissed off. Egg rolls away from the chicken and mutters, to no one in particular, 'Well, guess we answered THAT question!'"

She began to titter.

"There's that gorgeous smile. Like that one? Kid told it to me last night at work. Guess wit isn't completely lost on the DePaul crowd, huh? There might just be a smidgen of hope for Chicago's future." He held up an index finger. "And, if you think about it, joke makes people like you and me ease back from our excruciating quests to find answers for these massive, philosophical questions. Right?"

"Just a joke, Jake. A funny one."

"Exactly! Life's just life. It's not oppressive, but hilarious in that it's so out of our ability to understand it, control it, predict it, ultimately."

"You're taking it way too far, and oversimplifying. How we interpret life might seem like one of the few choices we actually do have, but many times it's not even an option. Least not for me. Sometimes life brings me so much sadness or anger that the emotion becomes its own authority, with its own mind, and I just its obedient subject."

Neither spoke. They gazed at each other with grave faces until Jake twitched one of his eyebrows. They burst into laughter. Camille looked at her shoes. Jake glanced around the café, checking out people on their gleaming laptops. In the wild, imaginative part of their minds -- that place which guides children but which adults come to ignore -- they both glimpsed at the landscape of their future together, as though they were standing atop a lofting precipice. They looked out on this fantastical land that was filled with unknown adventures and that brought them an ultimate sense of happiness because they were its only inhabitants. It was a thought that came upon them like a dream, quick, muddled, full of emotion and then scarcely remembered after it had passed.

"Can I kiss you?" he said.

"Can you *what*?"

"I want to kiss you. It's unconventional. Let's throw all decorum out the window and go right to the thrilling part."

"No."

"You don't like me?"

"I didn't say that." She chuckled. "Let's just take it slow."

"You're right."

"How about a walk?"

He stood up and she giggled at his alacrity.

She glanced over the side of her chair and reached for her purse, grasped it. "We could finish our drinks first." She looked around as she stood up. Walked past Jake and dumped her coffee in a slim garbage bin, continued outside where she dug into her bag and unearthed a Camel Light, lit it, puffed from the corner of her mouth. She gave sidelong gazes at the street.

The small shops on Sheridan were obscured by skeletal bushes and tiny trees that had been plotted on random parts of the sidewalk. Cars stopped for red lights, coasted through greens, swung into the parking lot of a Mobil across the street.

Jake, standing beside her: "Where we going?"

"I don't know," she said. She looked at him,

smoked. "The lake?"

"Great idea!"

They began to drift east, side-by-side, Jake observing her with eyes aslant, his lips curled into a mischievous smile. He watched her walk like a wave during low-tide in a tropical island, her every limb at ease, body mimicking her breath, which was steady, coming out of her mouth only when it had to. Her motion soothed him. He could think of no one else that made him feel this way.

Camille's every stir like a gleeful cry from a coloratura, he thought as he gawked at a Linden tree in the distance. He began to wonder if her sullen demeanor wasn't actually all just a posture, a great artifice, way to blindfold the populace to her secret, divine mission. He remembered how quick she was acknowledging her own foibles after he'd spoken to her at length, after he'd poured out all his carefully measured thoughts about her, as though what he'd broken his brain to find had already been so apparent for her it was now a top-ten cliché. But then he remembered how she'd shut herself down in the middle of speaking, beleaguered by her own dark reality that seemed like it had nothing to do with what was actually happening. He contemplated his complete inability to untwist the strands of another human being and then sniggered.

"I grew up in Ohio," he said as they came upon a small intersection.

"Why'd you come here?"

"Well, I went to school at U of I. Had a ton of friends who lived here. I'd come with them to visit. I really do love this city."

"That's funny," she said.

137

"What is?"

"Funny you'd hold such a fondness for a place so rife with pervasive individualism."

He whipped his eyes at her, gave a roguish smile. "Good memory."

They were coming to Inner Lake Shore. Cars moved faster, zipping onto the expressway, getting off. There was a small, concrete bridge in the near distance, the shape of a large vase, over a narrow road that ended in a cul-de-sac. Beyond that road a vast, flat park; beyond that the lake.

"Chicago has glaring flaws," Jake was saying, flapping his arms in the air, gazing at Camille. "But there's so much life here, so much diversity, so many different kinds of people, so many different stories. All being presented to our inquiring eyes honestly, all of which so far removed from that Tower of Babel the West Coasters are building to be unified in the latest pop-cultural trend, Tower of Babel on the East Coast to advance of some high-moralistic standard." He looked up at the sky, arms outstretched. "People here are all so unapologetically immersed in their many lives. They--"

"Jake!" she said. She reached out and grabbed his t-shirt, yanking him back.

Jake, oblivious, sky-high happy, had been wandering too far into the street. A white Honda Prelude was now swerving around him, its vengeful driver slamming on the horn. "Asshole," the driver's wind-smothered voice called out through an open window as the car whizzed away.

"Be careful!" she said to him, her eyes wide.

"Oops." He made his way back to the sidewalk, began to ramble along in front of her.

"What do you mean *oops*?" She was striding up to him now, staring at his profile as they walked. "Be careful. I'm serious. Or I'm going home."

"Yeah, I can be a little moony."

They waited for a walk signal, looked both ways, crossed the street.

"You could have been killed," she continued, shaking her head in the dewy, sewage-perfumed shadows underneath the bridge. "I don't know how you've made it this far."

"With the exception of that one time I almost got knocked unconscious by a hurling football in Eagle Creek Park," he said, "and the other time I almost got sliced open with a broken Bud Light bottle by that belligerent ATO at a bar my sophomore year, I'm happy to report I've made it out relatively unscathed."

"Serious," she said. "This isn't a laughing matter."

"I know, I know," he said, trying hard not to giggle.

They could see a backwoods playground, fenced off. A couple young moms were guiding their children up rubber steps. A six and seven year-old chased each other around a set of monkey bars until they fell on the bark-bespattered ground, laughing.

"Let's go on those swings," she said, suddenly, as she watched the ground-bound kids. "Come on -- it'll be *unconventional*." She took Jake's hand and they began running to the playground.

The park moms giving them quick, baffled looks as they jumped onto swings. As they began kicking themselves up until their feet were parallel to the upper frame of the swing set.

"I haven't done this in so many years," she was

saying, the wind throwing her red hair to and fro. She laughed.

"Me neither!"

She looked over at him, thinking of how silly he looked with his ecstatic grin, large body moving in the narrow swing. Yet there was something so comfortable about his lack of self-consciousness, a quality that made her feel he could do her no harm. That she was safe.

They let their legs go limp and cruised to a stop, dragging the tips of their feet across the bark, staring at the ground. They were silent a moment, catching their breath, grasping onto that almost-forgotten feeling of juvenile exhilaration coursing through their bodies.

"When I was in elementary school," she said, "I used to come to the swing set during recess by myself and swing as high as I could toward the trees. I imagined myself getting picked up in a limo by Madonna and taken off into a life of fame. Made me really happy." She looked at Jake and winced. "Does that sound weird?"

"No. Interesting."

"Things have been really hard for me."

"I get that."

She laughed. "I don't have a good relationship with my family."

"Don't know too many people who do."

"Well, what about you? What about your family? What are they like?"

He gave himself a push backward and began to coast with his legs up, gripping the sides of the swing. He was gazing at that curly slide a few feet in front of him as it got bigger, smaller, bigger, smaller. "I'm an only child. I tell you that?"

"You've said nothing about your family."

"Mom's real quiet. Just her nature, I guess. She was a seventh grade math teacher before I was born. Stopped working 'cause Dad wanted her to raise me, even though it meant less income. I remember her always being there. Always mild, gentle, concerned. I can't even remember her cursing. Not once. She didn't really have much of a life, though. Home, church, game nights, visiting or hosting relatives and then going out with Dad. That's pretty much it. Maybe she seems different to me now that I'm older, now that I'm far away."

"What do you mean? How?"

He continued to glide. "Like, maybe now I see that even though she seemed content, she wasn't genuinely happy. Maybe there was a part of her that really wanted to be wild, gregarious, promiscuous, free-of-mind, free-of-speech, but she just never had the courage to confront that about herself. Maybe she swept all those personal aspects neatly beneath the rug of "marriage" and "family" where she'd never had to look at them again, even though a part of her always longed to take them back. Maybe not. I don't know." He stared at Camille, grinned. "As I said before, I tend to lose myself in thought."

"What about your Dad? What's he like?"

Jake chuckled. "Thomas? A die-hard Buckeyes fan. Cut the man open, he'll bleed scarlet and grey. I swear by it. He used to take me to home games on weekends, even though I really didn't want to go. Silly part about all of it -- to me, anyway -- is that he didn't even go to college. He was a supervisor at a distribution center. Retired now. Dad's pretty loud. Goofy. Kind-hearted. He always had this go-for-it attitude. Eerily optimistic. He loves to sneak his Budweiser when Mom's not around. Never saw him drink around her. Never. Not once. When I think back on time spent with Dad, it involved me and him sitting on the couch while he watched State and I read.

"Case you haven't already discerned, Cam, I really didn't fit in where I came from. Findlay was way too small for me. Small-town mentality, small-town Christian values. Couldn't wait to get the fuck out. So now, flash forward, ten years later, most of my high school friends are married, have kids and haven't really gotten any further than Columbus. It's baffling, tragic."

"You don't keep in touch with anyone?"

He extended his feet upward and tipped his head back, but continued to swing. "Facebook."

She began to move her body, too. Stared at the six and seven-year-old as they'd now resumed chasing each other around an elm, the one girl letting out a hearty howl. "How long have your parents been married?" Camille said.

"Thirty-five years this September."

"Wow! I can't believe that."

"Guess it has been a long time. Never really thought about it."

The sound of their feet scraping piles of bark. The consolatory sound of no sound pervading the eastern realms of the woods. A western whisper from cars hastening here and there, almost completely extinguished by the massive park's timberline screen.

"That's like so unfathomable to me," Camille was saying, shaking her limp head left, right. She gazed at the ground. "My parents divorced when I was… thirteen. Dad moved to Florida. I grew up with a stepfamily I couldn't relate to, at all. Nevermind. New subject. No more family talk."

He started pushing himself higher. "You ever see that thing on Nickelodeon a million years ago, with that kid who swung all the way over the swing set and became 'inside-out boy?'"

"I used to love Nickelodeon." She propelled herself forward, back, trying to keep up.

"Let's see if we can do it," he said, now kicking himself as high as he could.

"Jake, this is crazy!" She was gripping the swing's chain so hard the skin on her hands began to tear. "What if we fall? Jake!" She let out a wholehearted laugh as she continued to dash forward and back.

"Only thing you have to worry about is what you're going to do when you become 'inside-out girl,'" he called out.

Their brisk motion soon dwindled into exhausted stillness. They were now two, panting bodies facing each other, giving out the last of the giggles.

"I must admit, Jake…" she said. "Wait. What's your last name?"

"Kellen."

"Jake Kellen. It feels good to be around you."

"You too, Cam. That's why I'm here."

November 3, 1994

Camille rubbed her bare arms and huddled her shoulders as she strode along Terri-Lynn Lane -- winter hissing its chilly breath at her. The way the long, hilly patches of grass between homes caused those homes to be observed as distant structures in the twilight had always made her feel like she was stuck in a rural horror film. She walked without direction. Kicking her blue shoes against grainy pavement. Listening to the tiny grating sound the pavement made; listening to that little echo clamoring for attention in the belly of Riverwoods' oceanic quiet.

She made it to Deerfield Road. A bright Mobil gas station appeared across the street like an Edward Hopper painting amongst the dark and vacant roads. *Jeff,* she thought.

Jeff, the aged hippie who worked there seventy-five percent of the time. His presence in this small town anomalous -- as though he'd left Woodstock twenty-five years ago in a faded tie-dye van that broke down in the middle of the Midwest, where, penniless and high, he'd had to figure out how to get back to San Francisco but became too lazy and instead made this his accidental residence.

She crossed the street; she pushed open the gas station's front door.

Jeff stood behind a narrow counter with a canopy above it that held multifarious cigarettes. His long, brown-blond hair was slicked back behind his small ears and tied into a pony tail. The hellish perfume of oil and gasoline seeped in through a glass door that separated this mini-mart from its adjoining garage, which lent Jeff, who was now leaning back against a wall and gawking at the pages of the latest *Car & Driver*, an air of primal ruggedness.

"Jeff," she said.

Jeff, still cradling his open magazine with both hands, shifted his dull brown eyes in her direction. He pursed his lips, widened his eyelids, raised both his beetle brows.

"What's up, Jeff?" she said, smirking. "Can I?'

"No." He shook his head, lips squeezed tight.

"Why not?"

"Cops have been in here *many* times." He put away the magazine and placed both palms on the countertop, his eyes freezing over as he stared at her.

She watched herself from the viewpoint of a hip and well-put-together contemporary who was observing her at her worst angle in this moment, in her worst light, and thinking about what a joke she was. Someone like Lexi Davis who would always give her that passing smile of lightsome pity as they walked by each other between third and fourth period, Camille secretly hoping Lexi would stop to acknowledge her, converse, that people would see them talking. Someone like Winona Ryder whose exquisite face always brought Camille into a state of benumbed adoration when it appeared on the screen, when she was watching *Edward Scissorhands* alone in her living room. The world so full of near perfection, reminding her time and again she was defective, humdrum. What the hell made her think she was cool enough to come to Jeff like this, a la suburbanite legend, get whatever she wanted?

"Could I possibly bum one, then?" she said.

Jeff continued to stare. He turned and began rummaging through a small pile of his crumpled clothes on the back countertop, unearthing a Marlboro from a pack in his shirt pocket, turning again, throwing it at her.

She gave a girlish giggle as she dipped down to pick it up; she situated the cigarette between her index and middle finger as she stood back up. Gazing vacantly at his face. "Got a light?" The words vibrated through her entire body before coming out her mouth, a Bacchanalian incantation that shattered her momentary bravado and displayed, from behind the rubble of her adolescent veneer, in a fleeting glimpse, that nascent animal within her, that young woman who wanted to attack this old, dirty man, right here, right now, under these loud lights, and make manifest all those licentious fantasies which had hitherto existed on a dark back-road in her mind.

Jeff plucked a small, orange lighter from a display case and flicked it at her chest.

Lighting up and tossing it back to him with a snigger and then rushing back out into this newly arrived night and she'd already forgotten what had happened: the sexuality which had been so present inside her now a distant memory, a vague notion of truth, a flash -- just a flash as though her whole life she was merely a character being portrayed by a mysterious actor who knew so much more than she did. The sting of smoke filling her lungs. Last scalding drag. Dead Marlboro sailing from her fingers out into the breezy night and into its final resting place between two sheltered gas pumps. Chilly, longing for more Marlboro comfort, she watched the Grim Reaper sauntering between the shadowy trees across Deerfield Road, whispering, "lung cancer" -- His voice amplified by the omnipresent wind.

She needed to see Michael.

Needed Michael's listening ear, sage words, sensitive heart. The tranquil home his company provided her, where she could finally escape this lone frenzy. Where they would laugh and be silly and she would close her eyes and breathe and reacquaint herself with herself, forget about the rustic, four-bedroom house that was behind her now, that wooden detention center within which she was measured, judged and censured by all the inhabitants, her brother with his iron-hearted wisecracks about her clothes, her mother with the constant reminders that her fantastical perspectives on life and art made people uncomfortable, her stepfather reminding her about her mother's reminders. She could have been dead to her stepbrother for all that one noticed. She would come to Michael now, feverish and forsaken, vulnerable, in secret, as she always did, come to him as the hostage from an old war between her two biological parents, still biding her time in this remote and loveless suburban forest.

How the fuck am I going to get to Highland Park?

She walked to a rusty payphone beside the gas station. Fishing through the front pockets of her moody-blue Levis. No change. Fondling the lump in her back pocket and pulling out her Velcro wallet. The tiny ripping sound the wallet made as she peeled it open: ten dollars.

She strode back into the mini-mart.

"*What?*" Jeff said, sighing over his magazine, his shoulders deflating.

"Need change." She pressed her crinkled ten dollar bill against the countertop with a brief, un-forecasted air of aggressive self-affirmation -- small shoulders now stiff, wide, blue eyes throwing off sparks of light, steady breaths ready to transform into defensive growls. Her air then waned into criminal-courtroom stillness before the sarcastic facial expression he gave her -- she was just a fourteen-year-old nobody from a small town who was awkward and hadn't even grown into her features yet, who didn't have the power to scare a fly. Michael understood her. Michael, with those pudding smears along the corners of his lips during lunchtime in second grade. Michael, her fellow angel made flesh. Michael--

"You moving in?" Jeff said.

Jeff had already been to the register, had already given her a five, four singles, four quarters. He was staring at her up close now, one brow raised, his breath a volcanic fusion of Bazooka gum, Marlboro smoke and dark chocolate.

"Thanks," she said. Grabbing her change and nodding, marching back out of the mini-mart. Back to the pay phone. Quarter dropping with a scratchy, metallic ping. The glacial phone against her ear. "Michael."

"What happened to you?" Michael said at the other end.

"Long story. Can I please come see you?"

"Of course. We'll have to be quiet, though. Where are you?"

"Mobil. Don't ask. I'll be there soon." Hanging up. Thinking. The coin slot at the top of the phone swallowing another quarter.

"Hello?" said a shrill voice at the other end.

"Janey. It's Cam."

"What's up, Cam-Star? How hot was Greg Albright in Bio today? Can you believe Lexi Davis gave him a blow-job?"

"No. I need a favor, Janey."

"Why you acting all weird?"

"Is your brother home?"

"Eww," Janey said. "Please tell me you're not

149

trying to go see Michael Parker. *Why* do you keep hanging out with him? That kid is so creepy."

"Come on, Janey."

Janey sighed. "Hold on."

Cam leaned against the gas station's brick wall, squeezing the phone. She suspected Janey's brother wouldn't give her a ride and became motionless – the hushed and infinite night around her now drawing attention to the loud, stifling desire in her heart, now shaking its giant, starless, omniscient head at her futile attempt to rebel against circumstance.

She watched a steel-grey Mercedes-Benz C-Class as it coasted up to pump two. A young man in a white, cotton button-down, carmine tie, black blazer and black slacks pushed open the driver's side door and swaggered into the mini-mart, touching his silky-brown hair. Out he came, a minute later, shifting a cursory glance at Camille, walking back to his pump, lifting the nozzle -- premium -- and then disappearing into the car, the door snapped shut. The hard-hitting bass from "Straight Outta' Compton" by N.W.A. began to resound from within the car's closed confines as though it marked the opening phases of wholesale, tribal warfare.

This is a war, Camille thought as she gazed at the car. *No longer will we be suppressed.* She imagined the BMW driver was one of the captains in the Great Youth Revolution and she longed to possess his young and wealthy fuck-you freedom.

"He said he'll drive you for twenty bucks," Janey's voice said through the phone, snatching Camille away from the countercultural anthem her mind was singing to that Mercedes.

Camille looked down at the concrete walkway,

shaking her head, squinting: "I can't, Janey. How am I supposed to get twenty dollars?"

"That's what he said. Why is it so important for you to go? You're acting so strange right now."

"Just forget it. I'll see you tomorrow."

Janey's phlegmy sigh: "Whatever."

The smacking echo of the slammed-down pay phone still swirled around Camille's ears as she began to make her way back along Saunders Road. The darker Riverwoods was becoming in its journey through night, the more she rubbed her arms and shivered. The natural warmth of her exposed skin being ice-bombed from every direction by an invisible temperature. *Arctic darkness*, she thought, *sneaky and commanding thief of Light, unstoppable black bandit. You suck away the Sun's bright generosity. Cursed cold. Cursed night.* She rounded Terri-Lynn Lane again, looking at all the somnolent cars and their sleepy driveways. Back in now through the front door which she'd left unlocked.

She started when she saw Mom standing by the kitchen doorway, staring at her, glowering. The fading aroma of meat loaf, gravy and steamed vegetables still wafted about the front hall. Cam's every limb froze.

Ellen stuck her finger in the air, pointing to Camille's room. "*Go. Now.*"

"Stop telling me what to do!" Camille said, her heart racing. "I can do whatever the fuck I want!"

Ellen stepped toward her, limbs stiff.

"Fuck you!" Camille said, darting to the staircase and sprinting up the stairs, into her room, door slammed behind her and locked. She could hear her mother's thundering footsteps getting louder and closer from her bed where she now lay prone with face buried in a blue pillow. Her door began to shake. Ellen's muffled voice: "Open this goddamn door, Camille. Now!"

She pressed her face further into the pillow: cool, smooth softness that countered the hot throbbing in her chest. *Is it just the pillow against my ears*, she wondered after a few minutes, *or has that horrible rattling outside my door finally ceased? Has the dragon gone back to her cave?* She pushed herself up and walked to the door, tilting her ear toward it. Nothing but the slow-motion cycling of secluded silence that enfolds middle-American suburbs. "Mom," she called out through the door, breath bated, "you're the scum of the earth. Why don't you take a trip somewhere and never come back?" Yet still nothing. She clicked open the lock on her door and eased it open, craning her head out into the tan-carpet hall, glancing around. Nobody. Door closed behind her again and locked – she jumped back onto her bed and picked up the phone.

"What's the address, ma'am?" she heard a gruff, bass voice saying on the line.

The fuck is this? What's happening? Motionless, upright at the edge of her bed, she continued to listen:

"We'll have someone over there in about twenty minutes," said the unfamiliar voice.

"Thank you, officer," her mother's voice said. "I just don't want her to run away again."

Cam hung up. She dropped the phone and stared at her window. Thoughts all scrambled now like eggs on a fiery skillet: *Get outta' here … Window … Jump … Police, jail, reputation … Sabotage*. She pulled up her blinds and unlatched the lock to her casement. *Probably about twelve feet*, she thought, gazing down at the wooden patio which was just a diaphanous sketch in the darkness. She edged forward, jumped, felt herself descending, the night's bitter chill attacking her bare skin, the all-present force pulling her to the earth – how she was powerless and *free* under its command... Tiny feet smashing into the patio's wooden slats with a profound smack that shot out into the backyard's evening ever-quiet and frightened two deer cantering amidst distant trees. The impact sent her toppling backward onto her butt whence she had enough of an angle to press her palms against the cold wood and stop herself from falling further. Breathless, palms still pressed to the patio, she took a moment to consider the severity of that sharp aching in her legs by sticking one leg out, then the other.

Just a bruise, she thought, standing, hopping.

Running around the house and back along the pavement of Terri-Lynn, the road's shape erased by the enveloping blackness. Jogging and panting, lost in this thick, autumnal nightfall: the shape of her life erased, too. Rounding Blackheath, then Saunders: she now seemed so little in this vast, rural patch of the world without a big house to warm her, cozy cars to take her around, hot food being put in front of her – a dwarfish wanderer of a formidable and uncharted planet who was waiting to meet a horrific death any moment.

The square-shaped lights from a Jeep Cherokee appeared in the distance like the ascension of a foreign moon. Whistling echo of coasting tires that laid claim to the forested silence. She shuffled onto someone's front lawn as the vehicle passed even though it had been moving nowhere near her. A keen, cold, paralyzing fear gripped her muscles, taking away that ache in her legs. *I can't do this*, she thought. *I need money. Need to be protected. Can't do this alone. Where am I going?* So her thoughts went until she annihilated them with a burst of spontaneity. Jogging along Saunders again.

This time, at Deerfield Road, across from Mobil, she turned right and headed west, deeper into Riverwoods' leafy bosom. *Why am I going to his house?* she thought as she moved, as intermittent cars whooshed past. She'd already turned onto Blackhawk Lane. The pavement had changed to gravel, the sound of her footsteps to scratchy gusts. For a moment, she couldn't remember which house it was. They all seemed hidden in the dark. *Which house?* she thought, mind now moving backward in time, to when Janey's brother had once taken Janey and her through this narrow, Dantean road.

She could remember the smell of lingering Marlboro smoke in Janey's brother's Volvo that night. Itchy back seats. Pearl Jam playing through fizzling speakers. Their high-pitched laughter. The way Janey's brown eyes crinkled every time she got giddy. *Janey*, she was saying that one night, as they were cruising along, *stop it -- seriously. Which house is it?* Janey's brother whining at them and then Janey: *It's five houses down on the left, Cam.*

"Five houses down on the left," Camille said to herself, remembering it now, stopping in the middle of the road. She turned and headed the other way.

She recognized the small, lacerated, stone gargoyles situated like sentinels upon the outer edges of James' driveway. A dilapidated, mint-green Chevy Caravan along one side of the drive, in front of a small garage with chipped, white paint and a sensor light. The house itself only one story with more length than width. A long front window, adjacent the front door, wanted to reveal the McPhersons' living room but was instead occluded by drawn blinds, the blinds casting a dark shadow over the window that seemed to deprive it of life. Even with the poor visibility of night, it was still easy to perceive the McPhersons hadn't attended to the dying leaves collecting around their shingled rooftop, stuffing up the gutter.

She remembered it now, where to go now, her feet moving around the side of the house as though her body was repeating the past -- that one night with Janey and Janey's brother in the Volvo. She was standing in front of another window at the back of the house that was designed like the one in front only smaller. It too had a thick set of blinds, which were pushed open. Inside, underneath the glow from a yellow-hued light, James sat hunched over his little wooden desk.

She tapped her knuckles against the window and James remained fixed upon his mysterious task. Began to rap. James whipped his head in her direction with a giant grin that displayed his large lips, wide teeth and that devilish twinkle in his deep, liquid-brown eyes -- as though he'd known of her desperation and knew she would come. Camille shuddered. *I shouldn't have come*, she thought, still panting, shivering, aching in the legs. She knew that this mutual gaze she was now locked into with James -- the attention she'd roused in him -- was akin to a witch's spell and that leaving was no longer an option. He was walking to the window, un-clicking its latch, sliding it open.

"Camille," he said, letting out a chuckle. "What brings you to my backyard?"

"My parents. I had to get the fuck out."

"Come in."

"Should I just crawl in through the window?"

James smirked, the pink hues over his big dimples. "We have a front door."

She cocked her head to the side, scrunched her brows. "Is that... cool?"

"Get your ass around the front of my house," he said, snickering. He'd already begun making his way toward the door with loud and decided footsteps.

His wide back as he moved, whale-like, and the faded-green, Zapatista jacket he wore in the warmth of his home as though it hadn't come off since the day he'd bought it: the witch-spell now in full effect, he'd seen her, she'd shown up -- there was no getting out of this. She looked to the tall, nighttime trees beside her and thought about darting into their depths where she would become invisible, thought about running like a stray doe -- leaves crackling beneath her swift feet, branches smacking at her rocking arms --, lost in that endless forest without promise of civilization, never to return, and safe, at one with the ghost of Thoreau. This imagined future, so full of hope, was then slaughtered into extinction by the realization that time was passing, James was waiting, that this present moment commanded her forth into some dodgy hideaway from a home too full of animosity. She walked back around the side of the house with shoulders sagging. Arrived at the front door.

James standing in front of her, hands buried in his pockets. He now had on his army bucket hat. She remembered the last time she'd seen him wearing it: when he was apprehended by Deerfield Police in front of their junior high for possession of marijuana.

"Want a cigarette?" he said, pulling out a fresh pack of Camel Filters from one pocket, a black lighter from another, lighting up two, handing her one.

She held the burning smoke behind her waist. "What about your parents?"

James put his cigarette between his gapped teeth and bit down on it, grinning. He walked toward her and grasped her small shoulders with his large hands. Began to shake her. "You are silly," he said, spacing out his words. "We are not going to get into trouble for smoking," spacing out his words again. "Okay?"

The night's dark wind, on the fading echo of James' imperious boast, usurped their will to make any more adolescent refrain. James gawked at the dented side-panel of his dad's Chevy Caravan. Camille stared at the side of James' round face and puffed her cigarette, wide-eyed. In that chilly, sylvan quiet, they were both confronted with the sobering realization that they'd just emerged into this life and that it wasn't what they'd wanted at all.

"Besides, my parents are *dead*," James continued, still looking at the Caravan. He turned to her with a baleful smirk. "My dad fell asleep with his cigar burning at our old house on Sanders and the whole place burnt to the ground while both my parents were in it." He nodded, widened his eyes. "I collected some of their ashes during the cleanup and drank them in a satanic ritual. You know anything about Satanism?" He shambled over to her, gaze resolute.

She shook her head like a lost, late-night cosmo, in the wrong alley, who was realizing she was about to become a victim.

"Just fucking with you," he said, laughing gruffly, patting her shoulder. "Dad's passed out right now on the La-Z-Boy in the den, watching 'Skinemax.'"

Camille tittered. *James' big, terrifying face*, she

thought. *We're this close, in this moment, – what will people think?* She needed him to stop touching her yet she knew this would happen, but still she'd come here like a naïve damsel unable to balance chaste reasoning with private passions. *You had nowhere else to go without a ride*, she thought. She affected a simpatico grin for him while inching away. Turned her body and puffed her Camel, all the while maintaining a nervous smile.

James squeezed the end of his lit cigarette like a joint, put it to his pouty lips and then sucked all the existence out of it with one heavy drag. He looked to the sky and let out foggy jets of smoke. "Check this fuckin' thing out," he said, reaching into his jacket, unearthing an eight-inch hunting knife with a brown leather grip and a rusty, curved blade. He held the knife straight up in front of her and continued to grin, eyes enlarged.

"James," she said, her heart beating quickly.

He turned the knife upside down, raised it again. "James!"

He jogged to a small tree and then plunged the knife into its bark with a grainy battle cry. Knife in tree, he turned to face her. "Wanna' try?"

"You're crazy," she said. She looked away and shut her eyes as she took the last puff of her Camel.

"*Crazy?*" He tilted his head. "You think I'm crazy?" He stepped toward her, grabbed her arms, shook her again. "I'm not crazy," he said, again spacing out his words and repeating them, still shaking her.

"Stop," she said, trying to giggle and shift backward. "You're crazy – I mean, you're wild – I mean, you know what I mean."

James, hands still wrapped around her shoulders, rolled his eyes upward so that all she could see was the wet whiteness of his eyeballs. His giant head began to convulse as if it was about to explode into shooting fragments.

Somehow he'd taken the breath from her and she had no ability to move. Somehow he'd made her the slave of his volatile whims. With James as God, she knew she'd be used up and then tossed away like a bag of fly-infested leftovers in a dumpster behind a city restaurant, all that radiance she'd once perceived to be emanating from within her extinguished and in its aftermath a cold, funereal body. *I have to get out of here,* she thought. *What's he going to do?*

James' eyes popped back into place as though a magician had snapped his finger and willed it so. His face became still. He laughed hysterically – a high, fierce, prolonged sound that wavered between the support it gave for the notion of his complete insanity and the notion of his genuine happiness. "Let's go in," he said, turning, plucking his knife from the tree, putting it back in his pocket. His manner now languid. He moved toward the front door.

She power-walked the other way and began running as soon as her shoes touched the gravel of Blackhawk Lane. *Michael, Michael,* her thoughts screamed into the wide, uncharted sea of night. *Why is it so fucking hard to get to you?* She stopped at the corner of Deerfield and Blackhawk, leaning forward, gasping, watching sporadic headlight beams sally to and fro. Thrust out her thumb at the tail end of a profound sigh, letting it dangle along in the cool, lightlessness. *Who the hell would pick me up?*

At that same moment, an old, brown Honda Accord, which had been whisking toward Edwardo's

Pizza, cast its narrow and faded headlights over her tottering body, frustrated face, outward thumb. Its driver, Jonathan Bellman, a Deerfield senior who'd taken the previous year off school to tour with Phish, hit his brakes and swerved in her direction, stopping about ten feet from her back-staggering body. Stepping out of the car to the pastoral jamming of *Me and My Uncle* by the Grateful Dead, which blasted on his CD player, stepping out from a heavy mist of dank, ganja smoke, Jonathan stared at Camille as she stood frozen in his car lights. He smiled: "What are you doing, girl?"

An angel, she thought, her eyes fixed to his face. She shrugged and cocked her head, puffing her lips. "Long story?"

"Get in here, loca. I'll give you a ride. Where are you going?"

"Highland Park," she told him as she got in. She watched him flip around and head back toward downtown Deerfield. "Is that … cool?"

He reached down into the little cove beneath his stereo as they moved along the 294 overpass, stereo now playing a live version of *Fire on the Mountain*. He pulled out a small, glass one-hitter and red Bic. Put the dark piece to his lips and flamed up, whipping stray strands of hair behind his small ears, all the while staring fixedly at the windshield. "It's no worries," he said with a strained sigh, letting out a faded burst of marijuana smoke which broke up and scattered along his windshield. He offered her the pipe and lighter with a gesture of the hand, still staring ahead.

She fondled the hot oney and watched the two-story homes along Deerfield Road -- all lit up by tall street lamps and presenting themselves from what used to be, what still longed to be, forest -- as they cruised past her window. She'd never smoked herb before: she could feel her heart beating. Put the bat to her lips, lit up. That heated, weedy sting at the back of her throat. The way the smoke moved into her like a thicker breath of fresh air. She let it out at the windshield, leaning forward and coughing hysterically, spitting, cheeks reddening.

"Take it easy," he said. He gave her a few gentle pats on the back, glancing at her and back at his windshield, chuckling. "Have you ever smoked before?" He took back his lighter and pipe and put them into the cove beneath the stereo. Gave his left hand, which was clasping the top of the wheel, a slow jerk and the car veered into the left lane of Deerfield Road, at Waukegan, beside a tiny plaza of antiquated, brick shops.

She gawked at the moving road in front of them and began to imagine they were in a fantasy epic: that this was an agrarian planet they were navigating in their tiny land-ship. *What is our mission here?* she thought. *What is it we are seeking to find in this world?* She stared at trees and shrubs passing the window, illuminated and shadowed by street lamps, and began looking for signs of foreign life.

Jonathan, glancing at the back of her head, began to laugh. "Where we going, sister?"

He's saying something to me. I'm in his car. Who is he? How did I get here? The one thing I can't tell him is that I'm too stoned to sound like I know what I'm talking about. She began to breathe rapidly. *Everything's fine. Just answer his question.* An image of her mother came to her, standing by their kitchen doorway, glaring. *I'm so alone.* She gazed at her legs. "What was your question?"

"What's the temperature on Mars today?" he said, pulling into a small parking lot in front of a White Hen. The Grateful Dead now shifting into a *Franklin's Tower* jam.

She was gaping at him as they parked.

Jonathan looked back at her, feigned a Janet Lee-Psycho scream. "Just fucking with you." He gave her a swat on the arm. "Good herb, though, huh? Purple Haze. My boy gets it from the west coast. Met him at the Phish show in New Haven. Dude was actually a roadie for the Stones back in the day." He nodded his head at the convenience store. "Wanna' Coke or anything?"

"Sure."

He leaned back, flashed a grin. "Sure what? Coke? Diet Coke? Slurpee?" He reached forward to turn up the volume on his stereo. "Just chill to this. I got you." Opened his door and ascended from the car like James Brown doing a soulful shoulder shrug. His slim figure disappearing into the store, hands flipping away stray strands of hair that kept fleeing from behind his ears and dancing along his cheeks.

She shut her eyes and began shaking to the music. Jerry Garcia's voice -- soft, simple and melodic -- was like that of a prophet, guiding quotidian minds away from embittered neurosis, inviting any and all to come back to a way of peace and happiness, a sweet arcadia, inalienable love communicated by our virgin nature. She swayed her shoulders side to side with the music's rhythm. She was a free-child, a flower-child. She'd tour through the country and make diverse friends, sleep on couches, play in fields, smoke pot, fall in love and then out of love and then into love again and it would be wonderful. *Roll away,* Garcia was singing, *the dew.* She leaned back against the headrest, let her chin drop to her chest.

Shaken from the fantasy kaleidoscope by Jonathan tapping her shoulder. Her eyes drew open, as though coming out of a long, undisturbed dream. She looked to him with a lustful smile that could have been exchanged between ardent lovers on their waking in the morning. Then she realized she was fourteen and powerless, that she didn't know him, that she'd run away, that... She straightened herself, glanced at her feet. Sorry, she wanted to say. I was just... resting. Yet still she was mired in that dense ganja bog which had formed over her consciousness.

"Two for the trip," he said, handing her a large bottle of Coke, a pack of Camel Filters.

She gawked at the gifts as she took them.

"Where we going?" He swigged his Mountain Dew.

"801 Thackery Drive."

"That off Green Bay?"

How'd you know? You're so smart, she thought. "North of, of, of..."

"Clavey," he said, shifting the car into reverse and gliding the wheel, jutting out his dimpled chin with an air of noble concentration. "Used to know a girl who lived over there. Keira." He shook his head and his eyes fell. "Sad story. Overdose."

Few more minutes of Bob Weir's guitar magic and the languid whir of nighttime, suburban road and their Honda had now begun to shine its lights on the winding pavement that was Thackery Drive, street even quieter than Camille's. The three-story homes with latticed windows and coiling driveways -- brand new sixty and seventy-thousand-dollar cars motionless atop those drives -- all seemed to sleep erect in the shadows, amidst manicured patches of lawn and bush.

"I remember these cribs," Jonathan was saying as he tilted his wheel. "Which one?"

She pointed left. "Two more. On the left. Wait! Wait, wait, wait!" She shifted her finger all the way right like a Jedi commanding motion with her hands. "Can you pull over here? And turn off your lights? And turn down the music?" She leaned forward, turned down the stereo.

Lights off and car stopped at the edge of a u-shaped driveway, adjacent a bulky lawn rock, Jonathan watched her as she fumbled to grasp her cigarettes and Coke bottle. "End of the line, my little sister," he said.

Everything happening so fast, she thought, looking at him, looking around the boxy Honda, *this car ride, James' place, cops, running away...* "Thanks," she said, shaking her head at the floor. "That was so cool."

"It's no worries. See you around."

She clicked open the door and stepped out into the breezing eve, gazing at Jonathan's vibrant, red taillights as they diminished and disappeared into the night's blackness. She swigged the Coke. Felt her legs aching again and rubbed them as she walked toward 801, now feeling in harmony with the whistling trees and conservative quietness around her.

Standing at the end of the Parkers' driveway, pondering her next move. A sharp, whishing sound emerged from behind and she whipped around to see Jonathan's Honda headed the other way. *New life*, she thought, gazing at his taillights as they vanished again. *Possibilities. Happiness.* She smiled uncontrollably, then turned back to 801.

Michael's white and dark brown house was two stories and stretched back for what seemed a quarter of a football field. A little chimney protruded from the center of the wide, triangular rooftop. Row of small windows were embedded just below the roof's lower edge. Below the leftmost windows, two selfsame, mahogany garages, side-by-side, like invariant business partners.

She didn't know how she was going to get to him. He lived somewhere upstairs, but it was only 8-ish. Could be anywhere in the house. She felt tingling through her whole body as she realized she was now dancing unrestrained to the rhythm of life, standing here without pre-planning or specific purpose, a bit high, a bit naughty, miles from that sense of self-imposed "propriety," or, in her case, subservience to the specious wisdom of authority. Her harrowing absence of ideas about how to get to him, smoothly, secretly, kept her wavering back and forth beside a vernal witchhazel shrub. "Fuck it," she said, throwing her Coke behind her. The grass-muffled thud it made on someone else's lawn. She began to stride forth.

Jogging alongside Michael's home with head down now and shoulders stooped, but imagining herself knocking brusquely on the Parkers' front door and Rachel Parker, Michael's mom, -- dark, curly hair, French hook earrings --, opening it, giving Camille a look of agitated puzzlement and then Rachel Parker looking out beyond Camille, out into the blackened street, and then back at Camille again and saying, What can I do for you?, and Camille responding, I won't let you keep Michael locked up in the prison of your craziness anymore! You could never understand his perfection. You're ruining him. Get out of my way. He's mine. We're meant for each other.

Get the fuck out of my way, you sorrowful waste of space!

At the back of the Parker home there was a thirty foot swimming pool in the shape of an hourglass, covered by a heavy, sky-blue tarp, which was ensconced in a large rectangle of brick paving and surrounded by a few scattered wicker chairs, small tables, just beyond a set of glass doors that opened up into a spacious atrium.

Staring at a solitary wicker chair and deciding the chair was inviting her into a moment of reprieve from her unavoidable need to figure out what to do, Camille strode over to it, fell back into it and gazed at the house. She reached into her pocket and pulled out her new pack of Camel Filters with a burst of glee, but then put it away when she realized she didn't have a lighter and was suddenly overwhelmed by disappointment.

A champagne-hued light flickered on from a bay window on the second floor of the house. She could discern Michael's small figure as he stood at the window's center in a bizarre, David-Lynchian composition of silhouette and definable feature. He then toddled out of frame.

Now, she thought, standing. Her shoulders tightened and she could feel a constricting pressure working on her chest. She walked to a line of trimmed shrubs alongside the atrium and bent down, brushing her palm against the soil, attempting to find a stone or pebble to throw at the window. The surface beneath her sweeping hands smooth -- nothing to project. She scooped her hand into a lump of dirt and yanked out a submerged twig.

Doddering beneath that window with the twig arched behind her shoulder, she flung it forward. The feeble stick moved through the night and made a soft, scratching click against Michael's center window pane, when, suddenly stripped of momentum by gravity's final bidding, it plummeted down into the dark green depths of shrubbery like a Fallen Angel.

Empty minutes moseyed past and the honey-hued window remained absent of Michael's figure. Camille gave an envenomed sigh. She walked back to the bushes and kicked them. The disrupted shrubs hissing in agitation. *Fuck it*, she thought, staring at his window, fists clenched. *I'll scream his name till he hears me and damn the consequences*. She could feel that wanton yell building in her throat, inflating her lungs, tingling at the back of her head.

Michael had now wandered over to his window and was standing there, unmoved.

She paddled backwards, spreading her arms out, jumping up and down.

Michael put his forehead to the window pane. He couldn't believe that was Camille flailing around in the middle of his backyard at eight o'clock at night. Looking at her, he was suddenly frightened – *Camille*, he was thinking. *Poor Camille. She's without a stable environment. Too young to be a friendless vagabond in this large, mysterious and merciless world, to be moving toward her own death like a confused piece of prey. I should just listen to her. I should just let her work out her problems and not react. That's the only way she can find clarity on her own. What is stability anyway? Everything's changing. Rome and the fall of Rome. Oral storytelling and then reading and then the television. I could get hit by a car tomorrow. It could be my mom, my dad. Then what would happen to this quote-unquote stable house we have? The only real stableness is the little piece of stableness we find in ourselves by accepting the unstableness of all things. Nothing's permanent.* He looked at his ceiling, smiled. *Impermanence was the last thing Buddha talked about.* He turned and stepped toward his door without entertaining the somatic need to rush. Strolled down a long, curvilinear staircase with his right hand caressing its banister, past Mom and Dad who were lying like litter on a windless day along two bulging, brown-leather sofas, watching *Pretty Woman* on their large-screen TV. Sauntering through an elongated, white-tile hall with multi-size modern paintings and opening the atrium door, the metallic whine of its knob barely audible underneath the sound of Richard Gere saying "Stop fidgeting!" from the loud Bose speakers in the distance behind him.

Camille leapt onto him as he was stepping out, the force of her contracting muscles pushing him back, causing him to let out nervous chuckles. She kissed his neck and put her chin on his shoulder and sighed into his ear. Wanted to give out all the emotions that had been eating her insides for years in that moment, in the last refuge his shoulder could provide her. When she opened her mouth to exorcise these haunting sensations, her head just fell onto his neck and she began to sob. "I can't handle all these horrible things happening in my life, Michael," she said.

Michael, holding her. "Let's go in," he whispered. He touched her shoulders and tried to free himself from the embrace.

She held harder, pressing her face into his chest.

He smiled, gave a low laugh, patted her upper back. "Cam," he said, trying to breathe through the tightness in his body. "It's okay. Let's just go in."

She clasped him more tightly and pressed with more force.

"You're squeezing too hard. You're hurting me. Calm down. Please. I'm a person, Camille. Not your Beanie Baby."

She tugged herself away and gazed at him, blue eyes frozen, brows furrowed, the skin of her slightly sloped nose crinkling with an emergent sneer.

"I didn't mean that. I…"

Chilling silence, like that of a witch's footsteps in the crepuscular shadows of a provincial town, surrounded Camille's countenance. The malicious energy from her expression drained, evaporated, and in its place appeared a profound sense of lack, attested to by her wily eyes that whipped back and forth as they wrestled with the hurtful information she was receiving. Her eyelids fluttered; she put her face into her palms and cried.

Michael whipped his head behind him at the atrium door, terrified his mom was now standing just beyond its threshold in a stance of preparative attack. He could picture his mom right there, watching them, immotile. *I knew you were no good*, she'd be saying with her censorious glare. *We're sending you to boarding school, Michael*, she would say. *Tell your friend to leave before I call the police*. The sealed and quiescent atrium door, however, firmly affixed at the center of some mighty reality that rejected Michael's wild imagination, appeared vacant, ghostly. He turned back to Camile, eyes large. "Stop," he said. "You called me and told me you were coming over -- I don't know where you are, how you'll get here, what time you're coming -- and then you just didn't show up." His inflection rose. "*Then*, I glance out my window, hours later, and there you are, jumping up and down in the middle of my backyard. My parents are in the den right now, Camille. Do you have any idea how much trouble we'll get into if they catch you here? How *did* you get here? Did you walk? Did you run away again? Jesus. Your mom's going to have a heart attack." He sighed. "Look, I know you're upset, but acting crazy like this is only making things worse. Why don't you understand that?" He touched her muddy hand, knitted his brow. "What happened? And where's your coat? Are you cold?"

"Nothing, I'm fine," she said, sniveling and looking away.

"Don't be petulant. Just come inside with me so we can talk, *now*, *quickly, quietly*. Sorry I said that thing about you treating me like a Beanie Baby. C'mon."

She gazed at him and began to tear. Her lower lip trembling. "Leave with me. We're better than this and you know it. We can get jobs, we're smart. Let's just leave this behind us. Right now. We'll be so happy, because we'll be together."

"What on earth are you talking about? You just need to calm."

"No, Michael. Why aren't you listening to me? Please." She held onto his flanks and was sobbing again. "Please, let's just go. Please! Please, please, please!"

He took a step back, whipping his head behind him, again gawking at that atrium door. *Mom heard that*, he thought. *Shit. She's coming – I know it*. He turned back to Camille, glowering, his small face taking on a florid hue. *Don't yell at her. Nam-myoho-renge-kyo. Nam-myoho-renge-kyo. She's just upset. Just get her out of here.*

"If you're going to act like this *again*," he said, balling his fists, "then you need to go."

A frigid glare eclipsed her face and dried out her eyes. She slapped him, quickly, as though an involuntary reaction to a needle prick.

They both stood stone-still, gaping at each other.

She turned and dashed off into the woods.

He rubbed his cheek and stared at that endless nightfall which had now swallowed her lamenting figure. *Let her go.* Disquieting chilliness started in his head, spread through his whole upper body. *What's going to happen to her? There's nothing you can do.* He looked back at the ground, still caressing his face. *It's not your fault, Camille.*

August 8, 2011

Jake kept watching Camille as she took a seat on one of his green sofas and crossed her legs. He stood by the front door, brooding. "Amazing."

"What?" she said, giving him a wry smile.

"Nothing." Swept away the thought with his hand, walked to the couch, sat beside her.

"You're so weird, Jake."

"No, it's just... the way you are."

Silence. Silence of expectation and immediacy. Silence beseeching them both to fill it quickly with their explanations, palliative banalities, anything that would erase the fear something horrible might be emerging in their relationship, a purposeful withholding of judgment, private feeling of superiority on one side or the other unspoken.

"Sometimes just watching you..." he said, putting his hand on her back. "You're very special."

"You always say that; you think too much of me."

"No." He touched her arm. "I know it. You--"

He was cut off when her winged mouth pressed his. Her small, full lips surging with warmth like beating hearts. She began sucking his upper lip. Jake remained inert as his mind struggled to process. He gripped her nape and began kissing back. Squeezed her stone-like breasts with his free hand. Her slim body jerked back and there was a sharp pain in his stomach. He let her lead, now returning dutiful strokes with his tongue. Began brushing his fingers against her thigh. Started massaging that warm hill between her jeans. Her legs clamped down on his hand; he could feel her moistening. Felt himself getting hard. His fantasy of her touching him, groping him, taking him out, giving him her mouth, saliva, juice seemed it was about to become reality.

"Jake," she said, pulling back, poising her needlelike fingers at the center of his chest.

He tried to force her hand away with his body, but she pressed harder.

"What?" he said gruffly. "What is it?"

She looked down at the cushions. "We're getting ahead of ourselves. We need to take it slow. Like an old, married couple." She looked back up into his eyes with unwavering determination, the implacable stillness of a native warrior confronting an imperializing army. "Okay?"

"Of course, of course." He moved back, face scrunched, eyes flipping left, right.

"You don't have to move away like I'm a leper," she said. She stood and straightened her mussed jeans, grabbed her purse from atop his coffee table.

"No, Camille, I wasn't… I was just…"

"Whatever, Jake."

"Why are you getting so mad? You were the one who wanted to do this all of a sudden. I did, too, but I wasn't forcing it on you."

"You think I forced myself on you?"

"That's not what I meant. Why are you standing? Are you leaving? What did I do?"

"Stop yelling at me," she said.

"I'm not."

She glared at him, cheeks taking on an increscent flush. "Maybe this whole thing was a mistake."

"What are you talking about? Because it got intense for a moment? I like you. This is silly. I thought things were going really great."

"I just need to go." She headed for the door.

Jake, following her: "Wait."

"What is this?" he said as she looked at him, scared, irresolute.

She let herself out, pulling the door shut behind her with a booming thud.

He stared at the closed door a moment, then turned and lingered in the same spot he'd been standing when he'd watched her on the couch, his expression again pensive, again full of fascination and puzzlement. Walked to one of the couches, laid on it awhile, hands behind his head, then decided to get up and go look for his phone. Shabby Samsung was lying just beside a dirty sink in his kitchenette. He called her and began to pace around. "Great to be with you today," he said after the quick beep at the end of her voicemail, "regardless of whatever just happened. Just want to let you know I can't wait to see you again. Call me whenever you're ready." He resumed his pose on the couch, now putting the phone on his stomach as though it was his first newborn and exhuming a remote from the cushion beneath him. He flipped on the TV, started watching an episode of *True Life*, but continually looked at the phone, wondering whether or not to call again, say something different, say more, deciding not to.

April 27, 1996

That intense, all-present daylight of a minimal Chicago neighborhood coming through Michael's Jeep Cherokee windows now, exposing the tiny, claret blemishes on Michael's forehead as he held the wheel with both hands, focused on the road, accenting the vibrant blue in Camille's eyes as she watched him and smiled.

"Can we please just listen to music?" she said. "This isn't fun."

"What's wrong with silence?"

"It's not silent. We can hear cars whooshing back and forth."

"Not completely silent," he said. "But silent enough to be more aware." He smirked.

"Aware of what?"

"The present moment."

"Are you an alien?"

"Our minds are so busy. We're always thinking about what we need to do or what we should have done or trying to write a story about who we think we are. But there's so much happening right now, if you can just allow for the silence and let all that other noise quiet down."

"What are you talking about, alien? What's happening right now?"

"The flow of this car on the road, the brand new late-morning we're a part of, so full of life, stories." He put a hand on her leg, but remained focused on the road. "This beautiful lady sitting right beside me. So much to get to know about her. An endless enigma. Always surprising."

"I don't know, Michael," she said, now pressing her feet to tip of her seat, hugging her knees. "Guess I always associated silence with depression, or, I don't know… Bad things." She let herself get hypnotized by the endless lines of Mom-and-Pop shops, the lusterless car battalions moving north and south.

"Silence is healthy and healing," Michael said as he took a left onto Sherwin: a modest street draped on both sides by the plentiful leaves from Shellbark Hickories, tucked away against the Lake Michigan shore. "Maybe you'll see that today." Right now, into a condensed parking lot with little pieces of errant gravel scattered across it. He parked the Jeep beside a beat-up Toyota Cressida with a bright-blue bumper sticker on its back right side that said "Coexist," killed his engine, stared at Cam.

Camille whipped her head toward the back of the car, at her window, at him. "Where are we?"

"I told you. Shambhala Meditation Center."

"Sham-what-uh-what-uh-what-uh?"

"The Sham--"

"I know, hon." Putting her hand on his cheek. "Kidding."

They stepped out, shut doors, click-click, and the quick chirp of Michael's remote-control alarm. Walked along a side of the building, Camille with her head up, mouth agape. The building before her appeared like a fusion of pagoda and long-standing, three-story, neighborhood home. Every level ornamented by dark brown, hipped roofing. There was a roomy, dusty veranda right at front, just above a small set of cracked, concrete steps, a space vacant, hushed, streaming with mellow energy, inhabited by peaceable ghosts that whispered of the many lucid moments once had right here, many esoteric realizations once come to, senses of home found.

"You know the craziest places," she said, still staring at the building.

"You're going to love it." He held the door for her after they'd walked up the front steps. "Something new."

Inside a stark room with white walls, the occasional framed picture of Chogyam Rinpoche. A soft scent of Blackberry Sage incense. Two elderly people sat side-by-side on a plain, beige couch, in pelagic silence, smiling at Camille and Michael as they walked in. The couple had long since situated themselves behind a wide, glass coffee table that had several issues of *Shambhala Sun* stacked in neat piles at center.

The couch couple greeting them, one after the other, and then the man, still staring at Michael and Camille as they inched forward: "First time at the Center?"

Cam didn't take her eyes off her friend as they sat and an awkward, get-to-know-you quietness followed Michael's response: "Yes, it is." Michael kept looking at the couple. The wide smile that had emerged on his face when they'd walked in still hadn't disappeared.

"Do either of you need guidance?" the old man said, looking only at Michael.

Michael, looking at Camille: "She might."

"Michael, no."

"That's alright," the woman said, her two words prompting prolonged silence. The woman turned to her husband and engaged him in low-pitched conversation, but their civil chatter was quickly broken by a middle-age woman now opening up and coming out a set of white doors to the bordering room.

This woman sauntering over to the couches, greeting the couple. She then introduced herself to

Michael and Cam. Kept looking at Michael and Cam with a languid smile. "Do you two need any guidance?"

"We're fine," Michael said.

"Everyone ready, then?" the middle-age woman said, her eyes moving back and forth betwixt the foursome.

Heads nodding. Murmuring assents. They all filed into the commodious room beyond the white doors, slipping off shoes. Four symmetrical rows of rectangular meditation cushions. An elevated floor at the room's far end. A cushion with a bronze Tibetan singing bowl beside it on one end of the far floor. Wooden altar with smoking incense at that far floor's center. Behind that alter, posted to the back wall, a cardinal tapestry with a large, black OM symbol.

Camille and Michael found a seat alongside a wall as the middle-age lady, who'd stayed behind to shut them all in, was now taking lotus posture on her elevated cushion. The instructor tugging at her drawstring pants, wiggling her hips this way, that. She fluttered her eyes, shutting them, opening them, smiling.

"I don't know how to do this," Camille whispered, grasping Michael's arm.

"Just close your eyes and focus on the breaths coming in and out of your nostrils," he said. He shut his eyes and demonstrated with histrionic breaths. "When you start thinking about something, let your mind finish the thought and then keep coming back to the breath. Try to do this from the time you hear the gong till the time you hear it again."

They gazed at each other, simpered.

"Sit like this," he said, giving her a little swat, showing her his lotus pose. He looked at the altar, crossed his knees and shut the eyes.

She was still moving her legs, jiggling her hips, trying to get comfortable long after the instructor had touched her mallet to the singing bowl and its soft, soaring ping had led everyone else in the room into a state of close-eye stillness. Bare feet planted on the floor, knees up, Camille put her hands on her thighs and shut her eyes, too. She kept flipping them back open. She would breathe quickly, look around, terrified she'd suddenly lost sight of how to think and feel the way she'd been accustomed to her whole life, that she'd plunged downward into a foreign and alarming plane where she was without identity, never to return, where she was amnesiac, infantile, powerless to defend herself from the world's caprices, especially her own imminent death. Started closing her eyes for longer now. *David!* she thought. *Riverwoods.* She saw an image of herself standing by a couch in the living room of her Riverwoods home, her mother right in front of her, their noses touching, but Mom's figure nebulous like a wraith. *Hell,* she thought. *Dim lights.* Now she was running up the carpeted staircase of her front hall, her hand brushing the wood banister. Stairs were without end; she kept moving in the same motion. Her mom behind her, saying something, trying to catch up, but it just wasn't possible for Mom to reach daughter. Cam's eyes flew back open. She took in a loud breath. Eyes fluttered, closed again. Now she was grasping at interminable blackness, trying to retrieve a thought, trying to remember. *Why is it so quiet? This is wrong.* She recalled Michael had said something about breathing and forced herself to continue. Images of Deerfield High School now. Those escalating radiators in B-Hall along a series of wide windows that overlooked the school's courtyard, the middle of a weekday, the whole place congested with handfuls of freshman, sophomores, juniors, seniors who were the elite, best looking, most popular. This mind-portrait inspired hope; it represented a world larger than her household, world of opportunity, a glamorous world, one that could, would embrace her fully. New thoughts now. Previous thoughts recycling. She squeezed her arms, nails pressing skin. Lost herself in a blitzkrieg of impressions and words. Flinched. Started when she heard the second ping from that singing bowl, flipped opened her eyes and remembered she hadn't gone anywhere. She felt a hand on her shoulder, turned.

"How do you feel?" Michael said. He was beaming.

"Strange."

"Why strange?"

"It's odd for people to just sit around like this, not saying anything."

They were cut off by another ting from the bowl. "Walking meditation," the instructor was saying.

"Could we go now?" Camille whispered, nodding at the entrance.

"Glad you did this," he said, taking her hand. They made their way out with brisk footsteps while the others formed a wide semi-circle around the cushions.

"I feel more chill," she said, waggling her way into sneakers on a couch in the front room.

Michael, right beside her: "Go on."

"Less bitchy."

"See how everything you observe is colored by your own crazy perception? How that creates almost all the stress?"

She smirked, shook her head. "You should write a book." Looked up at the ceiling now and crinkled her brow. "There is no other way. That's how we think. That's human nature."

"If you keep meditating, you'll understand you can just let all your wild thoughts fade away, like passing rain. You'll be able to see the world around you on its own terms instead of yours, always aware, learning, never judging. It's wonderful."

Camille now drumming her thighs, staring at her shoes. *Runaway train never going back*, she sang. *Wrong way on a one way track.* "We're still going to Mike's party tonight, right?" she said, turning to him.

"What about what I just said? Look, remember that screaming match you had with your mom last week?

"Please don't get me started."

"Just imagine going back to that moment and looking at your mom without any resentment or preconceived notions. Letting her react until she has nothing else to fuel her fire with. You'd be able to see that most of her anger comes from her own weakness and hurt and that it probably has nothing to do with you. You'd feel compassion." Michael snapped his fingers. "You'd be able to diffuse the argument in two seconds."

Cam chortled. "Have you met my parents?"

"When I see your mom and stepdad, I see two people struggling with their own moral codes, codes that were fixed upon them by their parents and fixed without meeting any opposition. Codes that suffocate them and leave them anxious. They love, Camille, but don't know how to love. I know you know what I mean."

Her eyes tossed back and forth as she watched him. She moved closer. A libidinous half-smile on its way to full arousal but not fully mature on her face. Her humid, successive breaths crashing into his chin. She put her hand to his nape, kissed him.

***

Midnight had now come to Highland Park. A large sensor light was all that lit up Mike Cardini's dingy back porch. Taylor Jennet sitting cross-legged, his back pressed to Mike's sliding-glass balcony door. He was singing *Hey Jude* as he played acoustic guitar. Most of the Deerfield and Highland Parkers who'd shown up for this party had already left. They were standing outside the twenty-four-hour Dunkin Donuts on Highway 41, smoking and grubbing, checking out the crowd and being checked out, or they'd broken off into smaller groups and were now gathered in someone's basement, passing a glass bubbler, playing *Ultimate Mortal Kombat 3*, making insensate comments about people they worshipped as being "so hot" and then passing out. Those that remained, this circle surrounding Taylor, watching him play, were all past the point of blundering intoxication. All stewed about in the giddy state of inanity that precedes heavy sleep.

"Play Pink Floyd. *Wish You Were Here*," Camille blurted out, her voice gruff from all the drunken yelling. Voice now a loud, scratchy whisper that Adam Steiner, the diffident junior three people to her left, would fantasize about later that night as he lay under his covers in his Deerfield home, masturbating. Cam's head fell onto Michael's shoulder as she continued to watch Taylor.

"'Ju-day, Ju-day, Ju-day, Ju-day, Ju-day now,'" Taylor sang, eyes shut tight, face in the air, head shaking back and forth. "'Nah-nah, nah-nah-nah-nah…'"

Everyone swaying, some singing with Taylor, some mumbling to each other, some just shutting their eyes.

Cam was nuzzling her head against Michael's neck. "I'm tired." She rubbed his scrawny stomach. Hand found its way to his thigh. "Let's go back to your house."

Michael's eyes moved around the circle and made contact with the one or two guys looking back at him, swigging their beer bottles and smirking. His cheeks turned red. He tried to nudge her off.

Still didn't know why he'd decided to come to this party. Certainly wasn't the type to hang around exclusive drinking crowds. Didn't like video games; hadn't even watched more than ten minutes of television since *Sesame Street* when he was in first grade. Not that he was obsessed with school or studying either. Michael just wanted to go home, lock himself in his room, read more about the differences between Theravada and Mahayana traditions, figure out which school he fell more in line with.

"Don't push me," Camille was saying as she tried to keep her head from falling from his shoulder.

He looked down at his leather wristwatch, brought it close to his face, gawked at it, gasped. He gripped Camille's arms and began to give her gentle shakes. "12:15, Cam. Past my curfew. Yours, too. Right? We gotta' go."

Her chin fell to her chest. "I'm not going home. *Ever.* I'm going with you."

"It's time to go." He helped her up.

Taylor continued to sing, but everyone else now stared at Michael and Camille.

"Later," Michael said, shrugging. He held Camille by her waist and guided her around the house as she stumbled. Put her into the passenger seat of his Jeep and pushed the door shut with three fingers. He strolled around the car and stopped by the trunk. Looked off into the darkness that had now subsumed Stonegate Drive. A terrible feeling of defeat came over him. He feared maybe he'd reached his highest potential as a human being. That maybe he'd finally divined the perfect, intricate science behind every aspect of his entire life.

The overt divide between actual and willed meanings, he thought, shaking his head. *The elaborate mind and word games people play to deny what they really want or need in any given moment. So much so that they become foreign to their most fundamental driving forces.*

He envisioned his mom trotting around their expansive kitchen, gabbling about how important it was for him to be more social, join clubs, go on dates, saying things like "I'm not going to have a son who cloisters himself away like a hermit." as she sifted through bundles of mail but then lost focus and continued to pace. There he was, in his thought-image, standing in a corner of that kitchen with head down, hands entombed in the pockets of his black corduroys, embodying his role as the misguided and repentant son but at the same time watching the both of them from a distance, weighing, considering and pitying his mom's implicit meaning. "I don't know what love is, Mikey," his mom was really saying. "I never loved and I've never been loved. I need you to look good so I can look good, so I can feel accepted by this community and I know I'm doing this... Well, I have the faintest hint I'm doing this to you and I fucking hate myself. Do you hear me? I hate myself! Hate myself so much I can't sleep at night without Valium and Vicodin."

But it's not my responsibility to go around healing everyone, he thought, now rubbing his tiny chin with his index finger and thumb. *I'm not God. I'm not a medicine man. No, it is my responsibility. That's the vow of the bodhisattva. I don't want that kind of responsibility. I never asked for this. Never asked to be so insightful, to be afflicted with the sufferings of all humanity. Did any of the great ones ask for their path? Did Buddha? No. The path asked for them, and they said yes, and they were... great.*

The Jeep Cherokee came back to his consciousness, the party, Taylor singing, drunken Camille, the touch and feel and smells and sheer, helpless, laughing insanity of everyone's direct immersion in their unfolding lifetimes. He continued around the car and got in on the driver's side. Turned the ignition, backed up, three-point-turned and snaked his way off the small street they were on.

He made his way west on Lake Cook Road, north on Waukegan, west on Deerfield, watching the other headlights around him -- little beacons in the night -- multiply, decrease.

"I love you so much, Michael. I..." Camille was saying, her head back against the headrest, eyes shut.

He kept watching the windshield and tried to let the subdued whish of road drown out her voice. He was finally creeping along Saunders. "You have to start taking better care of yourself," he said, turning right onto Blackheath. "I shouldn't always have to be around to help you. You need to start helping yourself." Neared the end of the street and turned off his headlights, turned on the interior light, so that it looked like their faces were part of a display case. He watched as she let her head fall to her left shoulder, as she grinned at him, batted her eyes, puffed her lower lip. "But I want you take care of me, baby."

"You *don't* love me," he said.

"Of course I love you." She put her hand to his cheek.

"You love that I listen to you."

Her eyes widened. She sat upright, poised her back against her door.

"Don't get all upset now. Just listen to what I'm saying. I care about you. A lot." He stopped himself and frowned as Cam's eyes were narrowing.

"You know what, fuck you, Michael. You just don't get it." She struggled to open her door.

"Don't get *what*? How could either of us get anything about each other when we can't even express ourselves honestly? When one of us doesn't even want to understand what that word means?"

"The *fuck* are you talking about?" she said. "Stop speaking in riddles. Only thing you care about is yourself. Your books and your meditation and all your weird, spiritual bullshit!" She'd now opened the passenger door and tried to lunge out, but didn't realize Michael had buckled her in. She gave a croaking yelp and then a frustrated growl as her seatbelt pushed her body backward. She whipped her face toward Michael as though he were that trammeling belt. The passenger door remained ajar.

He was looking at the windshield, shaking his head. "Calm down. You act like such a child."

188

"Why are you so hurtful? You're supposed to be my friend. I love you." She covered her face with her hands, began to cry. "I have no one. No one. I'm all alone."

He leaned over and put his hand on her leg. "You're getting yourself all worked up over nothing. You're wasted…" He stopped himself when he noticed a figure moving through the darkness by Camille's garage, his eyes widening in fright.

This was David Garner, Camille's stepfather, who'd been prodded awake by Ellen in their master bedroom. Ellen, naturally anxious, had been going in and out of consciousness for hours. She'd been laying with eyes half-open in the unmitigated dark of the bedroom as David filled up the space with his leonine snoring. She'd heard the faint and distant sound of her daughter's shouts from out front and had said "David! Wake up. That's Camille outside. She's screaming. Why is she outside? Go see what's going on." So now David, clad in a white, terrycloth robe, eyes baggy, receding salt and pepper hair disheveled, was about ten feet from Michael's Jeep.

"Camille, let's go, get out of the car," David said.

Camille, stunned, wiped her eyes. She continued to flash glances between David and Michael. Put her head down and unbuckled her belt. She didn't look at Michael, didn't look at David. Her head slumped and she got out. She stood before her stepfather in the driveway darkness like a plantation slave before their despotic master. Michael saw all this from the corner of his eye but continued to stare at the windshield.

"Goodnight, Michael," David said, shutting the passenger door.

She continued to repress her burgeoning

indignation as she followed her stepfather to the garage and listened to the sound of Michael's tires fading off. Her stepfather had again meddled in her personal life and hindered from her from her unadulterated exploration of her own raw emotions and aborning beliefs, from important time spent learning about who she was in the company of friends, all of which, if uninterrupted, would have been leading her toward becoming the person she was meant to be. She found herself voiceless, paralyzed as she waited for David to punch in the garage code, found herself in the same state she always did around David. They filed into the house, one after the other, in silence. Maybe she felt this way around her stepfather because he'd presented himself to her as the encompassment of all irreconcilable, emotional contradiction when her mind still needed to develop by first understanding concepts like "love" and "family" in terms of absolutes. David had married Ellen and situated himself in their private living quarters only a year after Ellen's divorce from Martin. David taken on the role of Ellen's loving intimate, Camille's calculating saboteur and model father figure all at the same time. He was intelligent, pragmatic and an ardent proponent of American bourgeois culture, a way of life Camille already knew she wanted nothing to do with.

You are the incarnation of everything I hate, she thought as she followed him through that kitchen dark, glaring at his lumbering body. *I see right past your goody-goody front. You can hypnotize the rest of this family into believing you're a stalwart savior figure, but you'll never fool me, you insecure, self-loathing megalomaniac. One day I'm going to put you in your fucking place. Just wait.* She kept her head down at the top of the front hall staircase, scurried to her room, closed the door.

David returned to the master bedroom.

August 15, 2011

Camille sat in lotus posture at the end of her bed, phone to ear, twirling her long, red hair with an index finger and half-looking at the frayed cover of her Penguin *Jane Eyre*, which she'd just put on the floor. "When you don't call me back, it makes me never want to see you or talk to you again," she said.

"I was just thinking about things," Jake responded to her over the phone. "You left me a message two days ago. Took *you* almost a week to get back to me."

"I got back to you that night." She grabbed a Camel from the pack beside her, fired up. Stood and began to stalk around in front of her bed.

"Text messages don't count."

"Of course they count. I was communicating with you."

Jake, a mile away, kept walking back and forth on his squeaky porch. He stopped rambling a moment and stared at the wide parking lot behind his building: the weathered, wood telephone poles and their drooping cords, the other aged three-story apartment building beyond the lot, its details scarcely discernible in the distance. A dreary, early-evening landscape not unlike that of Northern England's nineteenth century moors, he imagined, in terms of the sprawling picture it provided, with the post-rain murkiness that seemed to be depriving it of all lively color. He suddenly envisaged himself a Catherine Earnshaw figure, now looking out into the hazy expanse and trying to make sense of love felt for a mysterious paramour. He wondered how it must have been for lovers three hundred years ago, before electronic communication, when time spent apart was marked by so much quiet reflection. *So much time to consider the nuances of one another*, he thought, *perhaps through letters. To be consumed by the sublime flames of longing and then to have so much to offer each other when together, so much gratitude, tenderness and respect.* He continued to march around, head down. *What the hell has society devolved into? Everything so instantaneous now. No more room for thoughtfulness or weighty sentiments. We're all just a bunch of amorous animals.* He chuckled.

"What the hell are you laughing at?" she said. "What'd you just get quiet like that? What's wrong with you?"

"Sorry, I've been spacey today. I really don't want to argue with you. This is new; not getting right back to you was inconsiderate. What are you doing now? Want to hang out?"

She held the phone away from her ear, sneering at it.

"Cam."

"Don't patronize me, Jake."

"I'm not." He laughed. "You're upset because you think I'm not interested in you anymore, which is silly, because I am. Very much so."

She stood by her living room couch, smoking, jiggling her right leg. Tried to speak and restrained herself at the same time.

"You okay?"

"I gotta' go." She hung up, tossed her phone onto the couch, snuffed out her cigarette in the kitchen sink. Strode to her window and jeered. Her eyes dulled over as they bathed in the flinty colors of sky. *Such a waste of my time. You need to be writing. When's the last time you wrote?*

Jake, leaning against his balcony rail, had tried to call back twice now. He put his phone down and continued to walk around. *You're too forward,* he thought. *Too comfortable. She's sensitive.* He tried to imagine the world from her perspective and was suddenly absorbed in a state of stinging despair. *I have to be kind. Patient, caring, solicitous. That's what a companion's supposed to do.* Then he remembered how necessary it'd been to empathize with Cassie in order to justify her unpredictable temperament. He became filled with frustration, ire. *This is the same fucking situation. Stay away from her. Don't call her back, don't pick up the phone if she calls. What's wrong with you? Maybe I should just give up this life and join the clergy.* He decided to go inside and make himself a drink.

Jake's bantam kitchen situated just beside the back door. He stood before a lean, white fridge, glimpsing at the collection of liquor bottles he'd made on top -- some empty, some mostly full. His eyes locked on that bottle of Johnnie Walker Blue Label, still in its statuesque box. He grasped it and then a rocks glass from one of his wood cabinets, tearing the Walker case open with one hand as he made his way into the living room where his roommate, Tommy, was slouching on a couch and watching *Groundhog Day.*

Tommy craned his head toward Jake. "J. Blue, huh?"

Jake fell on the adjacent couch, tossed the mangled Walker box beside him, put the bottle and glass on their coffee table. He toppled onto a cushion. "Fucking girls."

"That's why we gotta' become MPUAs," Tommy said, gaping at the movie.

"Become *what?* "

"Master Pick Up Artists, man." Tommy, eyes still

195

transfixed by the television, waved his remote at Jake like it was a magic wand. "Read *The Game.* That book is the Truth. Trust me."

Jake smirked. "What's your point?"

"If you read it," Tommy said, now glancing at him, "you'd know that the Master Pick Up Artist can get any girl he wants, within two minutes." He snapped his fingers. "He's the ninja of all things pussy. Never has to focus on any one girl -- always another waiting right around the corner. No more LTRs. No more problems."

"The fuck is LTR?"

"Long-term relationship," Tommy said, glancing at him again, then going back to the TV. "A girlfriend. Go get the book. Actually, I'll give you mine. You better treat that thing like it's your dying grandma."

"You fascinate me."

"Serious, Jay."

Jake leaned forward, un-capped his bottle and poured a drink. He fell back, gawking at Tommy's profile, taking a long sip from his glass and then letting out a gravelly breath. "Maybe you're right. Maybe we're not meant to be the slaves of monogamy. Seems to go against our natural inclination not to satiate all these attractions we feel for other people." Another vigorous sip. "Why repress who we really are for one person? Because it makes us more civilized? Maybe. But is it worth all this anxiety?"

Tommy, twirling the remote: "Can you go host *The Montel Williams Show* somewhere else? Trying to watch this."

Jake stood up, drink billowing. "But Camille's such an angelic person beneath the surface. So unique, smart. So much substance." His glassy eyes now affixed themselves to a bristle dartboard hung against Tommy's closed bedroom door. "If she could just confront her demons, whatever the hell they are. Accept it, let it go, see how great she really is…" He nodded, scoffed. "*Much* easier said than done."

"Dude!" Tommy said, elbow now jammed into a couch cushion, palm propping up his head. "You're fucking killing me. Go away."

Jake turned, began striding back to the balcony. When he'd gotten outside, put down his scotch, looked at his phone and saw she'd called, he swelled up with bliss. Dialed her number:

"Hi."

"Look, I'm too confrontational, Cam. Sorry. I--"

"No, you're right."

Jake, who'd been trooping around in circles, stopped. "What?"

"I let my fears get the better of me. I was childish. I'm sorry. Can I see you?"

"Where? When?"

"Would you want to come over here? Now?"

"Give me twenty minutes. What's your address?"

May 15, 1997

"Wait-wait-wait," came a rough, high voice from the middle of the classroom.

Camille, gawking at the window, was disconnected from her daydream about a white-sand beach in Malibu, where she'd been strutting around in front of celebrities in a red micro bikini, where the serene rumble of water had been nuzzling her very soul, the bite of overhead sun turning her skin a more vivid shade of brown, the continuous whistle of the balmy wind -- that carried in it blithe, laughing voices -- making her forget all about time and date. She whipped her head around to find Josh Grier – big, curly-black hair, chubby, stubbled face – staring at their teacher with a look of pseudo-scholarly concentration.

"Did you just say *period* table?" Josh said. "That's disgusting, Kaczynski! I thought a tampon would take care of it. You're telling me you guys actually map it out with a *table*? You guys do vagina experiments, too?"

The entire class burst into a sudden and continuous peal of laughter. Even those feigning Picasso on their notebooks were jarred from the wild sketching.

Mr. Kaczynski stood right in front of the hubristic chorus: his balloon belly protruding from beneath a chalk-smeared button-down, dangling over a pair of tight, crinkled jeans that seemed to be scotch-taped to his torso with a leather belt; his bark-brown eyes forever fixed in a pose of subdued anguish, just above an unkempt, gray beard. He continued to stand hunched over and motionless until long after the echo of laughter had turned to silence.

"Dean's office," he said, eyes now locked upon Josh Grier. He pointed his tapering index finger at the front door.

"*Come on*, Kaczynski," Josh said.

Kaczynski didn't move. "Dean's office."

Camille, palm propping up her head, noticed how Josh's baggy eyes, once languorous, had now charged with rage. How the eyes were like two furious, green suns that stood upon Kaczynski and tried to burn up their sworn enemy. How his breaths had become quick and heavy, slicing up the stuffy air and longing to latch onto vehement words the likes of which would earn him an in-school suspension at the very least.

Grier broke from his predatory pose, stood. He muttered indiscernible profanities and turned with head down, shambling to the front door, kicking a vacant desk on his way.

Camille felt a hand tapping her arm as Kaczynski continued on about the elements of the periodic table. She turned behind her, flashed her eyes at Jennifer Ryman.

"Grier's kinda' hot when he gets mad like that," Jennifer whispered.

Camille, mouth agape. "What?" She glanced at the empty desk Josh had been sitting at, back at Jennifer, smirked. "No, not really."

"You going to Noah Bauman's party on Saturday?"

"*Course*," Camille said, scrunching her brow. "What time did he say to show up?"

They were cut off by a loud beep from a television mounted between two walls in the front, right-hand corner of the room. Jenn's eyes flipped upward and stared at it. Camille turned, followed suit.

The entire class watched as their dean, a lanky, bespectacled, bald man in a black blazer, appeared on screen, sitting in front of a blue wall. He gazed at the camera, expressionless. "Dear students," he said. "At eleven o'clock this morning, on the corner of Lake Cook and Waukegan, two Deerfield seniors, William Clemente and Ben Resdale, were involved in a very serious car accident. The accident also involved three students from Highland Park. These students are currently being cared for at Highland Park Hospital. I'm very sorry to have to report that one of the Highland Park students, Michael Parker, has passed away. We'll be canceling school for the rest of the day and our counselors will be available all afternoon. Thank you."

Camille continued to gaze at the television long after it had gone blank. *Has what? What?* Dean Kasen's words repeated themselves in her head, each syllable now protracted, working to solidify a more excruciating final point. *Michael Parker has passed away.* She tried to turn, but her body wouldn't move. The faces around her, the noise, the routine unfolding of hours -- no longer governed by forty-two minute periods, five minute breaks between classes, by the shrill intercom tones that defined beginnings and ends as day moved from early morning to late afternoon -- had all slowed to an irrational pace, dreamlike now, drawn out. She had no more lightness. Would've taken her an hour to cross the glaring classroom, if she could've gotten up. *Michael Parker has passed away. Michael Parker has passed away. Michael Parker has passed away.* She seemed to be flying backward now, into a fathomless tunnel, the scholastic atmosphere remote. The sound of her classmates stifled and in its place the steady booming of her insides, the frightened thump-thump-thump of her heart. Breaths moving so quickly she thought they'd whisk away from her body forever, leaving her helpless, panic-stricken and then a dead shell. Her eyes fluttered. She fell forward onto her desk.

She came to twenty minutes later, on a stiff cot in the nurse's office, head aching.

The nurse's pale, jowly face looming over her. The lady's bright blue eyes, now reddened, remained unmoved. "Camille?"

"What? What?" Camille said, shifting her head left and right, pushing herself up.

The nurse touched her arms. "How are you feeling, honey?"

Camille took a long, revivifying breath. The sudden news of Michael's death came hurling back at her like a ghastly nightmare she couldn't shake off. "Oh My God!" she said, jumping up, knocking the nurse back. She sprinted out of the office.

She ran down a long hall, mostly empty. Open doorways revealing vanished classrooms and the newly-emerged silence that had followed their wayward uproariousness. She slowed to a stride, all the fulgent windows and monochromatic lockers now blurred by her tears. Every so often a group of students or couple or someone on their own would pass by without looking at her. Each person with a mournful expression on their face. Each person stunned to silence.

She had to go. Get out. Hospital…

Why? Why is this happening? No! No-no-no-no. Michael! Please, God, no!

She was running again, into the school's courtyard, which had not yet been closed. It seemed she was surrounded by the ghosts of kids once scattered all over this courtyard. Seemed she could hear the echoes of their daily gossip. As though all that would be left of this formerly flourishing school after today was the somber, grass-patched memorial she was now moving through. Kept making her way forward. Swift footsteps across the screechy tiles of the front hall. Out into a gray and cloudless day.

She passed the cul-de-sac at the front of the school and noticed that most of the parking lots had already been cleared out. Couple of small, leafy trees shivering in the wind as she marched up sidewalk.

She went faster, her head down. Thought maybe it wasn't the school behind her now, gaining distance, but an opaque, black demon sent from the netherworld to consume only her, unravel her, begin the process of her destruction. *Breathe, got to breathe,* she was thinking. *Breathe, breathe, breathe. Don't die. Michael, where are you? What happened? Are you okay, my love, my heart, my twin soul? Where are you?* She stopped and gripped herself. Burst into a violent fit of choking sobs and then screamed: a high-pitched, window-shattering sound reverberating and dying in the gusty hollows of the vacant lot.

Everyone within vicinity turned to investigate the source of the noise. Some stopped mid-shuffle to stare at her. Others, further away, stood on tiptoes, craning their heads left and right, trying to figure out who'd made the commotion.

She caught her breath, stared at the ground, moved faster. Faster. Faster. Her body began to tingle. She felt weak. She'd made it to Waukegan Road now, started heading north. *Not going home. This didn't happen. Nothing happened. All a dream, a bad dream. How silly, life. Just silly.* She held herself, grinned. *Just walk. Just die. Everyone dies. You're Camille. You don't live here. Don't like anyone. Nothing. This silly, silly, silly life. Over. New. What happened? Nothing.* Cars whisking past her at forty, fifty, sixty miles an hour. She could feel blood and muscles in her legs pushing and laboring.

The Bannockburn Club sign appeared in the near distance -- a wide, wooden rectangle painted gray and white. She turned into its front lot, strode past shiny cars inhabiting the parking spaces. Stared at her shoes. Life just footsteps.

Inside the club a well-lit lobby, red-yellow ceiling lights as well as the daylight coming in from an oval ceiling window. Every now and again a sweaty, middle-aged woman with a headband, in some trendy spandex number, would strut through the lobby and up a winding staircase. There was an elderly, Jewish man now tottering toward a series of green, leather couch chairs by the check-in counter, dropping down onto one of those chairs like rubble from a demolished building. He hid his face behind a crumpled issue of *Chicago Tribune*.

That svelte woman with large, black-rimmed glasses behind the front counter was busy typing on a keyboard and staring at her small computer screen. She looked up at Camille. "Can I help you?" she said without actually saying it -- by raising an eyebrow.

Camille, standing before her, eyes rigid as fresh death: "Garner."

The woman clicked her keyboard, nodded. "Go 'head."

She moved into the club, along a small passageway, through the glass doors to the pool area. A place she always went when she came here, somewhere noiseless, secluded, where the hours would fly away like migrant birds as she sloshed around in the water, lost in all her bizarre ideas and feelings. The room, which consisted of a rectangular pool and Jacuzzi grotto at back, carried in it that thick odor of chlorine trapped in a greenhouse. There was a hairy, rotund man making his way back and forth across the pool, breast-stroking.

Kept watching her feet, moving toward the Jacuzzi, not knowing why. Never again would she listen to the terrible fracas of life beyond this room. She listened to the gurgling water, slipped off her sneakers and socks. *Warm womb*, she thought, gawking at the water's circular ripples, taking off her torn jeans. It was liberating to know she was exposing herself: her red panties -- the old man nearby doing what he called breast strokes. Off came her shirt. She stepped in, steeped herself. Her whole face. *Melt away, body. My fluids combined with the earth's fluids so that I'm everywhere and nowhere. Godlike. For all time.*

A constricting pressure began to push on her lungs, but she kept herself under. Her thoughts all muddled now in that hot, submarine scene, but her myriad thought-sentences, if they were to be filtered and organized into a logical form, would have been this: What's the point of going back up? What's out there for me? But some subconscious force just wouldn't let her leap into expiry. Up she came with gasps loud enough to confound that breast-stroking man in his most recent attempt to cross the pool.

The breast-stroker, now stopped, watched Camille convulsing by the hot tub. His wet, faded brows turned downward. He began to glide toward her like a bundle of logs milling about a swamp. "Are you alright?" he said, hands touching an end of the pool.

Camille coughed and heaved at the water.

"Young lady," the man said, clearing his throat.

When Camille didn't respond, but instead finished her coughing spell and was wading her feet in the water, the old man coasted back to the opposite end of the pool. Tugged himself out with the help of a small, metal staircase. He walked to a plastic chair and patted his large belly with a white towel. Wrapped that towel around his waist and made his way toward the pool entrance. The old man, standing wet and half-naked now at the front of the health club, found the bespectacled woman behind the front counter. She was still fixated on her computer.

"There's a very troubled young lady in there," the man said, pointing his crooked index finger at the pool area. "She needs help."

The woman peeked her eyes above the computer. "What's the problem, *sir*?"

It was as though the man had suddenly shaken off his ever-present, senile aspect and now stood gazing at that woman like he was thirty years younger, shrewd, lettered. "The young lady sitting in the hot tub is very upset. Too upset to be aware of what she's doing. You need to get someone in there to help her. Right now."

The bespectacled lady gave the old man a frown as she stepped out of the front office, shutting and locking the door behind her. "Excuse me," she said when she entered the pool area. Repeating it more loudly as she strode toward Camille.

Cam kept staring at the Jacuzzi and gripping herself. To her, the woman's voice had been like a faint whining from a mouse somewhere way beyond the bubbling water. Yet the voice kept getting louder and more apparent. Cam looked up.

"You can't be in here *like this...*" the bespectacled lady was saying.

Cam stared at this strange woman, then realized she was having an interaction with her. She looked down at her body, gasped, leaned forward and hugged herself to cover her half-nakedness. *Michael!* she thought. *Michael Parker has passed away. Hospital.* She jumped up and started collecting her scattered clothes.

The woman, watching her, found she couldn't glower or give a caustic facial expression. *If you don't get out of here right now, I'll call the police, you little shit,* the woman thought. *Why did I just think that?* the woman thought. The woman suddenly confronted by her own unwarrantable hatred for this soggy girl in the fleeting stillness that had followed her last thought. Woman sensed there had been a time in her own life, so far back now it was almost indistinguishable, when she too had allowed herself to *feel* so acutely. She wondered what it was she'd been spending all these years to build on top of her underlying humanity, what hideous and impregnable castle of self-denial. Envisioned herself a cruel, resigned older woman and was filled with grief. The bespectacled woman glanced around the rest of the pool area, thankful no one else was observing them.

Camille, cradling her pile of clothes, ran to the pool entrance. She felt the air-conditioning tickling her bare, wet skin as she headed to the ladies' room.

There was one other woman in that room, in her late twenties, standing in front of a luminous mirror, combing her glossy, chestnut hair with wide brush. The woman stopped, mid-brush, and gawked at Camille through the mirror. Continued to comb her hair so as not to draw attention to herself but all the while kept glancing

207

at Camille's reflection as Camille stepped into her jeans and wormed her way back into her shirt by a locker.

   She finished dressing and continued out of the changing room, past the bespectacled lady, who was now standing by the doorway with her fleshy lips parted. Cam made it to the parking lot, wringing water from her hair, shivering. She felt like she was right back where she'd started. Not at the Bannockburn Club or the beginning of the day, but back in the first moment she could remember -- Rain. Lashing rain. Rain bringing with it an eclipsing, mid-day dusk outside the Museum of Science and Industry on some random day back in 1983. Watching that rain in the harborage of Grandma Lana's arms, from beneath the museum's stone portico. How charming life at that moment, just examining and learning and being loved. She had no idea why she'd suddenly thought of this, but it made her feel light, free to imagine she'd had a completely different experience since that time and was now not the same person, was instead just a wayfaring poet passing through this part of the country, unknown to any of its current denizens. *Just head west*, she thought, considering what could exist miles down Half Day Road. Shelley's words still alive in her heart:

> Drive my dead thoughts over the universe
> Like withered leaves to quicken a new birth!
> And, by the incantation of this verse,
>
> Scatter, as from an unextinguished hearth
> Ashes and sparks, my words among mankind!
> Be through my lips to unawakened Earth
>
> The trumpet of a prophecy!

God, Jesus, Michael! she thought, twisting herself the other way, running south on Waukegan. She'd moved too far into the street. Swerved right into a thick patch of renegade shrubs as a cherry-red, Volkswagen Jetta roared past, bleeping its horn.

"Motherfucker, son-of-a-bitch!" she said, kicking the bush. "Fuck you!" she said as she whipped around to glare at that disappearing Jetta. She kicked her right leg in the car's direction. Then she couldn't move. Wondered if she was even going to make it out of the bush. Wondered whether or not this would be her end, right here. She pictured her little, rock-like gravestone hidden in an insignificant corner of Deerfield, this nearly map-less mini-section of the upper U.S. Her epitaph written in tiny, Gothic font: "Camille Carlyle. That radiant spirit never seen." She decided to lay down and looked up at the sky, her breaths swift, wheezy. *All I have to do is roll left a few times. Three, maybe four. The car would never see me.* She closed her eyes. *Get the fuck up, Camille. Get up. Now!*

Upward, onward, brushing herself off, hurrying back the other way, now staying mostly on the overgrown grass alongside Waukegan. She was trying to make sense out of a CITGO at the corner of Half Day and Waukegan as she cut left onto Half Day and jogged over railroad tracks. She ran and ran and ran, kept running, past Derrick Singer's place -- that broad one-story just beyond a long, timber fence, where many a weekend after hours she'd dawdled around the gravel drive beside Derrick's garage, chugging cans of warm Icehouse and hitting a glass pipe in the glow from an overhead floodlight with Derrick, Daniel, Kayla, Jancy, Greg, others. Always to remember Greg's beaten, gray Audi, "The Silver Bullet," their magic carpet. Always remember that night-screened laughter of theirs, flirting, their private jealousies. Today was the death of all "last weekends."

Turned at Wilmot, kept running, past the lines of hushful homes nestled into the woods, up a narrow, sloping street, past Ben Kingston's house.

All those hours spent sitting on Ben's stiff twin bed during late weekday afternoons, when she'd been alone in her house, incommunicado with her girlfriends, too uncomfortable to sit in the quiet, all those futile hours spent watching Ben, a year her elder, make fake IDs and play *Warcraft II* on his PC while she tried to mollify his ill temper with flattery, affected geniality so he wouldn't suddenly kick her out, or, worse, hurt her. Those encounters now just a dim remembrance, and dimming, forevermore.

She'd made it to her street, gasping and swatting sticky streaks of hair from her cheeks, punching in her garage code.

The house, at one-thirty in the afternoon on a Thursday, appeared vacant. Cleaning lady, Olga, had just left and had left behind her the pungent odor of lemon cleaning spray, bleach, left behind a living portrait of their home that was abnormal, immaculate and too fragile to be touched. There she stood, center of the kitchen, huffing, eyes flickering left, right, hands half-fisted and ready to hit or push or dial or do whatever they had to. There she stood, inert and dripping, that fleshly mess the house's cleanliness just couldn't incorporate. Ellen out doing volunteer work for the Deerfield Chamber of Commerce. David back downtown, brokering options on the Board of Exchange. His kids, Joseph... She didn't know.

She ran to the first house phone she saw, mounted to a wall at the edge of the kitchen, and yanked it from its base. *411*, her fingers commanded.

"This is Franklin, how can I connect your call?"

"Hospital. Hospital. Highland Park Hospital."

"One moment, please."

"Highland Park Hospital. How may I help you?"

"I don't... I," Camille said. She slammed down the phone.

Fuck-fuck-fuck; think-think-think, she thought, pacing around in the fore of the kitchen. *I need a fucking car!* She smashed her fist against the kitchen table, causing disorder to the formerly symmetrical feng shui of bamboo placemats, bride and groom salt and pepper shakers, the flowered napkins that had been blooming left and right from a scroll napkin holder. She pulled out a chair and collapsed.

"Camille?"

She looked up to see Cynthia, David's daughter, standing by the doorway.

Cynthia gazing at her with a look of cautious fervor. Cynthia's hair long, stringy, black, cropped in front so that two, twirling strands dangled along the far corners of her eyes. Her brows dark as her hair, and thick, shapely. Still the faintest hint of freckles along Cynthia's dimpled cheeks. "What are you doing home?" she said.

"There was a horrible accident," Camille began, but choked and burst into tears. She put her head into her hands and sobbed. Her head shaking back and forth. "I have to get to the hospital," she was saying, over and again, words muffled by her hands.

Cynthia looked around the kitchen, at the now

disarrayed kitchen table. Glanced at the miniature answering machine sitting on a corner of the kitchen desk, adjacent the wall phone, and remembered that she'd thought it was odd to have seen its red flashing when she'd walked back in from outside half an hour ago. *Who leaves a message at one o'clock on a Thursday?* she remembered thinking with a scoff. *Maybe a doctor's appointment or something.* She'd then returned to the guest bedroom and painted her nails vermillion, forgot all about it. Now she was convinced that message had something to do with Camille's pandemonium. She walked to Camille, bent down, put a hand on Camille's shoulder. "I'll be right back. Okay? Please don't go anywhere." Cynthia power-walked up the front hall staircase and into the guest bedroom, the wide room between Camille's and her parents where David's older kids would stay when visiting from school. She brushed away her detangler combs and powder make-up to make more room for herself on an edge of her plump bed where she now sat. Picked up a portable phone from atop a nightstand, kept fidgeting, looking toward the open door after she'd dialed Dad's number and was waiting for him to pick up.

"This is David."

"Dad, Camille's home. She's in the kitchen, crying. She's saying something about the hospital. Someone called earlier and left a message. Do you think that has something to do with it? What should I do?"

"Whoa-whoa-whoa, slow down. She's home? She's not at school?"

"Dad! She's crying. What should I do?"

"Alright-alright-alright, just calm down. I'll call Ellen. Go downstairs and stay with her."

Cynthia hung up, whipped herself out of the room and back down to the kitchen. Took the chair across from Camille, who was still writhing around, woebegone, in the same pose.

"What happened?" Cynthia said. "Do you want to talk?"

The house phone rang out over the remote sounds of their confusion.

Cynthia nudged her chair back with her butt, stood, jogged to the phone, picked up: "Hello?"

"Hi, Cynthia," Ellen said. "Can I talk to Camille?"

"Of course. Hold on." Cynthia putting the phone down, staring at Camille. "Camille, it's your mom. She wants to talk to you."

Camille didn't move.

Cynthia glanced at the phone, Camille, phone, Camille, phone. She picked the phone back up: "Sorry, Ellen, but I don't think she can really come to the phone right now."

"Apparently there was an accident involving some kids from Deerfield and Highland Park today."

"*Really*?"

"I don't know all the details, but I'm coming home. Can you stay with her until I get there?"

"Of course. Of course."

"Is Joseph home yet?"

"I haven't seen him."

"Can I get anything for you?" Cynthia said to Camille after she'd hung up and reclaimed her former seat.

Cam shot her head up, eyes barely visible from tears and puffiness. "Michael, Michael, Michael. I can't drive-hospital-no-no-no-no-no-oh-God-why?"

"Jesus, Camille." Cynthia said, standing. "Why don't you come lay down?" Cynthia walked around the table, helped her up.

She guided Camille into the living room and onto their cloth couch. Camille whimpering, muttering "Michael, Michael, Michael" as she faced the large pillows against the back of the couch and gripped herself.

Camille had now completely exhausted herself. She shivered. Was cold. Couldn't process another thought. Couldn't make a sound, could barely breathe. She shut her eyes. That ever-black soothing -- sweet, sweet reprieve. Sweet oblivion. She'd fall so deep into this sleep now upon her and never rise again.

September 20, 2011

They'd reached another long pause in conversation as a Muslim man and his son passed by. Both billowy-clothed devotees stern, the man looking straight ahead, eyes determinate. His boy, nine, maybe ten, scurrying behind him and staring at the ground.

"Can't believe I've never been over here," Camille said after another minute or two. She continued to traipse along the Devon Avenue sidewalk, looking around at all the brightly-lit ethnic restaurants and tiny markets. "Never even heard of it."

Jake kept gazing from window to window.

"What's with you today?" she said. She gave him a playful jab.

"Nothing, nothing." He was now pushing open the front doors to *Tiffin*. "This is it."

They were approached by a middle-aged, Indian hostess before Camille could say anything else. The woman, her ink-black hair tied into a chignon, was grinning at Jake.

"Just us," he said. He motioned to the inside of the restaurant.

Camille leaned toward him after they'd gotten sat at a wide table close to the back. "Seriously, what's going on? You're going to argue with me, *again*?"

"Can you just calm down? Why is everything a soap opera with you?"

"*What?* Why the fuck are you giving me attitude now?"

They were cut off by a tall, husky, Indian waiter in a navy blazer who was now standing in front of the table. The man couldn't have been any younger than fifty, his inanimate, brown eyes baggy and skin pockmarked. There may have been a time, long ago, when this man had a pate blossoming with ebony hair, but now all that was left above his brow was a barren hill marked by a few withering wisps, which he'd doused with hair gel and swept to the side. "Good evening," the man said.

Jake kept looking at Camille. He flashed his finger at the waiter. "Give us a minute."

"Don't speak to him like that," she said.

Neither said another word; both continued to stare.

The waiter lowered his head and walked away.

"Nothing's actually wrong, Camille. That's what's wrong," He was leaning back in his chair. Eyes had softened. A short, goateed Mexican man in a burgundy button down reached over the table and poured ice water into their glasses.

"What the hell are you talking about?" she said.

Jake, waving his hands to emphasize his words: "The two of us exist in a state of heightened fear, Camille. I don't seem to be embarking upon a nutritive and mutually beneficial relationship with you. I see now that I'm consigned to being your pillow to grip or tear or cuddle with or do what you will based on whatever whim it is you want to act upon at any given moment. How could we ever be normal, feel normal, if you won't allow the dynamic in this situation to shift? I absolutely refuse to repeat the last three years of my life."

"*What?* First of all, Jake, I've only known you for--"

"I've only known you for two months. Bla-bla-bla. Knew you were going to say that. You're always on the defense. How could you ever possibly understand what it means to be in love when you work so hard to avoid it?"

"I'm *flabbergasted* you're saying all this to me. What happened to that valiant knight who wanted to save me from myself? You're all over the place, Jake. And you're fucking crazy. You live in a beautiful, romantic, fantasy world where you just wander around, day after day, clinking tea cups with all your grandiose ideas. Meanwhile, you're completely oblivious to everything and everyone around you. P.S. Just because you're well-read does not mean you're cool."

"Attack me all you want. Doesn't change the fact that you ignored what I just said."

She glared at him, pursed her lips.

Their waiter was now stepping back to the table, standing overhead, gazing at them without expression. "Would you like something to drink?"

Neither looked back. It was that helpless, inalterable silence that overturns the comforts of civilized public locations upon them all now.

Jake, staring a wall: "I'm fine."

Camille, now looking at the waiter, her shoulders pushed up like two arrows poised in longbows and at the ready to deliver quietus: "Just please give us a few more minutes."

"You have so much audacity, Jake," she said after their waiter walked away. "You want some fucking truth? I like you, a lot. Liked you since I first saw you. You can sit here and call me *defensive* or a bitch or whatever other name you want to come up with, but the fact is I haven't allowed myself to be this intimate with *anyone* for a long time." She leaned back, shook her head, bent down to grab her purse. "This is what happens." Stood up, gave him a long stare, her eyes wet, tearing. "I just don't know what you want from me. I don't know why you bothered me in the first place. Just leave me alone. Let me be alone. *Please*." She turned and hurried out.

He resumed his gazing at the wall. Clenched his teeth. Jaw pulsed. Right leg began to quaver. He kept looking toward the front entrance, then back at the wall. He then slid back his chair, stood and started jogging after her.

Outside just the motile chains of people moving east and west on sidewalks, a street congested with fusty cars waiting for a light to turn, shining bulbs from modest businesses.

He paced eastward, weaving his way around a pair of ambling Hindu women, an Orthodox Jewish kid who was staring at the ground as he strode along. Jake panting. His eyes whipped left, right. He hoped, prayed, longed to see that jazzy red hair of hers, that peculiar gait. Finally stopped at Western to catch his breath, turned to look behind him, pulled out his phone, called her. Voicemail. *She got a cab,* he thought, not leaving a message. *I'll go to her place. No, I won't. I can't. I fucked it up. Just let her go. Why would you push her like that? Fuck.* He took a final glance westward and was now completely convinced she'd escaped him, lost herself in the city's labyrinthine vastness on purpose. Wasn't coming back. It had been said to him, for certain, by that comprehending sorrow which had made her eyes moisten when she looked at him just before leaving *Tiffin*. It was being howled at him now by this busy metropolis she'd ordered between them. He put his head down, hands in his pockets, started to rove. Wondered if her plaintive face would be the last image he'd ever have of her, to keep his heart ablaze with her suffering, a despondency he'd actually wanted to share with her. *Why did we meet in the first place? Was there a reason? Have I made her life better, worse? Will I get to see you again, seraph? Will you let me? Is it up to fate? Is there fate?*

May 1, 1998

Camille was about to take another hit off her Marlboro, stopped. She flashed her eyes at Kayla. "Don't you dare even try to talk about that."

"We have to talk," Kayla said, tucking a tuft of brown hair behind her left ear. Her gaze hadn't moved from Camille. "It's been a year. I'm shocked you actually answered the phone when I called tonight. How many more weekends are you going to stay locked up in your house? All we have left is this summer, Cam, then everyone will be at school. We'll barely see each other."

Camille hit her cigarette. She looked out the extended windows of Denny's at a small, semi-vacant parking lot surrounded by short bush and illuminated, in random pools, by the white halogen lights from a Shell station just up the highway. It seemed to her she was part of an inconsequential town trying to keep itself alive and identifiable amidst the all-present nighttime darkness. Seemed the town's weakly attempt at lighting itself was inspired by fear and denial about the town's own insignificance in the nocturnal decree of Nature. She understood Michael's physical body was now dissolved, but she wondered if his spirit had become part of that dark. *He would've liked it that way. Complete release from all corporeal restraint.* She let out a suppressed laugh through her nose. Found it bemusing that what she remembered were the deeper truths about his personality, the aspects of him she'd been too emotional to realize she'd known while he was alive. Her cigarette had now burnt to its butt and was singeing her fingers. She dropped it in a glass ash tray, shook her hand.

"This is exactly what I'm talking about," Kayla said, still staring at her, leaning back against their booth. "How long have we been friends? Why can't you just talk

222

to me?"

"Drop it," Camille said. "You're *really* starting to piss me off."

Kayla looked away, her curvy brows turned downward, which gave her a momentarily sinister appearance. "I wonder where the hell our food is?" Kayla began to glance around, now noticing a group of teenagers packed into another booth diagonal from them, Deerfield sophomores, all of whom smoking and picking at red, wicker baskets of onion rings, sandwiches and fries in front of them. She twisted her zaftig body more and looked at the umber-carpeted hall that ran alongside a broad counter with worn stools affixed to the ground. Some of those stools occupied by elderly men, scruffy truckers in straight-brimmed baseball caps, sipping coffee from grainy-gray Denny's mugs. Their server, an older lady with kinky, red hair and sunken cheeks, was lingering by a tiny kitchen window, waiting for more food to come up. Kayla felt her beeper vibrating against her thigh and unclipped it from her bell bottoms. She gazed at the translucent device. "I gotta' use the phone." She squirmed out of the booth and gave Camille a sardonic smile. "If our food's not here when I get back, I'm going to be really pissed."

Cam kept looking the window. "Can't believe you still have a beeper."

"Blow me," Kayla said, turning and shuffling along the hall, toward a small area between two sets of doors that led outside. Her baggy pant legs kept scraping the floor and once or twice she tried to hike the old jeans up with an insouciant tug. She'd reached that area between the doors, picked up a greasy payphone, put a quarter in, punched numbers. Waited four rings for Janey to pick up and all the while stared at the ground, thinking about the fact that she'd already smoked most her eighth, that they needed to get to Dakota's place in Lincolnshire so she could get more of that Super Skunk.

"Sorry I didn't call earlier," Kayla said after listening to Janey's nasal hello. "I been with Cam -- trying to talk to her."

"Where are you guys?"

"Denny's."

"How's she doing?"

"Not good."

"Should I come?"

"Just let me talk to her."

"Are you still going to Kevin's?"

"I don't know," Kayla said. "If I can get her to go…"

"I'm really worried about her. Like -- serious this time. Still can't believe… Well, will you guys just come pick me up when you're done?"

"I'll call you," Kayla said. "I don't know what's up yet." She hung up. Was halted by three Highland Parkers now coming in, single-file, as she turned to head back into the restaurant. They were all squinty-red-eyed, gazing at the ground, sniggering. Last one bumped Kayla's shoulder.

"Watch it, dip-shit," Kayla said.

The boys continued to walk on as though she'd said nothing.

Kayla glared at the doorway for a few seconds after they'd gone in, then shambled back in herself, eyes attached to the floor. She lost herself in a blustering fall tree of thoughts. *Cam. Fucked up. Teenagers, school, herb. Go to Dakota's.* When she lifted her head she was back at the table, but the food hadn't arrived.

"What the fuck's wrong with the service here?" Kayla said.

"It's Denny's."

Kayla smirked, sat back down. "Should we just go?"

"I'm hungry."

"For a salad? Have you been eating, Cam? You look bony."

"Who beeped you?"

"Janey."

"What did she want?"

"We were supposed to hang out. Remember?"

The redheaded waitress finally plodded up to the table holding two, red baskets in each of her hands like they were dead fish -- in one basket a ham, egg and cheese on sourdough with heaps of slightly burnt french fries alongside it, in the other deep-fried, ranch-doused barbeque chicken strips and wilted carrot straws that sat atop shredded lettuce. "Moons over My-Hammy?" the waitress said, raising the basket in her left hand.

Kayla seized it. "Took long enough."

"Buffalo chicken salad," the waitress continued, in monotone, putting the other basket down in front of Camille.

Camille started plunging into her mound of lettuce, giving that food her unwavering attention. Before Kayla could finish half her sandwich, the basket in front of Camille already appeared hollow, save for a few globs of barbeque sauce, the occasional forsaken leaf. Camille leaned back against the booth like she hadn't eaten anything at all and kept staring at the window.

Kayla waded a bushel of fries in a ketchup pond.

225

"Michael Parker, Michael Parker, Michael Parker. *There*. I said it. I said his name. You have to talk to me. You can't keep bottling this all up."

Camille glowering.

"I really don't care what you have to say right now," Kayla said. "This is more important. I *know* how much you cared about him. It's a fucking tragedy. There's probably no one who's going to understand how sad it is like you. Maybe his parents…"

Camille scoffed.

"Maybe not, I don't know. Point is there's nothing we can do to change it. We just have to accept that he's gone. That's it. He's gone. He's fucking gone. You just shut yourself off. You're a completely different person than you were last year, and you're hurting all these people who care about you by abandoning them. We all miss the old you."

"The fuck? What is this? Thought we were just going to hang out, Kay, have fun, party."

"Yeah, 'fun.' Not staring at the window and weeping."

"Please. Give me a break. Weeping?"

They were cut off by the presence of a Highland Parker -- one of the kids Kayla had seen walking in earlier -- as he now stood in front of the table, glancing at them with an awkward smile and then looking back at his two friends who'd taken up the booth across from them. The boy was sporting a Highland Park Giants jacket, half-open. Had sandy brown hair that was curly and thinning. Cheeks welled outward, slightly, but were finely curved and rounded the way a porcelain doll's would be. His eyes a vibrant hue of green almost supernatural. "Could we borrow your ketchup?" he said.

Kayla, glancing at Camille, glancing at him: "Fuck off, preppie-bitch."

"Wait," Camille said. "What's your name?"

"Paul," the boy said, shifting his malevolent gaze from Kayla to Camille, then letting his countenance lighten up.

"Why don't you guys come sit with us?" Camille said.

Kayla was now gaping at her friend.

Paul looked behind him, back at them, blushed.

"We won't bite," Camille continued. "Too hard." She gave a supercilious laugh and shot an involuntary glance at Kayla, trying to connect smiles, but Kayla's facial expression hadn't changed; she hadn't moved. Cam turned back to Paul. She leaned forward to hand Paul their glass ketchup bottle. "Kayla and I are going to this party tonight -- in Deerfield. It's going to be the bomb. Why don't you talk to your friends and see if they want to come?"

Paul, shrugging: "Okay."

"The fuck are you doing?" Kayla said to Camille as Paul was walking away. "Why are you acting like this? I don't want to hang out with those douche bags."

Cam grinned at her friend, continued to gaze at the boys.

Just get out of here, Kayla thought, staring at the table. *This was a mistake. Fuck her. No, you can't just leave her. God! She's so fucking hard to deal with.*

When it had become clear Paul wasn't coming back, Camille slid her way out of the booth. She ignored Kayla's hissing and grunts and sashayed over to the three boys. They were all picking at mozzarella sticks, looking at their menus, slurping their half-consumed drinks. The

227

ash tray center of their table clean, polished, and it was clear from the way the boys didn't make eye contact with it that none of them smoked cigarettes, perhaps never had. The boy to Paul's left porky and rosy-cheeked with a 'fro of curly, jet-black hair. His eyes beady. There was a sexy-cool to him notwithstanding his cast, perhaps on account of the washed-out Dave Matthews Band tour t-shirt he was displaying, which announced to all observing that he was wrapped up in the culture of massive jam-band shows, or perhaps it was the way he'd been smiling at his friends and appeared unconcerned with anything or anyone else. The boy to Paul's right tall, thin, short dark hair, light blue eyes, small and well-shaped nose. He was the first to say "Tell us about this party." while his friends were darting their shy eyes around the table when Camille came up.

"What?" Camille said, still staring into the thin boy's eyes, rubbing her bare hip bone that protruded from her low-waist jeans.

"The party?"

She out let out a nervous, high-pitched laugh. "My friend Kevin. Two kegs -- Honey Brown. You guys should totally come."

"Kevin who?" said the boy with the fro.

"Markowitz."

The thin boy, smirking: "Where is it?"

Camille's cheeks reddened. "Why don't you guys just follow us?"

Thin boy, glancing at Paul, glancing at her: "So you don't actually know?"

"Course I do." Camille glimpsed at Kayla, back at the boys, Kayla, boys. "Like over by Shepard; like Deerfield and Waukegan." She nodded in Kayla's direction. "I should go check on my friend." She turned and walked back to her booth without saying goodbye, eyes downcast, now realizing how outlandish it was to have just left their table like that.

Kayla continued to nibble food, ignoring Camille as she sat down. She watched her last three fries darken with ketchup. "I'm just going to take you back home," Kayla said as Cam lit a Marlboro, blew a misty smoke stream at the window.

"Thought we were going to Kevin's…" Cam's eyes widening. The skin over her nose scrunched. Tiny gusts of smoke chugging out her nostrils.

"Not if you're going to act like this."

"Like *what*?"

"You're acting crazy. One minute you're a vegetable. Then you turn into Jessica Rabbit when those jerk-offs arrive. I can't keep up."

"So what, I can't have a little fun? I'm too wild and reckless? Or was it too weepy, Kay? Too bony? Which one? What kind of friend are you? You're worse than my fucking mother. I'm going to this party. I'll hitch-hike."

Kayla shook her head. "Hitch-hike? Where do you think we are, Woodstock in the late sixties? Who's going to stop for you? A Highland Park mom in her new Audi?"

"Fuck you." Camille took a last drag of the Marlboro and batted it against the ash tray as her shoulders tensed and eyes flickered right to left. She slid toward the end of the booth.

"Don't go. I'm sorry," Kayla said, grasping Cam's arm before she could get up, looking into those exanimate eyes. "Chill. We'll go to Kevin's."

Camille stuck out her index finger. "I don't ever

want to hear you talking about what we were talking about again. Got it?"

"Chill."

"No. Dead serious. It's none of your fucking business, Kayla. You stay out of it."

June 3, 2012

It seemed like the placatory wind, an atmospheric Jesus, had kissed away the leafy deaths of the Norway Maples and was now restoring them all to a verdant vigor with every airy touch. *Still can't believe summer again, already,* Camille thought. She continued to walk along the lakeside pathway to Foster Beach and looked toward a skate park she hadn't seen before, to her right, just past the Montrose exit. Skinny kids with long hair or faces half-obscured by beanies were dipping down into what looked like a waterless pool with their BMX bikes and Baker skateboards, arms flailing. She watched them for a few minutes, taking note of the way in which the kids on the outskirts of the skate pool were at a standstill, totally absorbed by what they were observing. Reminded her of middle school, standing on the sidelines of that undersized basketball court at the back of Mitchell Park with Janey, Ali, Marissa, other girls, watching the shirtless boys in their grade play a game. She began to muse that they could never return to the world they'd once created on that Mitchell Park basketball court, because they'd all been partners in adolescence then and "adolescence" was their prolonged and euphoric first epiphany. Adolescence a quick and enchanted unfolding of years just before their adult lives would isolate each individual one of them, set its draconian terms and then leave them alone to cope. She wished she could capture her thoughts in a well-polished stanza now, which would preserve those thoughts so they could continue being offered to thousands of others making the transition from child to adult.

She stared at her burnt sienna sandals and kept strolling. *Wasn't it just as tempestuous for me then as it is for me now? In a different way? Why do I keep longing to return to some embellished time I can never go back to? Ageing is inevitable, Cam. Maybe not bad. Maybe not good. Maybe just something new.*

She suddenly remembered a random day during the summer last year. Rain had been pummeling the city on and off all afternoon. Remembered sitting on one of Jake's frowsy, green couches, next to him, tensing her shoulders almost every time she heard the far-off thunder. Tommy sitting on the opposite couch. A half-eaten box of Lou Malnati's pizza and crumby, tomato-smeared paper plates scattered along the coffee table between them. Tommy singing the theme song from *Dawson's Creek,* in soprano, every time Michelle Williams appeared on screen during the movie they'd been watching. They all kept laughing hysterically, like elementary school kids. She'd been so comfortable with the two of them at that moment, so fulfilled. *Wonder what Jake's doing now? Probably has a girlfriend.* She thought about leaving Jake that one night at *Tiffin,* then ignoring all his successive calls, erasing his messages without listening, until he'd just stopped completely. She shook her head. The way she'd behaved too juvenile to accept.

She looked up and caught sight of a young, honey-skinned girl darting south on the opposite side of the path, on rollerblades, half the girl's head shielded by a large, purple helmet, her elbows and knees covered with black pads. The rollerblading girl now zipped past. This girl seemed to exemplify that same quality Camille had perceived amongst those kids at the skate park: this keen sense of being spellbound by the present, in the case of the rollerblading girl not because the girl had peeled apart all her layers and come to the tranquil center of herself, but because the girl on wheels was too easy of heart and

233

fearful of mind to reject that which was right in front of her -- whirring wind, the exhilaration of moving fast -- for the prospect of lofty perspectives not yet felt or seen. Camille envied her this. Camille longed for just one drawn out moment of pure, stupid simplicity.

Her legs moved faster -- two reluctant horses being whipped by her avid reflections. She became so enwrapped in her meditations that when she gazed up again, she was already at the mouth of Foster Beach.

This pale-sanded strand small. It curved outward in the shape of a windswept mainsail. Beyond a row of dwarfish trees and bush that surrounded the beach and beyond an almost unseen-unheard car parade that zoomed back and forth on North Lake Shore Drive were a series of mid-rises that were spread out, dissimilar and seemed as though they represented the unique, artistic structures that had rebelled against the orderly positioning of Chicago's skyline.

The beach was somewhat crowded, but people had organized themselves with enough room to create distinct personal space. This unlike Fullerton Beach, just four miles south, which was a ceaseless, post-graduation attempt to keep the spirit of an outdoor frat party alive. Here at Foster Beach people had wandered away from their weekly labors, their administrative and secretarial positions, check-writing and envelope-stamping and laundry-washing, had brought their motley deck-chairs and large beach towels and dinged-up iPods and SPF 15 sunscreen to a setting where they could finally just sit and bask in their own little piece of nature.

She began to walk along the lake's undulating edge. Lifted her right leg backward and reached around to pluck off her sandal from her right foot. Did the same thing with the other foot and let the two sandals dangle from her fingers as she glided her toes in the water. The breezy openness of the beach, within which ring-billed gulls coasted from spot to spot and the lake continued to let out its booming hiss, now reminded Camille of those late-summer mornings in Miami as a kid, when she'd roam the deserted beach in front of her father's apartment, tickling her bare feet against the foamy lips of the Atlantic, when she'd felt like a girl whose life had guided her away from the affluent vacuity of the Chicago suburbs and taken her to a tropical land within which she was to learn a new way-of-being.

But what good is all this thinking doing me now? Her bare feet faltered in miniature peaks and troughs of sand but prevailed forward, toes kicking out teeny sandstorms on the way. She couldn't help but to envision herself twenty years hence -- as if framed in a medium shot amidst the denouement of some old, noteworthy drama. She was wearing a loose, satin, pearl-white dress with a matching Kentucky Derby hat that she fumbled to keep on her head in the wind. Was walking on this same beach in the same way. Was alone, never-married, happy. A woman respected -- a modern-day Virginia Woolf. As Camille neared the end of the beach, she realized how refreshing it was to toss back and forth between individual fantasy and collective reality in a space like this, place where people didn't have much claim over the natural earth around them.

She caught sight of a half-naked couple lying beside one another on a wide, navy beach towel, near the sand's bordering footpath. Though the girl she saw had well-defined cheek bones and bay hair cropped just below the earlobes, Camille couldn't mistake the feeling aroused in her on beholding the girl: a sharp burst of puerile excitement attached to a memory of chattering with her in the hallways of Deerfield High School sixteen years ago. This was Kelly Patrelle -- she was certain of it now.

She continued to stare at them, astonished by the way Kelly had metamorphosed from a pudgy, coral-cheeked teenybopper into this lithe vixen over the past decade. She tried to glance away and keep walking, but found herself constantly stopping, looking over, playing with the idea of making direct eye contact. *Fuck it*, she thought, putting her sandals back on, and turning her body, pacing toward the twosome.

Neither Kelly nor her best friend Jimmy discerned Camille's approach. Both laid out like cadavers, gazing up at the descending sun with their big sunglasses. Wasn't until Camille blocked Kelly's sunlight that Kelly finally sat up, flipped her glasses to her forehead with her index finger and tried to make sense of the shape that was Camille while shading her eyes with an open palm. Kelly's expression shifted from stupefied to acknowledging before she exhibited her garish smile. "Camille Carlyle? It's been three hundred million years. How are you?"

Jimmy rolled over and propped up his head with his left arm. Hard to distinguish the exact object of his gaping from behind those pitch-black shades, but still pretty obvious from the position of his head he was gazing at Camille.

"Been a hot minute," Camille said, simpering. "You live around here?"

Kelly pointed behind her. "Edgewater. We just moved in."

"Are you two... married?"

Jimmy and Kelly looked at each other and laughed.

Kelly, looking back at Camille: "We--"

"I'm gay," Jimmy said.

"Oh," Camille said. "Sorry." She looked at the sand, shrugged.

"Gay," Jimmy continued. "Not a cancer patient." He giggled and leaned forward to shake her hand. "Jimmy. I'm her best friend."

"Camille. Sorry, I didn't mean--"

"You're so timid now," Kelly said, stealing Camille's attention. "What happened to you? Did you go off to India and have a life-changing experience at an ashram or something?" She giggled. "Cool hair, by the way."

Cam fingered her swooping bangs. "Thanks. Yeah, something recent..."

"Come sit," Jimmy said, patting their towel. "Want to smoke a bowl?"

"No -- I gotta' get going. This thing with my brother..." *Brother? Why the fuck did I just say that?*

"You sure, girl?"

Cam glanced up at the polychrome sky, letting its intense colors flood through her eyes and rinse out her mind. She squinted, nodded. *Stop running. Just stop. This is life. It's here. Now. Enjoy it.* She looked back down at them. "Guess I could be a little late."

"There you go," Jimmy said, falling back.

"Well, fire it up," Kelly said. She began to rake through an oversized beach tote bag by her legs, unearthing her bleach-blue, ghost-fumed glass pipe and tiny Bic. "Just like old times, right Cam? Remember when we used to clam-bake in Kayla's Impala on those late-arrival days?" She fell beside Jimmy, chuckling. Held the pipe between her lips and lay still, used one hand to light and the other to cover. Away came her hands like descending seagulls and the hunky ember at the end of the piece could now be seen sparkling, even in the sunset's dusty light. A smoke flood barreled out of Kelly's mouth after one of her drooping hands returned from the sand to rescue the semi-cashed piece. "God... Kayla... I wonder what the hell she's doing now?"

Cam kneeled in front of them. She put her clutch purse beside her, smiled. "Seems so long ago, right. Like another life. Take it you didn't go to the reunion. I didn't." She glanced around the beach, noticing voluminous families, toddlers and pre-teens in swimsuits bolting to and from the water, constructing sandcastles, bouncing beach balls. "Sure it's okay to do this *here*?"

"You bitch," Jimmy said, tilting his head toward his friend. "Did you just smoke it all?"

Kelly let out a resounding cough. "We still have half an eighth."

Jimmy grabbed the lighter and moribund pipe. Took a thunderous hit. Kelly grasped it back. She returned to the bag, re-packed. Hugged her knees and gazed at the water, now extending her right index and middle finger -- the pipe and lighter sandwiched between them -- to Camille. "Reunion?" Kelly said. "Fuck that shit."

Cam hit it, then lay down alongside Kelly, Cam's eyes crinkling, lips breaking into a grin. "Remember when we saw Trisha Hauser walk into that pole in D-Hall?"

"That was the funniest thing I've ever seen in my life."

The girls tried to explain the remembrance to Jimmy, cracking up, taking more hits of the White Widow. Their mirth, in which Jimmy had now partaken, started phasing out into a short-winded quiet.

"Are *you* married?" Kelly said to Cam.

"No," Camille said. She became motionless, stared at her feet.

Kelly, gliding her sunglass-clad face in Cam's direction: "Isn't love awesome? At least you're not following the crowd."

"What do you mean?"

"Have you bumped into anyone from Deerfield recently? I have. Married, pregnant, works in marketing. Same thing, over and over. How about the way all those people now have two last names on Facebook -- their maiden name and their married name? 'Marissa Paige Welby. Janet Dorler Guzik.' How about all those stupid fucking pictures of their little dogs and their weddings everyone now has to look at? Feel like I grew up on an episode of *Leave it to Beaver*."

"You just wish it was you," Jimmy said, still lying unstirred. "That's why you care so much."

Kelly rolled over and slapped his arm. "Yeah? Who's the one who wouldn't eat anything except yogurt and wheat bread, alone, in his apartment, not answering the phone, watching Lifetime movies, for almost three weeks after breaking up with 'Gay-Gay-Jay-Jay?'"

"Stop calling him that," Jimmy said.

"Who's 'Gay-Gay-Jay-Jay?'" Camille said.

Kelly turned to face her. "Jimmy's *super-fabulous* ex-boyfriend. He hated me."

"He didn't hate you," Jimmy said, sighing.

"Why'd you guys break up?" Camille said, her

dulcet voice now invoking a momentary speechlessness between them all.

Jimmy: "He found out I was cheating."

Kelly: "Plates shattering, grown men screaming, floods of tears. It was like reality TV at its best. Jimmy's neighbors almost called the cops."

"What happened?" Camille said. "You were there?"

Jimmy rolled over, held up his head with his hand, gazed at the both of them. "Not to be all Oprah on you two, but... Moral is if you really love someone, *really*, and you know when you do, then you have to give yourself to them entirely, or you'll end up regretting it."

"I hate when he gets like this," Kelly said to Camille. She rolled toward Jimmy. "You definitely did not love Jason."

"I did."

"You were *always* bitching about him -- 'We're going out tonight. Fuck that little queen.' Or how about that time you said Jason needs to get kidnapped by guerillas, shipped off to the Amazon and then slaughtered. How many times did you get other guys' phone numbers when he wasn't around?"

Jimmy let out a weighty sigh, shook his head. "All part of what I'm talking about, Kell. To *truly* love someone means to make yourself vulnerable by giving them your trust, which is scary. Terrifying. It's much easier to act like you just don't care, so that if you do get hurt it won't be that bad. But you're actually making yourself more alone, even while it still might be working with that other person."

Cam started to become ruminant. Kelly and Jimmy's chatter now just a faint hum beneath the vigorous clap of water. *It all boils down to non-will*, she thought. *Letting these feelings, these apprehensions, these irrational fears, this residue of erstwhile impressions flitting around my subconscious, these whatever the fuck they are, just be whatever they are. I don't own you. You don't own me. I'm filled with you and then I'm empty again. You're a part of my physical being. Just like everyone else. Everyone carries their past impresses and future aspirations with them to the present. It's one big cluster-fuck of mental vertigo when we all commingle and it's okay. It just is. Jimmy. God speaking through him, to me. Give myself. Just give myself. Don't get hurt. Not again.* She could now hear the reverberations of horrific screaming from a thirteen-year-old girl trapped in a strange Highland Park apartment, the shrieking of a frazzled teenager to her fatigued mother about her father's permanent disappearance, standing there, in middle of 1993, in her stalwart pose of defense from any more unforeseeable events, center of a small, carpeted living room with fists clenched, and then she realized it wasn't a sound at all but the ruthless and recurrent pounding against her worn-out heart. Her eyes squinted with budding tears.

"Are you alright?" Kelly was saying, body now twisted toward Camille.

Cam wiped her eyes with the back of her left hand. She pushed herself up. Bent down to grab her purse, stood, glanced at them. "Just thinking. Life. You-know. I should probably get going. My brother..."

Jimmy slapped Kelly's shoulder. "Why'd you start talking about all this?"

"No-no," Camille said. "Not that, really. I'm going to be so late. Great to see you, Kell. Strange, huh?"

She nodded at Jimmy. "Nice to meet you." Sniveling, gripping her purse: "You're both on Facebook, right?"

April 13, 2000

Camille still couchant on the frayed settee she'd bought with Tyler, her roommate, at Salvation Army. She was gawking at their wood ceiling fan as it turned like a languid Ferris wheel. "Why do you keep wasting your time with all that shit, Tyler?"

Tyler, back still propped against the wall by their kitchenette, legs still spread out in front of him, eyes still locked upon the pages of *Self-Reliance* by Ralph Waldo Emerson, said: "It's true wisdom." He took a slow sip of oolong tea from his plastic mug.

She shot her eyes at him and smiled broadly. "You're so funny."

"Yeah?" He flipped a page.

"You're not even paying attention right now."

Tyler raised his eyes. "Pay attention to what? I don't have time for this MTV-Spring-Break persiflage. I have an exorbitant amount of reading to do." Both hands returned to the book, as did his eyes.

Persiflage, she thought. *Cool.* "It's a beautiful day. Let's hit the pool. Ooh -- then we'll get Publix subs and catch a flick at Miracle 5. Little disco nap at eight and we'll be good to go for Irish Pub tonight, buddy. You owe me a shot of Jager."

Tyler shook his head, chuckled.

"See!" she said, sitting up and stabbing her finger at him. "You totally agree. Life's meant to be lived. Not read."

He let the book drop to his lap and looked up, smirking, fluttering his eyes. "How do you...? How do you get such good grades? When do you do your work?"

She nestled her head against her open palms. "Tyler, Tyler, Tyler. Gotta' learn how to play the game, my friend, or you're never gonna' make it in this society.

You're too much of a purist. You really want end up stocking books in a public library when you're 45? Maybe coming home to some mangy apartment you can barely afford, where your two unruly kids are wrestling each other and you're fat, angry wife is yelling at you? See how far Transcendentalism gets you then."

"*What?* Where do you get these preposterous ideas? Enlighten me, please: What does 'make it in this society' mean?"

Her eyes sailed back and forth. "How is that even a question?"

"You can't articulate it, can you?"

"We just don't live in a world where sitting around reading is profitable."

"Who said I'm seeking profit?"

She rolled over and closed her eyes as though petitioning the subconscious to come wipe away this intellectual toil with a big, pacific dream-slideshow. "You just love to argue."

"No. I just don't think you think things through."

"Whatever."

"I'm not trying to fight." He picked his book back up, rumpled his brow. "This is for your own good. You've been brainwashed into revering absolute ideals by the media and capitalism. Time to wake up."

She glided off into sleep. Could now see a prolonged image of her father, his face adorned by a pair of oval glasses, hair thin but wild and wavy. He was wearing a long, crumpled t-shirt and a pair of tight, threadbare jeans that accentuated his heavy thighs. He was at the center of a thick darkness, like it was his third day freefalling through a well that stretched to the center of the earth. Now she perceived herself to be in the back of an old car, something from a drive-in movie lot in the 1950s. Couldn't move her head left, nor right, nor could she distinguish what was directly in front of her. Could only speculate that the car was full of passengers, and, from the quick flashes of gray-skied farmland along the corners of her eyes, that they were probably traveling on some interstate in the rural Midwest.

Next thing she knew she was thrust back into a sharp, stable reality. There was weight attached to her breathing which had not been applicable in the world she'd just come from. Her body ached and tingled as though she'd been wrested from the deep of a warm pool. She looked at the timber entertainment center in the middle of their living room and remembered that familiar itchiness of the couch she was laying on. She lifted her head, blinked at Tyler, still reading in the same position. "How long was I out?"

"I don't know," he said, shrugging, eyes fastened to the book. "Twenty minutes?"

"I love sleeping." She put her head back down, cast out her arms and gave a small yawn. Tumbled off the couch, landing on her back. After a minute or two, she rolled again. She now lay prone at the living room's center with arms outstretched like she was mocking the Rood. "Tyler! Let's go to the pool."

He smacked his book shut, pressed his palms to the floor, jumped up. "Alright-let's-go!"

"That's the Tyler I love."

They met each other at the front door, Cam putting her hands on Tyler's shoulders, staring into his eyes. "I knew you'd finally see the light, Reverend."

"The Lord hath spoken to me."

"What he said, Reverend?"

246

"That you should buy me a buffalo chicken sub."

"Well, if it be His will, missuh," Camille said, twisting the front door's ramshackle knob and flinging it open for them.

They strode, single-file, across a white oak porch. Down a set of squeaky stairs, their feet banging the wood, giving out a plangent song about the unconcerned lightheartedness of being young. Camille led them to a narrow parking lot instead of the pool. A few rundown cars scattered around the space. Cam's shiny, dark-silver, Ford Escape parked backward and diagonal across two spots.

"Where we going?" Tyler was saying as he let his fingers hover beneath the Ford's passenger side door handle.

"To the moon," she said. She unclicked the car's locks with her mini remote, yanked open her door and swooped in. Flipped on the engine when they'd both situated themselves inside. Reaching down now with her right hand to turn on the stereo. Gazing at the windshield. The car started to boom with twanging bass. *Music is the answer, to your problems*, Celeda was singing over high-powered beats. Camille nodded to the music, jerked the gear-shift lever into drive and gave the gas pedal a hasty push. They lurched backward as the Ford swerved out of the lot.

"Easy, tiger," Tyler said. He reached down and lowered the volume.

"What are you doing?" she said, one hand atop of the wheel, the other grasping for the stereo.

"Too early for a rave."

"This is Danny Tenaglia. One of the best DJs in the world." She gawked at her roommate and pointed to

247

her CD player, stunned. She then took a quick glance at the windshield and whisked them left onto a small, oak-tree-lined street outside their apartment complex. Looked over at Tyler. "Could you imagine partying to this at a club in Ibiza? Four o'clock in the morning, shoulder-to-shoulder with hundreds of people, lights flashing, music bumping." She started rocking her fisted arm to the music, bouncing her shoulders, swinging her head, squinting at the windshield. "You're all sweaty, rolling, kissing some French person you don't even know while those beats are just fucking everybody…" She stopped grooving a moment and closed her eyes, opened them, smiled. "Ibiza… I'm coming to you."

Tyler, gazing listlessly at the Chevy Silverado drifting along in front of them: "We still going there this summer?"

She veered right. "We have to figure all that out -- soon." She knew she wouldn't actually take that trip, though. That she couldn't afford to lose one efficacious summer spent doing an internship for an ad agency in Chicago and making her resume glitter more dazzlingly than all of her contemporaries' combined, so that it would be easy to get that coveted career right out school, so that she'd be "on her way." *I'm only twenty, though,* she thought. *Just go with him. I said I would. It's fucking Ibiza. You're so young. Fuck an internship. To hell with it. I'm going. No, I can't. It's the wrong decision. Yes, you can. No, I can't.*

"Where we going right now?" Tyler was saying, interrupting her private hysteria.

"Wanna' see what's at Miracle 5."

"Is *Wonder Boys* still out?"

"That left theaters two months ago," she said,

chortling.

They came to a forlorn parking lot surrounded by depleted shrubbery. Center of the space a mid-sized plaza with clay-tile shingling. "Miracle 5" a row of bubbled, blood-orange letters announced to them above a windowed entrance. There was a bright, white image of theater masks alongside the lettering.

"This city is so fucking desolate," Camille said as she curved into the lot, parked crookedly, took up two spaces.

Both of them now gazing at the vacant box office as Camille killed the engine.

"Are they even open?" Tyler said.

"What time is it?"

He lifted his forearm and looked at his digital watch. "1:30."

"Let's find out." She shoved open her door, stepped out, hurled it closed behind her. Pranced over to the box office window and put her forehead to the glass: a milk-white home office desk with ruffled invoices and a torn copy of *All the Best, George Bush* sprawled out on top of it. A Dell desktop computer and mouse. Swivel chair turned sideways in front of the desk.

"Why don't you start by looking at the showtimes?" Tyler said. He'd come up behind her noiselessly and was pointing over her shoulder, at a pepper-colored magnetic board posted to the back wall of the office. "First movie's not till 5."

"Shit-fuck," she said, putting her head down. "Wanna' get a sub?" She was already striding back to the car.

Few more minutes of high-volume-house-music-car-stereo-party-time and they were now cruising into a parking space in front of the Publix on Blairstone Road.

"Can't wait to sink my teeth into a big, toasted buffalo chicken sub," Tyler was saying, lifting his head toward the car's roof, shaking his hands like Martin Luther King.

"I shall bring you this offering, my lord," Camille said back, giving him a credulous gaze as she turned off the engine. She made her exit from the car the same way she had at the theater.

Both of them now pacing toward the store's front entrance, side-by-side. The sky an abandoned pencil sketch, smudged with furious, gray steaks from the artist's previous attempts. The mid-day air had developed a constricting chill, which was prompting the scowling locals and bumptious students flowing into and out of Publix to move along more briskly. This abrupt cool made to feel even more villainous by the fact that the sun's buoyant hues could be observed but remained locked behind the medieval rampart of ashen clouds.

Inside Publix, Tyler and Camille were thrashed by the gusty air conditioning, met by long aisles jam-packed with foodstuffs and presented to them under fierce, white lighting.

Tyler looking left, right: "Which way--"

"I know," she said, cutting left. She strode past resounding check-out counters and came upon the deli, tucked away in a southwest corner.

There was a tubby woman in a mint-green apron and baseball cap behind the sandwich station, her plastic-gloved hands pressed against to a stained cutting board. She was staring at Camille and Tyler in a dopey, livid-eyed, ever-pose of defeat.

"This one's on Dad, right?" Tyler said as he

shuffled behind her toward the counter.

She turned her head toward him. "David isn't my dad, Tye. You know that." Turned back to the sandwich lady and pointed her thumb back and forth between the two of them. "Two buffalo chicken subs."

"Bread?" the woman said, lifting her thick hands, straightening the crinkled gloves.

"Wheat."

"Wheat? What? Why?" Tyler said softly, patting Cam's arm. "That takes away half the flavor. White."

"Okay, wheat and white," Camille said to the lady.

This Publix employee couldn't seem to construct one single part of their subs without first giving them her comatose gaze and awaiting instruction. She didn't just squirt ranch dressing and buffalo sauce on the bread, but completed a kindergarten, arts-n-crafts oil canvas. Didn't just sprinkle on a little lettuce, but forged hills of disheveled grass. When it came time to incorporate the breaded chicken, however, the theme of the entire sandwich, she was very careful to lay down *exactly* five pieces, as though rather than being informed by the Law of the Christian God, it was the "Fear of Publix Policy" that regulated the lady's actions.

Nowhere to sit and eat, so Camille suggested the car. Would have been an uninvited foray into the spheres of lethal asceticism for either of them to have waited the ten-minute drive home before devouring those warm, redolent sandwiches now in their hands. They bid their quiet, condoling adieu to the wit-bankrupt sandwich lady, checked out with the blue AmEx Cam's mom and stepdad had given her before she'd left for school and then made their way back across the breezing parking lot.

251

Once settled into the Ford, Tyler took a monstrous bite of his lunch, dabbed his little chin with a Publix napkin and gazed at the windshield. "Why'd you come all the way out here from Chicago? I forgot."

"Film school," she said, mouth full of liquefied chicken. "Least that's what I thought when I came." Her eyes wrinkled. "You know all this."

Tyler, smiling, taking a few more smacking chews. "Why not L.A. -- the epicenter of the entertainment industry?"

"Why are you asking so many questions right now?"

The car became choked with silence. Tyler took another Herculean chomp.

"You should be more honest with yourself," Tyler said.

"What the hell are you talking about?"

He put the remains of his sandwich down onto the wrapper across his lap, glancing at it, sorrowful he'd opted to part ways with the food a moment. He stared at the windshield. "Martin lives in Miami. You came to FSU so you could be closer to your dad."

The last lively spark in her eyes had now perished. She sneered at him and held the look. "Why the fuck do you think you have the right to talk to me about my personal life like that? I take you over here, buy you a fucking sub and this is the shit you're going to say to me, Tyler? Fuck you." She smashed her sandwich wrapper over her half-eaten sub and tossed it behind her without looking at where it might have gone. Was glaring at the windshield now, firing the engine, cranking the stereo, flipping the car into reverse. She hit the pedal; they lashed backward.

"Calm down," he was saying, whirling his head back and forth, covering his sandwich. He reached forward to turn down the music and let out an uneasy laugh. "This is ridiculous. *Why* would you react like this? Just wanted you to consider a different perspective."

"My dad's an asshole," she said, jerking the car left onto Blairstone.

"Why, though? Martin's great. He loves you."

"What kind of fucking father just leaves his two kids, Tye? Absolutely none of your business."

Silence. A sudden and Socratic silence of weighing and considering occasioned by Tyler's non-response. Camille turned the music back up, full-tilt, and they both allowed themselves to be stripped of the heaviness attached to hushed introspection. Tyler gazed out his window, fondled his squashed wrapper and brooded. The early-afternoon light, now tinted charcoal-gray, snuck through high leaves and made ripples on his angular face.

"We definitely need to go have some fun in Ibiza this summer," he said. "This town is just too drab and dreary."

June 13, 2012

"Funny on one level," Jake said. "I guess." He took another long sip of black tea and his eyes coasted upward. "If you think about it, though, what improv actually presents us with is this extended demonstration of how closely connected yet slightly different human beings are." He glanced out the window of Melrose Restaurant. "Think about how instantaneous the improv process is, how much those guys had to rely on each other's like-mindedness *and* uniqueness and then think about the elaborate webbing of ideas that had seamlessly emerged from it all. It's a wonder everyone was hooting after the show and not just sitting around in a state of silent reflection."

The girl across from him nodded and continued to stare at her iPhone.

"What do you think?"

"It was funny," she said, still gazing at the phone, tapping it. "Short."

"Why are you so in love with that device?"

"Sorry -- my friend Jamie," the girl said, flipping her eyes up, back down at the phone. "Her boyfriend just broke up with her."

Jake began to glance around the bright, semi-crowded diner, mouth agape, his eyes two wandering orphans searching for an affectionate family. He noticed a pair of couples taking up a booth, all of them gazing at each other with impassioned interest, giggling, making goofy noises, scarcely even touching the food in front of them. *So connected; so happy*, he thought. Like they'd all just suddenly appeared from a lotusland he'd only been able to access in films like *Jules and Jim*. As though he could reach across the room and run his hand through their black and white pixels. He turned back to his date, put his mug to his lips, took a loud, boisterous slurp.

She looked up at him and grimaced.

"Beautiful," he said. "Definitely a face to the inspire the dreams of all men."

The girl's hazel eyes widened. She looked back to the phone.

"Dear Jamie," Jake said, now mimicking her. "OMG! You'll never believe this boy I'm with. What a loser! Call me in ten so I can make an excuse to leave, kay?"

"You can pay this check," the girl said, looking back up. "I'll be leaving now."

Jake stuck his hand in the air and gazed at the waitress -- an older, hoary-haired woman with a crew cut and jittery eyes. Waitress hurried over to the table.

"I'm sorry," Jake said to their waitress. "This date is just going abominably." He pointed to the girl, but kept looking at the waitress. "C'mon. Is she not the symbol of our devolution from human back into ape? Why would I go out with someone like this in the first place? Loneliness. Anyway, that'll be all -- check please."

Waitress stood there a moment, staring at him, brows knitted.

"Just the check," Jake said.

"You're a real asshole," the girl said to Jake after the waitress strode off.

"Yeah, I don't do well with married women."

"I'm not married." A breathy, fuddled laugh.

"What about your iPhone?"

The girl fleered at him, then reached down to snatch her white-leather purse. Tossing her phone in that bag, standing, purse straps now slung over her right shoulder. She turned and flounced out the restaurant without looking at him again.

He leaned back against the indurate booth after the waitress had returned with the check. Eyes anchored to his now steam-less tea mug. He thought about that severe and oppressive affront of absence the girl had just given him, an anti-gift he'd received from several women since he'd moved to Chicago, perhaps because city living, with its vast stimulus, offered people the liberty to just de-value and disregard those they knew and those they didn't, or perhaps it was him -- that he was too frank, convoluted. Maybe it was because he really wasn't seeing these women he'd been choosing, who they were, which meant what he'd been seeking from them was something he wasn't giving himself. *Which is what?* he thought, rubbing his Vandyke. *Acceptance? Why do I have such a low self-esteem?* He sighed, snagged the bill, stood, shambled to the check-out counter.

The old man behind the register had a wide, sloping nose, withered, olive skin, a gold necklace with an owl pendant being exhibited on account of his half-unbuttoned, flannel shirt. Man chewed a toothpick and was looking down at a fuzzy, vintage TV, watching an episode of *Modern Family* with an austere gaze.

"Last time I pick up a chick at Hub 51," Jake said, slapping his check down on the glass countertop. "Women. Like a slow, ambrosial venom."

The cashier flashed his eyes at Jake, narrowed them, looked down at the bill. He took the check, turned to his register and punched numbers. After completing the intensive calculations, he stared at Jake again. "Six dollars."

Jake pulling a crumpled ten from his wallet: "Keep it. Pleasure talking to you. Pleasure talking to everyone in this town." He turned and shoved open the front doors, strode out into the night.

A nine-thirty pm air of hopeless distraction to the corner of Broadway and Belmont now. The aged apartment buildings all being back-staged in a darkening penumbra from the showy lights of franchised, commercial shops. There were dwindling groups of wearied, well-groomed young professionals still tarrying at bus stops, tuned in to their phones or gaping at the sidewalk, many of them longing for just one benign thrill before getting up to do it all over again tomorrow morning -- a desirable purchase made, yoga DVD they could utilize to become more toned, greasy restaurant they would let loose their appetites at, sexy boy or girl to stalk on Facebook, maybe even send a message to. A Chipotle on the southeast corner of the intersection shimmering like it was the daughter of Studio 54. A high-ceilinged Walgreens right across the street answering back with even brighter bulbs, lights that were now making Jake bat his eyes as he walked past the store, along Broadway.

He looked across the walkway he'd had to stop for as cars tossed to and fro and saw Camille standing at the other end. Felt his heart speed up. He stood awestruck, limb-locked.

All those times he'd come upon some random corner in the city over the last year, filled with excitation, because he just knew he'd bump right into her, knew from the way he felt around her that they'd been put on this earth for each other and that their reunion was stitched into the weaving of Divine Design. That short, silent film of their startled encounter which kept playing in his head just before he'd come to Wabash and

Washington, North and Damen, Broadway and Lawrence, Clark and Foster... With uncontainable tears falling from their eyes, a long, inexorable kiss -- their two fervid tongues offering damp apologies for mistakes that couldn't be undone, making sodden promises they'd never leave each other again. But what he'd met with every time was an inauspicious breeze or an unknown face or another vast stretch of night that reminded him she was hidden somewhere amongst a vastness he could never comprehend, let alone gain mastery of. How his shoulders would then deflate; he'd sigh through his nose, look at the ground, scuff along. All those times he'd made an excuse, any excuse, a jog, restaurant he had to keep going back to, just to pass by her building in hopes of catching her on the way in or out, just to see her, but only finding her lonesome and abraded front pathway, the trimmed bush. Or those fugacious quarter-minutes in the midst of a crowd, in bars, on trains, when he'd espied a head of plush, red hair, standing out like it was an incarnated nymph in a den of slovenly hobos, and he'd been so sure it was her and felt his breaths speed up and the face turned and it was foreign.

Never could have forgotten her, never would. That delicate face and curvaceous body and self-commanding manner of hers, the amplified sound of her intimate laugh followed by the words "I love you so much, Jake." that preyed upon his daydreams over and again these past twelve months. No, couldn't forget her then, couldn't now, here, in this consummate moment, in the flesh. *Her hair*, he thought. *Different. Face thinner, jaw more pronounced*. This change in her appearance suddenly reminded him of how much time had passed since they'd been a part of each other's lives. She'd been a *real* person during that time and not just the misty sylph frisking through his thoughts. She'd been carrying on without him, getting haircuts, and was probably now absorbed in a relationship with someone totally different, someone less plainspoken, more sensitive. She was fulfilled and he wasn't even a memory.

Camille continued to look down at the sidewalk, her brow crinkled. When she got the walk signal and looked up and saw Jake, she squinted, then shuffled to a sudden stop, which caused the gay, twenty-something behind her to crash into her shoulder, flash her a quick look of frazzled repugnance and then keep walking. She collected herself quickly and resumed her brisk gait, not looking at Jake, instead scrunching her lips and staring at the street.

Finally standing in front of each other by a small shrub on the outskirts of Walgreens, wide-eyed, smiling.

"How are you?" he said.

"Good, I guess…" She touched her chin. "This is different."

"Yeah, figured it was more appropriate for my demeanor," he said, rolling his fingers along his goatee. He pointed to her hair. "What about you? When did you do that?"

"Just a change."

They then found themselves wordless and nodding, heavy of breath, two figures stopped in a Lakeview night with that galvanic conversation that just wouldn't transpire between them. Camille, smiling, glancing past his shoulder, back at him: "Jake, I just want to apologize for the way I acted… It was really hard for me to be more open to you, then." Her eyes dropped. "I'm doing a lot better now."

He put his hand on her arm. "I was way too imposing. Something's wrong with me, Camille, not you. Look, I go around like nothing bothers me, but that's because I'd rather live in an illusion about who I am than face the fact that I feel worthless, and lonely, all the time. I miss you so much. You don't know."

She pursed her lips, let out a lengthy breath. "It's-it's really great to see you, but I have to go." Nodding at Melrose. "I was supposed to meet Mere at 8:45."

"Wait," he said, breaking from speechlessness, as she was already a step and a half away.

She halted, turned, eyes fixated, frightened in the candid glare from a store light.

"Can we see each other again?"

"I don't know, Jake."

He stepped toward her, locking eyes. "Why don't you come meet me after Mere?"

She looked to the restaurant, back at him. "Well... I..."

"Don't even think about it. Just come. I'll be waiting for you at Caribou, right across the street. I'll be that overwhelmingly handsome guy just sipping his caramel macchiato, pondering."

She giggled, looked at the ground. "You *could* just call me."

"You won't pick up. Besides, I don't even know if your number's the same."

"Same."

"Well, come because whatever preternatural force it is that has handed us this moment is now leaving it up to us to decide once and for all whether or not we want to make us into something long-lasting."

She giggled again. "Don't be dramatic."

He clamped his hands into prayer position. "Okay, come because--"

"I'll think about it," she said, fighting to keep down a smile. "Tell you what, if I'm not there by ten, I'm not coming. Just call me."

He pulled out his grimy phone, gawked at it. "Ten o'clock?"

She lifted up both her hands.

"Ten o'clock," he said, stepping back, blowing a kiss. "Ten o'clock. This is great, I'm so happy. Best night of my life. Ten o'clock: When all things past are dissipated in the mystical music of our presence." He turned and then waited for a dragging band of cars to pass so he could cross the street. "Say hi to Mere," he shouted, now striding along Broadway. "Haven't seen her in a blue moon."

November 11, 2007

Camille remembered standing in front of Grandma Lana's ornate mirror in one of her grandmother's crocheted dresses, remembered slipping bare her shoulders, moving her head left, right and comparing the contours of her neck to a swan or perhaps a duchess in a stately portrait. The powerful mustiness in that basement -- that preserved scent which would bring her closer to history and intoxicate her. Remembered her sudden fantasy of grand corridors and silk-clothed banquet tables, of inhabiting a distinguished position in an epoch busied with pressing matters of court.

It was the summer of '06, two weeks after Grandma's death when she'd gone to Grandma's one-story in Skokie with Mom and Aunt Paula to help box up Lana's former possessions so they could be kept, sold or parceled out to the rightful friends and relatives.

She'd now taken off the dress and begun to wander up the basement's rickety steps. She strolled across Grandma's bare living room and then made her way toward a framed pencil sketch of State Street in the 1920s, still hanging center of a small wall alongside the dining area.

The gradated rendering conveyed a wide, fissured road dotted with torch-like street lamps that lofted upward. Old-fashioned Fords, Chryslers and trucks formed regimented lines on both sides of the street. Skyscrapers shooting up into a sky no longer visible in the urban smog. The buildings surrounded the roads, locking them up in hefty prison bars.

"Chartered streets," Camille said, nodding at the picture and turning toward Ellen, who was now on her haunches in a living room corner, beside a wide window, placing dusty, blue-rimmed plates and sterling flatware into a large cardboard box. "Blake said it best."

Ellen stopped, gripped both sides of the box and turned to Camille. "*What*?"

"I've always thought this city was like one big, concrete jail cell," Camille continued, pointing to the sketch, smirking. "I think this picture expresses it all for me."

"Take the picture down," Ellen said, her voice vehement. "Your aunt and I need help now." Ellen looked back to the box and shifted plates.

Camille stared at the floor. An evanescent quiet had now swept across the room like a protective shade from an itinerant angel's wing. This silence her most genuine friend. It was acceptant and not tyrannical.

She listened as Ellen's footsteps began striking against the squeaky floor, getting louder, closer. She watched, breathless, as Mom gripped both ends of the picture frame and yanked State Street from the wall. Watched, wide-eyed, as Ellen strode back to the box and returned to her task, the picture now lying face down on the floor beside her.

"You're such a bitch," Camille said.

Ellen, stopping herself, turning to Camille, trim, dark eyebrows shifted down, roseate lips hung halfway between an incredulous smile and trembling frown. "Get out! Now!"

"*Get out*? We're in Skokie, Mom. Should I walk back to Lakeview? Hitchhike? You know what, I'll just prostitute myself from suburb to suburb. That's about how much you think I'm worth anyway, right?"

"Get out! Get out!" Ellen said, her shrill voice resounding through the passageways of the small house.

Paula, who'd been examining the turtlenecks still

265

dangling from hangers in the sliding glass closet of Grandma's bedroom, started and turned to the doorway when she heard her sister's shrieking. She stepped out into the living room and took up an empty, far left-hand corner with an expressionless stance, hands on her hips, bespectacled eyes coasting back and forth between Ellen and Camille. She glanced at her sister as her sister glared at Camille, then walked over to Camille, touching her back, guiding her out of the living room.

"You're polar opposites, but that doesn't mean she doesn't love you," Paula was saying, looking at the ground as they walked, single-file, out the front door, out into a windy, sun-lit day.

"She's fucking crazy!" Camille said, thrusting her index finger at the door they'd just come from, her eyes gravid with tears. "You heard her…"

Paula touched Camille's arm. "You make each other crazy." She lifted a subdued smile, spoke before that smile could hint any sense of joyful concordance: "You *both* need to relax and try to understand each other. Emotional sensitivity is not one of your mother's strong suits. You, baby girl, are an artistic soul. You're all emotion. The two of you need to find some happy place in the middle."

Camille looked away, wiped her eyes. She gazed at a gable roof house across the street, watching two girls in teal dresses as they ran side-by-side, squealing, in their embowered front yard. She looked up and winced at the brilliant sun.

All my tempestuous feelings in that moment with Aunt Paula, Camille thought, a year later now, as she stared at a soaking sky through her apartment window, as she recalled the beautiful, horrible ignorance of those two young girls she saw in their front yard that day, as she remembered those pitiable, laughing girls who'd not yet seen what lay beyond childhood. *All my tempestuous feelings in that moment. All the yelling and miscommunication which surrounded that day at Grandma's like an Egyptian plague means nothing now. A memory, that's it.*

She listened to faded car honking outside her apartment. Listened to the remote ruction of city as if it were a postmortem sound wave reaching her in a celestial realm. Shut her eyes and let that terrible music resounding from cars down below rush into her ears, air-raid her inner-being.

The most profound peace I could ever know if I just jumped out that window, if I swan dived into death. The only way out of this ill-fated life. A solitary image of Michael now came to her, the last time she'd seen him alive, 1997. Shutting himself into his Jeep in the vast parking lot of Northbrook Court mall. Buckling his seatbelt, turning to look both ways as he reversed, so cautious, driving off, disappearing. Off to transmute into the ageless sprite who would be haunting the backlands of her mind for the rest of her life.

She flipped open her eyes.

That last idea; the notion Michael had *not* ceased to be, but was instead living on in the thoughts of all those lives he'd touched, in a glorified state because he was now the bearer of some recondite understanding about what existence meant, gave her goose bumps. She'd follow him, all the way beyond that ancient car crash of his.

The last few nights she'd had a recurring dream

267

about Michael:

It was as though she'd been Antonioni behind the lens of a camera. There was a widespread desert without rocks or crevices. A blanched-blue, cloudless sky. A sharp horizon line where the limitless ether mocked the patchy earth like it was a lauded canvas rendering by some once-alcoholic-now-dead cowboy who'd attempted to express the rugged realism of the American Southwest. No heat, coolness. Michael, a scarcely discernable figure just before the horizon, was sprinting toward nothing. She couldn't move, talk; could only watch. Long, obsidian bat-wings appeared from Michael's sides and flapped, once, twice. He lifted upward, glided into the blue, disappearing from mortal bound. He--

Camille jumped as her tatty RAZR phone started vibrating on the table behind her.

The ringing now reminding her that she had a relationship with other people, that those people were watching, evaluating, helping to define her. *My suicide would kill a part of all them, too*, she thought. *My living presence, voice, smile, laughter, storytelling suddenly wrenched away and never to be reclaimed.* She smirked. *How the fuck does that feel, you heartless wretches?*

Her eyes fell to the floor, shoulders sagged. She jogged to the phone, picked up:

"Hello?"

"Can't believe you didn't come," Joseph said.

"It's between Mom and me."

"You made it everyone's business. Do you have any idea how your actions affect the people who care about you, or are you just totally oblivious all the time?"

"I'm warning you to stop persecuting me," she said. "You have no right to call like this."

"We're your family. When family needs you, you show up. That's the way it is. You're one of the most selfish people I've ever known in my whole life. Tell you what, if you hurt Mom again, I'll fucking kill you."

"You don't…" she said, tearing.

He hung up.

She started sobbing, her small phone being squeezed in her clenched hand. Breathed in, out, dropped the phone on the table and turned to face her window again. White-framed window, little cynosure, portentous gate between her and the all-powerful voice now beckoning to her from the other end, a voice that could have stilled the rain if it wanted to, voice whispering, *You don't belong, Camille. Just leap out here. Come to me. Come to happiness. Find your freedom.* She took another step toward the window. *You can suffocate at these celebratory Sunday brunches for the next twenty years by yourself, Joseph,* Camille thought. Another step. *What the fuck do I care that Cynthia's pregnant? Who's she been to me? What do you care? Who are you? Traitor. Sell-out. All of you sitting there feigning family over bagels and lox, trying to flee from your own inescapable inner hells by telling yourselves that the perdition is just a standard discomfort of the white-collar worker.* Another step. Another step. *Slurping your coffee and spouting out your pointless, everyday anecdotes and talking really to yourselves -- not each other -- and passing that silver tray of scrambled eggs and pretending that this is what love is.*

She was lifting her window all the way open. Pattering rain hitting her hands, her face. She tilted her chin up, closed her eyes, took in a long breath of the moist air through her nose. Leaned forward, eyes shut tight. The water beating her cheeks, her temples. Hands pushing the sill, she could feel her bare feet coming up off the floor. *I can't, I can't, I can't!* she thought. *Broken body, blood, mortal smack!* She flicked open her eyes, came back onto the floor, slammed the window shut.

Eyes closed again. "Hope you're at peace, Michael, my love. I'll be there soon, don't worry."

She spun around, glanced at her apartment. A quick look at the spare, pine-colored couch she'd picked up from a second-hand shop, with old copies of writing trade publications and little bottles of nail polish now strewn across one of its cushions. The two French Impressionist paintings that hung center of parallel walls, dreamily rendered settings that reminded her of her ongoing quest to transform raw reality into art each morning, images she'd had framed cheaply. That heaping pile of two-week-old laundry still deserted at the fore of her kitchenette. This her snug and meaningful living quarters, her concealed space that biographers were supposed to comment upon with phrases like "humble beginnings" in the "Early History" section of her encyclopedia page fifty years hence.

Not safe. Go. Now. Paris. London. Take nothing. Anonymous. No second thoughts.

She strode to her laundry mound and flung off her taffeta negligee like she was an amorous virgin on a midnight grove in a Dionysian ritual. She jiggled into stinky jeans, wormed her way into a wool shirt, teetered as she tried to furnish her feet with dirty, pink socks, then snagged a set of keys from the kitchen counter, collected her phone and hemp purse from the dining room table, went to the tiny front hall closet for her ruffled jacket and low boots. Out the front door -- shut, locked behind her.

Jogging down her tubular hall, her puffy coat making rasping noises as she moved.

"C'mon, c'mon, let's go," she said to herself as she punched the elevator button and listened to the mechanistic wail of its ascent. She looked left, right, bounced.

The poorly-lit machine finally appeared on her floor, snapping into place with a catastrophic hiss. She snatched open the front grating, closed herself in, jabbed at the lobby knob. Started to creep downwards. The elevator jolted just before it hit the second floor, then stopped completely.

"You're fucking kidding me," she said. "Again? Now? Of course. I hate this building!"

She kicked the call buttons and the elevator gave a slow rattle. It continued to descend.

At last freed from the braced mouth of that defected contraption, she was hastening outside. The rain had now remitted from a soppy wrath upon the earth to a more gloomy and disjointed sprinkling. Intermittent pockets of sluggish, Sunday people around the sidewalks were still galloping toward building awnings and entrances with pulpy city newspapers hoisted over their heads, or, devoid of any makeshift coverings, were making histrionic twisting movements and high-pitched moans as they scampered to bus shelters, or, those that possessed umbrellas, were striding along and scowling at the ground from underneath their somber canopies.

Camille plunged into the back of a Yellow Cab, the knavish gusts of wind tossing her hair. She leaned toward a scratched partition to tell the swarthy face on the other side where to go, but then just fell back against her stiff seat. She stared out the window. *Europe? Really?*

What money? Still have to get my fucking passport. Her fisted hands tensed. *Geography's not the problem, or the solution...* "Um, um..." she was saying to the cabbie. *Where, Camille? Damnit, where? Tell him something.* "Landmark Theatres," she said, now remembering that *Love in the Time of Cholera* had just come out and longing to transport herself into that late 19th century love triangle, yearning to feel Florentino's heartbreak over Fermina. "Clark and Diversey, please."

The driver, peering at her in the rearview with his blunted eyes, nodded. He clicked his car into drive.

Her head dropped. She sighed. Watched as vapory, brown-brick apartment buildings moved past the window. Watched grassy hillocks and diverse families of trees, all indistinct and glistening. Everything now becoming just a dull dance of color, melting out of the "shapes" humankind had assigned to them, appearing less classifiable. All these objects now emancipated from that strict, scientific framework which had been imposed upon them, the consensual and conspiring taxonomy on account of which the human species could revel in its delusive power to subjugate the planet. An old, cracked, pallid building with a bright, white marquee now appeared before her window as though it were the last American sliver of antiquity left untouched by time.

"This is it," she said.

Her shoulders jerked forward as the cab swerved to the side of the street and came to a halt, the reckless motion reminding her the driver cared not a fig about her gentle, drifting reveries, only about attaining as much money as he could. She handed him a ten and stepped out into an ashy, post-rain coldness that now enveloped Clark Street. Looked down, flipped up her furry hood as she crossed the road toward the theatre: she was surrounded by scatterings of people all in transition, but not realizing it -- no one would remain over time, nothing lasted as long as hopes could promise, no friendship, love, lust, financial fortuity, no exchange of troths that at one point might seem so incorruptible... She turned at the alcove beneath the theater's marquee and surveyed city dwellers moving back and forth, youngsters in groups, halfway through telling clamorous stories, an intent homosexual man with hands inhumed in his trim, black peacoat pockets. *All your firm self-conceptions*, Camille thought, turning again and heading into the building. *Just a hundred weakly stakes wobbling around a volcanic terrain called The Unknown.*

She watched the white-tile lobby of the indoor mall fall further below her from the glass window of an elevator, her head slumped against it. Stepped out on the fourth floor, turning her hood down, maundering toward a dark box office situated up a carpeted ramp.

She noticed there was a heavyset woman to her far right as she was approaching a ticket attendant -- the woman's black-clothed figure silhouetted in the low lights behind the candy counter. The woman staring at an open magazine on the countertop below her with squinted eyes, puckered lips. *That woman's raven hair*, Camille thought as she nodded at the box office man in front of her and looked up at showtimes: *her dark brows: her pale face: It's as though that woman's the steward of a small chamber in a mild and lesser-known section of Hell.*

Camille observed how that woman kept moving her eyes and brushing away streaks of hair that clung to her cheeks and glancing at her and then glancing away with fumbling subtlety and then -- *Poor woman locked in*

your meek and reclusive life here, Camille thought,
*you've got to fight to be yourself! Or die, or you're the
living dead. You can't listen to them. They're all brutish.
You're the sensitive one, the gem, the shining spirit, and
your purpose is to lead. Never submit. Never surrender.
Come away from that magazine and be dauntless. This
won't be easy, but there's no other choice* -- and then
Camille staring at the ticket man again and saying, "*Love
in the Time of Cholera.*" She reached into her back pocket
for her wallet. Getting a ticket and change for her twenty
and making her way through the lusterless lobby and
stealing a final glance at that woman, who was now
running four fingers through her hair and focused on her
magazine like it was an emergency broadcast from the
president and Camille thinking, *See you on the front lines,
you beleaguered divinity*.

Camille walked up another ramp into the high-
ceilinged house of theatres, coming upon an employee
slouched against a ticket check stand.

The boy short, scrawny. He continued to swat at
long strands of oily-brown hair that dangled in front of
his unshaven face while he gazed down at his open book.

"What's the point?" Camille said as he looked up
to tear her ticket, did it.

The boy's glassy green eyes two motionless cows
trying to make sense of a small road between fields. He
smirked.

"All these civilizations we've formed in hopes of
vanquishing the chaos of Nature through our ability to be
organized, but how many times has that titanic enigma,
Nature, risen up, roared, and shown us how utterly
ineffectual we actually are? How long can these inane
cycles of society continue?" She glanced at his book.

"What are you reading?"

The boy shrugged. He picked up the text and looked at its cover. *"The Stranger."* "'Maman died today,'" she said, staring at him. "'Or yesterday maybe, I don't know.'" She smiled without suggesting joy. "Camus gets it. The nature of our existence is *not* appealing, nor will it ever be explicable. Let's just *stop* trying to package all of life up and wrap it with our little pink fucking postulation bows, just start accepting the contents themselves. Simple, but complicated at the same time. How else are we going to evolve? Right?"

The boy shrugged, smirking.

She narrowed her brows. "What do you think?"

"I'm just reading it for class..."

"I see," she almost whispered. Her eyes sailed away. "Thanks." She strode on.

***

A frigid and galactic blackness had come to claim the streets of Lakeview by the time Camille had gotten out of the theater. She couldn't tell how long she'd been floating around in the street-side darkness punctured with store light. Was still trying to let those gleaming traces of film-story disperse from her present awareness and her eyes still blurry with tears.

Unbelievable! she kept thinking, now bumping shoulders with a portly Iranian man on the sidewalk, continuing on. *What a sacrilegious interpretation! Who is this director? Get Inarritu to do it. Someone with an artistic eye, who actually understands the magic of Marquez's literary landscapes. Fucking Hollywood! But why am I crying?*

She found herself standing by an old cash register amid the loud lights of Yummy Yummy Asian Cuisine, drying her eyes with the tips of her fingers. A little, Chinese woman, who'd been sitting in a chair behind the front counter and watching Fox Chicago News on the outmoded television propped up at the top of the wall across from her, stood and seized a laminated menu when she saw Camille walk in. The woman offering Camille her quick, friendly smile. "Just one?"

Cam gave her a chary nod.

"Wherever you like," the woman said, now shuffling around the counter and motioning across the vacant space with her stubby arm, waiting for Camille to choose.

Cam drifted to a table at back, dropped down into one of its firm chairs. She let go her purse on the seat beside her, but kept the jacket on. Was staring at a glass of cloudy ice water that was now poured for her, the menu, thinking, *This is just too exhausting; I'm living in my head; I can't think; I have to go home*, and suddenly she could feel a hurricane that had been crashing about her inner-person come to a momentary calm. She closed her eyes and took in a protracted breath. *Don't think. No thought. Blackout. Respite.* Her eyes flinging back open. *You can't not think. No hiding place. I go home, I go home, and how long till that fervent, spellbound worship of the workaday here in Chicago causes me to feel excluded again, worthless, estranged?*

The Chinese lady now stepping up to the table. "You ready to order?"

No, she thought. *Obviously I'm not ready for anything. And Fermina wasn't ready for Florentino, because she was hypnotized, too. Just like everyone, always, how sad. And I'm the shameful apostate. And that's what everyone has made me into. Can't you see that's why I'm here, alone? Please just listen to me. Listen!*

"Whatever *you* like," Camille said, closing her menu, handing it over.

The Chinese woman now holding that menu like it was a wilted bouquet. She hesitated, smiled. "I'm sorry?"

Camille looked up at her. "Just the pad thai."

"What type of meat you like?"

"Shrimp," Camille said, glaring at her water.

"Spicy?"

"No."

"Anything to drink?"

"That's it. Go away. Leave me alone."

The woman bowed her head and scuffled to the kitchen.

It was the lady's phantasm Camille was staring at now. *I'm so sorry.* Her heart beat wildly. *There wasn't enough time for me to think about what I was saying. Please forgive me.*

She gawked at the table and girded her temples with her hands, thought: *There wasn't enough time… There wasn't enough time. Wasn't enough time, Michael… I think you were the only person I've ever really given myself to, fully: the volatile, uncontrollable nature of my mind, my life story -- then --, my lips, body… How tragic this life without you, for me and all humanity. Why? Why do these things happen?* She shut her eyes and soared into literary history, seeking out a lofty spirit to console her, finally gliding over seventeenth century London and sojourning in the consciousness of Shakespeare. *Michael was a player*, she thought; *We all*

*are. He made his appearance on this intricate stage,
offered us an extraordinary energy, but was then cut
short by a director none knew.* Eyes open, head lifted, she
looked at the restaurant's tall front window and smiled.
*Maybe you're boon with all those great minds now,
Michael. Maybe you're all a troupe of phantoms
swooping through the firmament, heightening that
crystal-blue summer day, or accenting the bleakness of
this early-winter eve...*

Severed from her ongoing musings by the soft
scrape of an oval dish as it was now placed down on the
table, below her, hot, peanut-scented steam rushing into
her nostrils and fumigating all transcendent meditation.
She looked up to thank the Chinese woman, but that lady
had already paced away, so Camille belied her attempt at
kindness by shifting glances between the food and front
counter, as though she'd only been doing what she'd
always done in public places, checking everything out.
She picked at her food in slow intervals, ten minutes
passing, twenty. Kept trying to embrace that bliss of
buttery fish sauce in her mouth, the soothing charge of
her stomach as it took in clumps of rice noodle, but she
kept pausing and tensing her body every time her body
started emitting too much vim.

Another hour and she'd long since left Yummy
Yummy and was now sitting on a chilly bench at a bus
stop just east of her apartment building, not waiting to go,
instead watching those that came and went, hood back up
so she could be incognito. She couldn't help but let the
vigor born of her digesting Thai food quicken upon every
part of her and was finally forced to recognize just how
unhealthy she'd been this last week by only eating one
paltry meal a day, if that. Food had just been meaningless

substance ever since their nasty fight, since that incessant heartache. Nicotine sustenance enough. Her mother's harsh closing words still rang through her like it happened yesterday: "You're a burden on everyone."

You're my mother! You're all I have, had.

She looked down and started rummaging through her purse, found an empty pack of Camel Lights, crunched it. "Fuck!" Looked back up and flashed her eyes around the tiny crowd still lingering by the bus stop. *Smoker, smoker… Who's a smoker?* She fixed her gaze on a bony, Indian guy with a leather messenger bag, then the woman behind him who kept shaking her nappy head and smirking as she stared at a BlackBerry, now imagining that both figures were resuming their former postures, condescendingly, after denying her a cigarette when she'd asked. Imagined both now considering her unorthodox approach in the asylum of their customary personal space and thinking: "A cigarette? What a filthy and desperate girl. Smoking? Really? Disgusting. She must be homeless, a druggie. Thank God it's not me."

What if I was homeless? Camille thought, looking at her jeans, shivering. *What if I did have a drug addiction? Why would your first impulses be revulsion and not compassion? Fuck you. What is everyone pretending they're not afraid of? Has everyone gone mad? Why can't we all just try to be more open and loving? Can't we accept people the way they are?* She glared at the woman who was still looking at her phone and now deciding not to stay and marching off and Camille could hear the knifelike echo of "No! You're nothing. Shut up." in her wake, could envision that echo tossing around with the sporadic wind, traveling into and out of other people's minds all over the city because the echo had actually come from the icy air itself, had been birthed during the boom of manufacturing and retail on this landmass back in the 1840s.

　　She remained seated a long time, long after the Indian stranger disappeared into the 145, until the bus stop had become unfrequented and buses ceased coming every fifteen minutes or so, when the random, outlying chirp of a bird could be heard, sitting there depleted and still, leaned back, her hands in her pockets, observing. Her eyes kept drawing shut and eventually she fell asleep. Came back to consciousness fifteen minutes later with a panicky gasp, sitting straight up, whipping her head left, right. She let out an extensive breath and her cemented shoulders softened. No negating the fact that the sudden sleep had assuaged her squalling emotion. Unzipping her purse and combing her fingers through tampons, hairbrush, wallet, cell phone -- nothing filched. *Take it,* she thought, almost disappointed now, pushing the open purse along her legs. *I don't want any of this. This what we're all working so hard for, killing ourselves for, killing each other for? This why we're all so inhumane? Products? Take it, someone, anyone. Please. Do me the favor.* Wasn't a noble lightness she was feeling with those scant, sacrificial possessions on the altar of her knees, but rather lassitude, surrender. She zipped up the purse, stood and swung its slender strap over her shoulder, wiped her coat.

　　Stopped when she took note there was now a couple in matching hoodies cuddling and kissing at the far end of the bench, both of them gawking at the shaded grass in front of them, static, as though they'd just finished a mammoth bong. She thought about sneaking up behind the lovers, putting her purse beside them and then dashing off -- her last bequest to two remaining believers in the potential of human connectedness as *she* sprinted off into the midnight, alone, directionless, to shed all final traces of identity. She started strolling past them and tightened her grip on the purse, glancing, glancing away, then just kept meandering toward her building with head down, with a smile.

STASIS?

"Caribou closes at ten," Jake said, touching Cam's knee. "Let's go have a drinky."

Camille, smirking, legs crossed center of a suede chair: "You drink every day?"

"Every other. Occupational hazard. You don't drink much, right?"

"Time and a place for everything."

"How 'bout now?"

She shrugged.

He drummed his hands on the side of his chair, then gulped down the cool dregs from his macchiato and hopped upward, reaching out his hand. "I've got the place. Let's go!"

A sinewy, French woman in a tight, black tank top was now looking up from her Apple MacBook at the wood table behind them, smiling.

Camille standing and staring at Jake's eyes. "Into this starless unknown."

Jake shaking his head. "What happened to you over this last year?"

"Shh," she said. She put her forefinger in front of her lips. "Let's just go."

She followed as he strode out the front door. Stood beside him at the edge of the sidewalk, clutching her purse, beaming, while he held his hand for a cab. He was on tiptoes and gazing into the darkling road, still alight, slightly, from an occasional store open in the near distance, or the fluorescent-orange puddles being made by high street lights, or a periodic car with its headlights materializing in the murk as though from a vacuum, making its way past. One such set of southbound lights veered right, pointing its rays at them as it came close.

Jake opened up the Flash Cab's back door and slid

sideways to let Camille in.

"Parrots. It's on Clark and Wellington," he said after they'd situated themselves inside, their legs now adjoined, Jake's forehead pressed to the partition. He fell back against his seat as they pulled forward and threw his arm over Cam's shoulder, his eyes shuttling before hers. "Still can't believe you cut your hair like that."

His features masked by the night and by shadows and the vague outline of his face a voguish screen upon which Camille projected pictures from her imagination: she fancied it was Johnny Depp talking to her now, that she was famous, Johnny's egotistical plaything in the back of some limo.

She leaned in, kissed him. Helpless, free, hand on his round cheek.

He pressed his chest to her breasts. Muttered "Want you so…" at the half-open gate of her lips. Could feel her trying to drive him away with half-hearted pushes that perhaps meant she actually liked his strength, liked the game of victim-victor and wanted him to exert more power. He did. He tugged himself off and then collapsed against his seat, sealing his eyes, opening them, grinning. "'Nor am I the captain of my soul; I am only its noisiest passenger.'"

Her ultramarine eyes intent, would throw off sparks if they could. She breathed like a demoiselle in labor pains. Tendered a fathomless eroticism in her proximal pose of mute placidity.

"I love you," he said, touching her cheek.

She simpered and looked to the opposite window.

"What?" Smirking, his brow contracted. "What are you thinking about?"

She was looking at the tapering gleam from a

street lantern as they'd now turned onto Halsted and were whisking south. Chortled when she thought about how they were encased in this cozy vehicle that allowed them to fast-forward past the sense of being small, being locked into a wide and mazelike city with only one's beating heart, brain and limbs to attain desired destinations.

He leaned over and tickled her.

She turned, leapt onto him, thrust her lips back to his.

He offered a final, prolonged peck when he felt the cab slowing to a stop, then inched forward and put his finger against his window, pointing to a red-brick building across the street. The poinsettia-colored sign of a parrot perched on a dangling tree branch, just above a narrow window with neon beer logos -- candescent reminders that hedonism was still a great way to forget in this darksome neighborhood peopled by the young and working and anxious. Jake gazed at the back of the driver's head: "That's it; this is it."

Cam tilting toward the opening in the partition to pay the cabbie before Jake could pull out cash.

"*No*," Jake said. "Why? I got it."

"Take a load off, kid," she said, winking, smiling.

They bid the driver their flippant, unified "thank you" and tobogganed out. Stood side by side now in the same posture, arms lank, lips parted, gaping at the nondescript building across the way as their cab zoomed off.

"I didn't even know this place existed," she said.

"It's great," he said, voice booming. He took her hand, looked both ways, guided them forth.

The bar appeared austere to Camille, unique, like

it was only moonlighting as a tavern, by day would resume its function as the community's long-standing dentist's office. She could now see, through a depressed front window with ruddy blinds drawn, a singular, multihued glow over a chalk-smeared pool table from its overhanging light, while the rest of the room lay hidden in shade. She turned to Jake and chuckled. "*Why* do you know this exists?"

"Because I am Isaiah Kellen and I have already seen all that was, is and will be to come."

"Shut up," she said, giving him a dig.

They made it to the front door. Inside were met by an extended, wood-paneled room devoid of any tables or pictures, that focalized a small bar with five or six rusted stools. No music, jukebox. Just the intermittent report of a tarry throat being cleared, pint being guzzled. There were only three occupants, counting the bartender. The farthermost stools taken by two jowly, middle-aged men whose relationship couldn't be distinguished on account they weren't talking to each other, weren't talking at all. Just scowling at their cigarette packs and beer. The bartender, meanwhile -- short, stocky, curly-brown hair to her upper-back --, was facing glass shelves of liquor bottles with one hand on her hip, thumbing out a text.

They sat beside the older men, who didn't look at them. Nor did the bartender turn to say hello.

"Something fruity, right?" Jake said, staring at Camille with a smirk.

"Screwdriver please," she said, looking at the bartender's back.

The bartender, still texting: "Don't have vodka."

"That's *right*," Jake said, slapping the bar-top. "Only the liquid bane. I forgot."

The bartender turned around now, phone clenched in her right hand. "Whiskey and scotch. And beer. That's it."

"Two shots of whiskey," Jake said. "Worst you got."

"Jake..." Camille whispered. "I can't..."

"Shh," he said, clasping her thigh. "Let's just drink."

Bartender snagged a bottle of *Old Crow* from the middle shelf and was now pouring out two shots, positioning a tarnished glass in front of each of them. "Six."

"Six? That's it? I love it," Jake said. He reached behind him to fetch his wallet.

Booze burning their chests, bartender back on her phone and facing the liquor shelves, Jake looked at Camille and said: "I love when you're uninhibited, Cam. Frees up that angelic quintessence of you for all us mortals to marvel at."

She watched him, her lips caught between smile and gape. "Wanna' do another?"

"Two more," he said, thumping the bar-top.

Another round of shots, then two Old Crow and Cokes.

"Let me show you the rest," Jake said, now standing with his second cocktail cresting, dribbling on his fingers.

"Is it scary?"

"Fear not." He touched her shoulder, waved his glass across the bar. "I will take you to a room flowing with vacancy and pool accoutrements."

She followed, single-file, gripping his shirt, simpering, as he made his way through a narrow hall. To the back room, tenebrous until Jake swept a wall and flipped the light switch. That pale dirtiness Camille had perceived through the bar window earlier now came to life. This room like the one before it, but more claustrophobic, as though the wood-slatted walls had been pressed toward each other by some epic creature in an abrupt attempt to re-configure the world. Dowdy pool table center of the space, couple stray stripes and solids and two beat-up pool cues sprawled out across its felt; that boxy, acrylic light dangling overhead, commanding a shiny, inspective beam upon the equipment. There was a forsaken trio of walnut-wood tables and chairs along a wall, the circular tabletops garnished with plastic ash trays full of deceased cigarettes.

Cam slurped her whiskey. "Reminds me of the movie *Vanilla Sky*."

"That's one I haven't seen, actually."

"There's this moment where Tom Cruise is running through Times Square in the middle of a weekday morning and it's completely empty. No cars, people. The monstrous electronic billboards still flickering, behemoth skyscrapers still aglow, like they could never let up. Cruise stops right at the center of all commerce, all of twenty-first century civilization, looks up -- a godless David facing a malevolent Goliath of his own creation--, throws out his arms and then howls when he finally understands he's left to live with the tremendous mistake modern humanity has made through this indefatigable project of mass industry. That he's a spiritual prisoner without possibility of escape." Another slurp. "Feels like it is just us here. Like it's now up to us to deconstruct the wrongs that were and build a more honest terrene for all posterity." She jumped onto the table and played pendulum with her legs, drink splashing.

"It is in our hands," he said. He held her thighs, steadied her.

"I wasn't alluding to our *situation*. I just meant sometimes when we're together I'm reminded we're like two, allied souls in a decaying country of unknowns and that we get to work out our special purposes together, which is such solace."

"Do you believe in Providence?" he said, tone buoyant. He lifted himself onto the table behind her and lay back, brushing balls out of the way. Rested his glass on his stomach and started revolving it. "Doubtless we have this abstruse connection that seems to go beyond the need for years of involvement. Beyond that host of mutual sufferings and felicities two people eventually succumb to as a means of growing together or apart. Is it fate that brought us together, Cam? Fate that brought us to this pool table right here, right now?"

She hunched her shoulders and started to muse that all the people she'd known, knew, would know were humans, yes, but perhaps also emanations of some Almighty Force, which were being jostled against her, others, one another, so that everyone could struggle and develop as they were supposed to, a notion assuring for the lack of open-endedness it offered, but then also dreadful in that it meant no one navigated life by way of their own will. "Maybe, maybe not," she said. "What's most important is that we *are* here. That's what counts." She edged forward and bounced up. "Off-off. Let's play a game."

Jake, rolling over: "You play pool?"

"No, never." She walked to a table below the window, put down her drink. "But tonight is the renaissance." Strode back to the pool table, flicking her hand at him. "Off. Let's play."

"I'll rack," he said, jumping up. Started to unearth his wallet. "You get us more drinks."

"Round's on me."

"Sure?" he said, clasping his wallet as she moved toward the hallway, disappeared.

She chuckled when she returned with their glasses to find the pool balls organized into a tidy triangle at the table's far end, cue ball just a foot away and positioned center, two billiard cues of disproportionate height, upended, side by side, against the table rim. As though Jake had surmounted the disastrous cave they'd been in and from its disorderly elements had forged for them a kempt, little domain.

She sauntered toward him with drink, her eyes electric. Strutted back to the table upon which she'd placed her previous cocktail to put the new one down, twirled, gazed at him. "How do you play?"

"You don't even know?"

"Help me."

He strode toward her, taking up the smaller stick on his way, proffering it as he stood tower-like in front of her, peering into those orphan eyes. "You mean to tell me that in all your thirty-two years, you've not taken one shot on a pool table?"

"Just play with me, Mar--" She shook her head, giggled. "Jake."

"Who's Mar?"

"Play," she said. She gave him a frolicsome push.

He walked back to the table and seized his stick. "Rack 'em, crack 'em, sack 'em." Leaned over, worked the cue between his index finger and thumb and then gave the cue ball a vigorous thrust. The ball flew across the green and tore the triangle, sending balls in all directions, 12 into the bottom right-hand corner. "Stripes." Determined, loose-of-limb, he sank three more before missing a long shot on the 9. "*You*," he said, now looking up from his error like he was rousing from an uninterrupted dream. "Come here. I'll help you shoot."

She sipped, let out a scratchy breath, put the drink down behind her without looking at what she was doing. Hip against the fore of his crotch as she was bending forward now, parallel to the table, stick wavering in both hands. "Am I doing it right?"

"Wrong ball, redheaded adulation." He nudged closer, distended stomach resting on her flank. Put both hands over hers. "First of all you hold the stick like this. See that? See *that* ball over there? The white one? Always want to shoot the others with that one."

She nodded, let him glide her furthermost hand back, forth.

"We'll do this first one together."

Tautening his grip over hers. Angling. *Clack* -- 2 went rolling into the lower right corner.

"Yay-yah!" she said. She waggled her body, then dropped the stick, spun round, held his arms and started kissing him, hungrily. "I want you inside me."

He looked toward the hallway. "Right here?"

She grabbed his shirt, pulled him back to her. More kissing. She sprung onto the table and wrapped her legs around his waist, unbuttoned his fly. "Wait," he said with his lips touching hers. "Shh," she said back. His Levis fell to his shins and she rolled down his boxer briefs so they hung center of his brawny thighs. Stroking him now with firm, circular motion. He could feel her filmy g-string, humid, as he kneaded her. *She's perfect*, he thought. He wrestled off her jeans, ripped those panties from her body. Theirs a hysterical confusion of flesh, whist meld of blood. Fortuitous sanctum of two, foundling souls. Kissing her deeply, he continued to labor between the extended legs, the sweat misting his hair, coming down his nape in lawless streaks. He cupped her mouth as she grunted, groaned. Kept the noise muffled, squeezed harder, whimpered, let himself go. "Perfect," he whispered. Pants and underwear at his legs, bare, clammy ass on display in the indiscreet lights of the room, Jake stuck his cheek to hers, shut his eyes. He breathed like a tortured horse. "I love you," he said.

"Think I love you, too, Jake."

She gave him a prod, stood, raised the jeans and zipped up. Bent down to sweep her mangled panties from the floor, then cupped herself, giggling. "I'm dripping."

"So now the enchanting tale is consecrated with our ink."

"Put your pants on, silly," she said, looking all around.

They teetered alongside each other in silence. Smoothened, dusted their clothes.

"Let me take you somewhere classy," he said. "Treat you like royalty."

"I have to be at work early."

"Lunch shift?"

"No, I work at Loyola now."

"You *what?* Since when? What are you doing?"

"Library Assistant."

"How--"

"No work talk tonight. Let's just go. I'll go."

Twenty minutes later they were pulling up in front

of the Peninsula Hotel in another taxi. Jake leaning forward to pay the driver, Cam stepping out underneath the hotel's tinctured awning. They paused with their hands on the hotel's gold-rimmed, revolving front doors, both having the same simultaneous fantasy they were now a high-profile power-couple walking out into the night and lights like they'd never seen any of it before and needed to acclimate. Both carrying on the fantasy, without voice, as Jake motioned Camille into the hotel with his arm extended, taking a little bow, as Camille, on her way in, shot him a cocksure look that could've bespoken decades spent in cradle of the public's affections.

The lobby lights subdued. Space cool, peppered with modern, Asian furniture, everything symmetrically placed. No music. Just that serene air of nobility being preserved. A suited attendant stood erect behind a long, marble desk to the right, eyes fixed down, desk enveloped in shadows save for a single, studious beam of light from a jade lamp with a scalloped shade. The attendant continued to annotate a Chicago brochure as Camille and Jake breezed past, through the Persian-carpeted room, toward an elevator bank.

"Isn't this *so* cool? Aren't we *so* cool?" Jake wanted to say as he pushed the up button, but didn't. Didn't even look at Camille. Just let the experience croon its chic lyrics to them.

"I come here sometimes," he said inside the elevator, his arms outspread, legs crossed, fingertips pressed to the wall. "Great haven for self-communion."

Doors coasted open with a ting and they were met by a long, lambent hall, the ceiling arched. Rows of glass-encased cupboards -- all filled with ornamented dishware and time-honored livery -- lined both sides.

"No one I know would ever have enough culture to figure out I'm here, nor enough aplomb walk in if they actually did," he continued as they strode past a vacant concierge desk. "I can hide in a tiny island of the rich."

They came to a black-oak hall, which opened into a commodious barroom, umbral, yet irradiated by the lucent panels of beveled glass from behind a rangy, burnished bar, by single-shade chandeliers, a zigzag of broad, tableside lamps. Were now surrounded by tall, sanguine walls, stepping on an unblemished, honey carpet, staring at that onyx fireplace at the far end of the room, its crackling flames bedimmed. The bartender, a twiggy man in a single-breasted, ebony vest, was gazing at them from behind the bar, smiling. Only two other people, reclining by the fireplace -- an elderly man in a pewter suit and the voluptuous, young, Asian woman curled up beside him, rubbing his chest with her petite hand.

"What may I get for you two this evening?" the bartender said to Cam and Jake as they stepped up.

Jake: "Do you have tea?"

"Tea?" Camille said.

"Certainly, sir," the bartender said. "What did you have in mind? I recommend our Genmaicha. Very relaxing. Has an interesting popcorn flavor."

"Genmaicha's great," Jake said. He touched Cam's arm. "You'll love it."

Bartender motioned toward the crepuscular expanse behind them. "Anywhere you like. I'll bring the pot right over."

"Tea?" Camille said again, now simpering. They were taking seats across from each other on a pair of plum-colored, suede chairs. She looked at herself. "Are we even dressed to be here?"

"You could be wearing a garbage bag and still be Chicago's idée fixe." His eyes narrowed. He fondled his Vandyke. "Tea's calming. Tea drinking has actually been around for almost five thousand years. Medicinal purposes, initially, but around nonetheless. *What?* Why are you looking at me like that?"

"You might be the only cerebral autodidact who has ever come from Ohio."

He poked his finger into the darkish gap between them. "Fibber. What were you really thinking about?"

"Nothing. Just someone you remind me of..."

"Who? Tea wallah? Winsome disciple of the Buddha?"

Interrupted by the bartender, who now conveyed a set of cast iron cups, coasters, a clay pot with steam slinking out its inflected nozzle from a maroon tea tray he was carrying onto their table. "Anything else I can offer the two of you right now?"

"Fine, thank you."

"Don't even try to prevaricate," Jake continued, cutting Camille off as she was about to say something. "Tell me what you were thinking. Remind you of whom?"

She gazed at him, the eyes dormant, constricting. "What?"

The eyes now aqueous.

He reached across the table, stroked her arm. "Sweetheart, what? I was just having a little fun with you. What is it?"

Her face curdled and she broke into tears. "Why did he have to die, Jake? Why did he leave me alone? I didn't want to live. Not for this. Oh God, so much time! Fuck this life!" She screened her face with her hands, kept sobbing.

"Jesus, Cam, what?" He rubbed her quivering shoulder. "Who? Why did *who* leave you alone? What are you talking about? Where's this coming from?"

She stood, now masking her mouth and nostrils and reaching down for her nylon purse. "Please excuse me, Jake." Voice atremble. "I'll be back." She scuttled off toward the hall from which they'd come, disappeared.

He continued to assess that hallway in her wake, his brow scrunched, finally deciding just to turn around and tend to the tea. Slurped his torrid Genmaicha as he peered across the room at the fireside couple, both of whom way too self-involved to have noticed what just transpired. Sipped again, looked down, thought: *The hell is spooking her like that? Where did that come from? Don't say anything when she gets back. That's what you always do. Just shut the fuck up. Let it be. Is she coming back?* He whipped his head toward the empty hall.

When she did return, ten minutes later, straggling to the table, surprising him, her eyes baggy and mascara slightly smudged, she resumed her former sitting pose, looked down at her tea cup, trifled with it. "That was embarrassing," she said, still looking at the tea. "Sorry. It was something silly; it was a person I knew a long time ago. I was just a girl." Her voice shaking again. She took a protracted breath through her nose, eyes still fixed on the tea. "Michael Parker -- that was his name. Michael Parker." She chuckled. "He died. He just died. I loved him so much; I loved my father, too…" She looked up and wiped tears, looked back down. "What ails me isn't all that, Jake. Not anymore… It's the heaviness I carry.

The residue. The unmitigated realization I'm left to bear about things as they actually are. Powerless to go backward in time and console that little girl, me, wrap her up in my arms, whisper that life would be full of hardship because it just would and that it wasn't her fault, that she was loved, so very loved. Powerless, and in my heart I hear her unalleviated torments every minute of the day. Can't move forward. Can't move at all." She stared at him, snuffled. "This is a savage world, my friend. You can induct yourself into as many nouveau schools of thought as you like, imbibe your heady perspectives, blur consciousness, sleep, dream, but the truth will always be right there waiting for you -- that we are irrelevant, forever wobbling along the barranca that separates life and death no matter how loudly we lament, no matter what we do. 'Rage against the dying of the light' or just open your arms and let that ever-night take you as it will. There's *nothing* to hold onto and God or Nature or whatever you want to call it doesn't care. We're all unendurably alone." She lifted a frail smile. "You're so quiet now."

"Just listening."

She sipped, squinted. "Does taste like popcorn." Sipped again. "You're *too* quiet, Jake. Say something."

"Remember when we were at Starbucks and you were talking about where you grew up, how oppressive it was? Remember when you mentioned Chopin's book. What's it called? *The Awakening.* You were talking about suicide, and then you just became pallid, speechless. Remember? Why, Camille? This friend of yours, Michael... Did he kill himself?"

She looked off at the tenantless room, nestled the tea cup. Back down at the table. "I got uncomfortable then, because I'd unintentionally taken myself back to a despondent time when I almost jumped out the window of my apartment. It was a while ago now."

He kept staring at her, his eyes starting to water. "What happened?"

"Just came to seem like the most assured form of liberation from an ongoing pain I felt I couldn't cope with anymore."

"What actually *happened*, though? Was there a specific incident?"

Her breaths shallow and eyes petrified.

He wiped his face and smiled. "You know what, let's not even talk about it. Just want to know as much as I can about you is all, because I really care, because I love you. I'm not going anywhere, so you can tell me whatever you want to in your own time, lamb. I'll do my best just to listen, empathize. God knows I need some practice at that."

She chuckled. "That really means a lot to me."

He began to tattoo his fingers on her hand. "This place seem a little too eerily gothic to you? Like the disquieted apparition of some baron's once-immured-but-now-departed first wife is about to materialize from a wall, scare us out of our wits…? Should we just go?"

A smirk; her smirched eyes crinkling. "Where now?"

"Now it's time to play 'Follow the Walk Signals,' ladylove."

He lifted his hand and held it for her to take. They ambled to the bar, paid, made their way back through the hotel, out onto Superior Street.

"This way," he said, pointing west. "See that walk signal?"

"But where are we going?" She was giggling, trailing behind. "What time is it?"

"I don't know and I don't know."

They ended up in the caliginous, tree-girded park across from Newberry Library. Jake jogging along the sidewalk: "Catch me, catch me, catch me."

"Jake, slow down," she was saying, pacing behind, grinning. "I can't see."

He rounded a corner and jerked right, but then kept moving forward. "I'll stop when you touch me and I become *it*."

"Not chasing you anymore." She turned and strode toward Dearborn Street. Got less than twenty feet before she felt a swift impact on her body and felt herself being hoisted upward. He'd grabbed her by her reedy waist and was now balancing her on his shoulders.

"Jake..." she was howling, the rest of the words supplanted by a high-pitched laugh, snort.

He staggered with her to the corner of Walton and Dearborn, then let her down and wobbled back, falling onto a shrub. There he lay, spread-eagle, breathing deeply.

She hitched out her arms, gave a jesting death-rattle and swan-dived on top of him. Landed on his chest with a forceful clap and they both rolled off each other, moaning, laughing. She rolled back over when their groaning raillery vanished and that bare, vitalizing need to experience each other's bodies came forth, snuggled up in the nook between his arm and ribs.

"Let's stay right here, just like this," she said, closing her eyes. "Like we're hiding from the rest of the class during recess, holding each other in the breeze beneath a vernal arbor, two awkward darlings fondling, fumbling their way into the aurora of their lifelong love."

"Mind if we skip to high school, when it's time to give our virginity?"

She gave him a sportive whack. "Bear."

"*What?* Ours would be ethereal, unforgettable. Like there we are pulling up in front of your house on a brumous, autumn midnight. Headlights off. Parents slumbering. I turn to you--"

"Just shut up, Jake. Just hold me."

Their words expired. Two locked bodies and a cozy conversation of hands. That privy minuet of masculine and feminine effluence. The soft, nocturnal, summertime winds speaking now, murmuring of an arcane wisdom from eons past. Sibilant leaves; the chorus surrounding that drafty affirmation and exalting it. They surrendered their sight to the sweeping after dark and no longer concerned themselves where an arm concluded, finger commenced, where the patter of that squirrel was coming from, how the childly scent of skin commixed with the vegetal fragrance of grass, if it was him or her who had the taste of burnt seaweed, because both were now emboldened to be impotent by the powerful actuality of their togetherness.

"Is this all a dream?" she whispered, now weary from their necking, her dropping her head down just beneath his chin.

"In a sense, yes." He listened as she began to snore and then started stroking her head. "A dream we were always meant to experience with each other." He clicked his cheekbone to her pate, took in a lengthy breath of lavendered hair and was then asleep, too.

Made in the USA
Lexington, KY
18 June 2015